SLICED VEGETARIAN

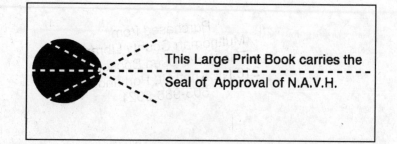

A DAISY ARTHUR MYSTERY

SLICED VEGETARIAN

LIESA MALIK

WHEELER PUBLISHING
A part of Gale, Cengage Learning

GALE
CENGAGE Learning·

Farmington Hills, Mich • San Francisco • New York • Waterville, Maine
Meriden, Conn • Mason, Ohio • Chicago

GALE
CENGAGE Learning·

Wheeler Publishing Large Print Cozy Mystery.
The text of this Large Print edition is unabridged.
Other aspects of the book may vary from the original edition.
Set in 16 pt. Plantin.

LIBRARY OF CONGRESS CATALOGING-IN-PUBLICATION DATA

Malik, Liesa.
  Sliced vegetarian : a Daisy Arthur mystery / by Liesa Malik. — Large print edition.
    pages ; cm. — (A Daisy Arthur mystery) (Wheeler publishing large print cozy mystery)
    ISBN 978-1-4104-8266-2 (softcover) — ISBN 1-4104-8266-9 (softcover)
    1. Widows—Fiction. 2. Retired teachers—Fiction. 3. Murder—Investigation—Fiction. 4. Large type books. I. Title.
  PS3613.A43576S58 2015b
  813'.6—dc23   2015026535

Published in 2015 by arrangement with Liesa Malik

Printed in the United States of America
1 2 3 4 5 6 7 19 18 17 16 15

For Chloe, my brilliant and
favorite budding author,
for my wonderfully supportive
dancing friends at Colorado
DanceSport, and always,
for the pets.

ACKNOWLEDGMENTS

It is my firm belief that no book is written entirely on one's own, and this is particularly true in my experiences. Thanks to the generous spirit of the following people, *Sliced Vegetarian* is finding its way into print. "Thank you" cannot possibly say all that I feel, but I hope everyone who reads this knows how special they are:

Beta Readers Thank you to these readers who caught typos, misspellings, plot problems and unintentional character twists, then helped to correct them. My beta readers were Melissa Butler, Kathryn House, and Winnie Kesteloot.

Special Experts Not every piece of information can be had with a Google search. Thank you to the following who gave special expert information: Sherry Davis, for introducing me to the existence of the Smaldone family; Eric Scott of King Soopers, for helping me understand the grocery business better; Susan Michalakes of Bethesda Lutheran Services, for reviewing what life is like for adults with developmental delays; and Steve Cominsky for help with my restaurant management questions.

Friends No thank-you would be complete without acknowledging my writing friends and communities: The Ladies Suppah Club, Rocky Mountain Fiction Writers, Rocky Mountain Mystery Writers of America, and the great team at Five Star Publishing. Particular thanks to my supportive friends: Daven Anderson, Ian Ballard, Sandy Branning, Elizabeth Hall, Sharon Henning, Jennifer Harrelson, Trish Hermanson, Michael Hope, Mindy McIntyre, Laurence MacNaughton, Deni Dietz, Alice Duncan, Tracey Matthews, and Tiffany Schoefield. Wishing you all many stories with happy endings.

CHAPTER 1

Doggone it!

Everything moved in slow motion, but I moved even slower. Pens, paper, books, and tea flew out of my hands to arch in the air over my soft, worn quilt. That's what I got for trying to bring so much stuff to bed with me.

Georgette had exercised one of her seldom-used miraculous leaps to launch her overgrown belly from the floor. It was a great move for a middle-aged cat, but in the process, she bumped my elbow. As everything blasted into the air, I was left holding an empty saucer, and staring at a huge bedtime mess. My cup of tea became a brown river flowing across the quilt and over copies of this week's submission to my writing group.

Quick as my stiff, fifty-something legs could move, I ran to the bathroom for a towel and returned to see my cat indulged in a good lapping of tea.

"Georgette! Hsst! Go away, you overgrown fur ball."

Georgette turned to look at me with a what's-your-problem attitude. She blinked once, and I scooped her up — none too gently — then dropped all sixteen pounds of her onto the floor. My cat wandered off, not at all intimidated.

I turned toward the mess on my bed and quickly sopped at the papers there. The tea had missed several but flowed menacingly over one particular set. I glimpsed angry red critique lines bleeding into the rest of my copy and felt a split-second twinge of satisfaction.

Dan Block's review of my work looked like it might be a casualty of tea wars. I smiled and called to Georgette.

"It's okay, Georgie-Porgie. Accidents happen."

Dan Block.

That man must go through a pen a week with all his slashes and other graffiti-like comments. I detested the way he would rip and write in huge letters across a page, "Too fat, trim," or worse, "Delete!" Sometimes he made my pages look like silver screen World War II letters, with redaction lines through just about everything.

Dan joined our wRite Stuff writing group at the beginning of the year and had made my life an uncomfortable array of editing slashes and exclamation-pointed rebukes since. He even tried to "correct" the spelling of our group and I had to explain that the capital R and S were for members no longer with us, and we spelled it the way we did to honor their memories.

Honestly, I was glad the tea attacked his work. I dabbed up the mess as best I could and took Dan's notes to the bathroom to dry in the tub. I heaved a sigh and returned to bed.

My bed. All mine, now that Art was gone to that great sports channel in the sky. *I miss you Art,* I thought, and grabbed at a locket around my neck.

Seven years ago, when Phil Mickelson was swinging toward a second Masters championship, Art started yelling for Tiger to get back in the game. Then Art grabbed his chest and I dialed 9-1-1. Since then, I've left his seven iron in the umbrella stand at my front door as a small memento and reminder to never watch golf on television again. But I also became friends with the gravestone business owner up in Denver, who told me how I could have my Art's picture burned into a piece of porcelain that would be encased in a gold locket for lasting memories. I could wear the necklace whenever and wherever I wanted. If I wanted, I could even wear it in the shower.

The small case had a rose on the front in honor of our daughter, and Art's picture inside. I started wearing the locket again after that horrid murder last fall, and whenever I was faced with an uncomfortable situation, I grabbed hold of it and felt better. It was kind of a protective good luck charm and felt like I was keeping Art and Rosie close, for whenever I needed family.

I gave the locket a small squeeze. No use crying over spilt tea. I kissed my family good night, turned on the heated mattress pad that had replaced Art's snuggles and threw off the tea stained layer of my bedding. Then I climbed in under the remaining blanket, and ordered and stacked papers next to me for a read-through before I slept. The nightstand clock showed after eleven, but I liked to read the critique group comments before shut-eye.

This week's reviews felt similar to other recent efforts: "Does this passage need to be here?" "Great description, if a little over the top." "Love your work, but you may want to drop a few adjectives." Overall, they were satisfactory remarks. I reached across to turn off my lamp and caught a glimpse of the bathroom door standing ajar.

The gloom of the night crept from behind its opening, and a grimness called from the shadows there. Dan Block's review had not been addressed.

How I loathed Dan. I cringed at his forthright comments and confident, sparkling work, week after week. Even his first submissions had a terse, powerful feel, and I knew Dan would be a published writer much sooner than I.

Dan was employed by one of those large delivery companies. I'd have to guess he lifted boxes all day because his shirts seemed to strain over broad shoulders and his large, deep brown hands were callused. He was always impeccably dressed in simple jeans and golf shirts. And unlike my dearest Art, there was no bulge around Dan's middle, just a hardness that left me uncomfortable in my middle-aged pudge.

When I chatted with him about becoming a member of our group, Dan said he had wanted to be a political activist in his youth but, instead, married his high-school sweetheart, and went to work without a college degree. But he loved to read, and writing came naturally to him. So after twenty years with Express Parcel Service, he joined our group and began writing suspense novels with Ernest Hemingway crispness.

Okay, so he was good at *his* kind of writing. What did he know about the romance novels that I focused on? Bet he couldn't make a love scene happen for all the Pulitzer Prizes in the world.

As I dug into work on my second novel and struggled with each page, I had to admit I was jealous of the ease with which Dan seemed to write. I also loathed his critiques. Zero tact.

I did not want to go to my bathroom in search of his "This makes no sense, chop!" comments. Reluctantly, I pulled the blanket from around me and slipped my feet to the floor.

A pounding sound came from the direction of my front door.

Bang, bang, bang!

I turned on my heel and jumped back into bed. Who would come to my door after — I checked the clock — after midnight? I pulled my blanket up to my chin.

The pounding reverberated through my house once more. For the billionth time I missed Art. He was only an average guy, but he was my hero. If he were here, I would have poked him from his sleep and made him slink into the dark to see who was there. He might have grabbed his golf club if the noise was too menacing, but he would bravely go where no retired special education teacher like me dared tread.

Bang, bang hit my ears again. The glass in my front door rattled. I grabbed a fuzzy pink slipper for protection and slowly crept into the dark, toward that awful noise.

I hoped the clamor was Georgette diving into the trash again, or that whoever was out at this time of night would just go knock on someone else's front door. By the fourth time the poundings came, I was sure they were meant for me. My stomach nose-dived as I crept slowly toward my front door.

There was a shadow in the window portion of the entry, silhouetting someone on the other side. I dropped my slipper and reached for Art's golf club in the umbrella stand. Sometimes, mementos paid off.

I grabbed the club and squeaked out as firmly as possible, "Who's there?"

"My Daisy," shouted a familiar voice. "My Daisy! Please. Open up."

I put down Art's seven-iron and pulled open the door. "Ginny?"

Ginny Caerphilly was the daughter of Gabriel Caerphilly, my Littleton police lieutenant and ever-so-slowly-emerging love interest. Ginny had been my special needs student a few years ago, right before I retired, and I loved her completely.

As I opened the door, a bundle of arms, golden straight hair and tears launched themselves at me.

"Oh, My Daisy," cried Ginny. "We in trouble!"

CHAPTER 2

I bundled Ginny inside and turned on a light. She blinked at me from a tear-stained face, so I knew I had to take my time with this situation.

We walked into my living room, where I encouraged her to sit on the sofa, which she did, but then immediately jumped up to pace the floor. Ginny kept shaking her hands as if to swat at unseen gnats, and murmured "We in trouble" over and over again.

I took the young woman's hands. "Ginny, what is it? Why are we in trouble?"

Her face crumpled. "Are *you* in trouble too, My Daisy? Oh, no!" Fresh tears welled up.

"I don't know. You said 'we' so I thought . . ."

I took a deep breath. "Let's start over. At the beginning. Ginny, *who* exactly is in trouble?"

"I in trouble. Bri-Ann is in trouble. My daad will be reeeally mad. Mad Daad. We in trouble!"

I played a hunch. "Ginny, does your dad know you are out this late at night?"

Ginny hung her head.

"And he doesn't like you out past a special time?"

She hid her downturned face in her hands and more tears came. "Ten o'clock. 'Cept when I work. Are you gonna tell on me?"

"First, let's figure out what's going on. Then we'll decide what to tell your dad. Who, Ginny, is Brian?"

"Bri-Ann is my boyfriend. I love him. But I f-ink Bri-Ann did sumpin' bad."

"What did Brian do, Ginny? Did he hurt you, dear?" A thousand thoughts flew through my mind, none of them good. I'd call Gabe when things were clearer and under control. Whoever it was, that man, Ginny's "boyfriend," would wish he hadn't fooled with a police lieutenant's daughter.

Gabe was a no-nonsense kind of guy who saw the world as full of bad-guys or good-guys, and not much in between. I often thought the jury was still out as to where I stood in Gabe's narrow spectrum. It was important to get Ginny's story straight before calling him.

"Ginny, sweet, you have to tell me what's wrong, or I can't help you."

"I don' know. I don' know what's wrong, My Daisy. Bri-Ann called me on my cell-telephone. He said 'help' and I went to work and I founded him. I said we should go to my friend, My Daisy, an' he said 'okay,' an' so we camed here on da bus. Bri-Ann is a good guy. I love my Bri-Ann. Can you help us?"

"Of course, I'll try to help," I said, "but Ginny, where did Brian go when you got off the bus?"

"Silly. He camed here!"

"Here?" I looked around.

"Yeah. He is outside. Can you make him come in? He is so scared."

Curiosity won out. I went back to my front door, opened it, and called out to Brian. No answer. I told Ginny to stay inside and I stepped out onto my front porch, closing the door behind me. Didn't want my young friend to hear what I had to say to a no good "boyfriend" who encouraged Ginny to stay out past curfew, and do heaven only knows what with him, then leave her to take care of his problems.

"Brian, whoever you are, I know you're out there. If you've hurt Ginny in any way, *any* way, I think you should know, her dad is a police officer and you are in deep trouble." There. That sounded nice and firm.

A rustling of evergreen shrubs in my front yard let me know that I had been heard.

"Please show yourself," I continued. "Let's discuss this situation like adults." At least one adult — me — and possibly one creepster — this Brian character.

The silence dragged for a few moments.

"Brian? Look, you. It won't do any good to hide at this point. Come out from my bushes." I may have stamped my foot on that note.

A long wolf-like howl emanated from the shivering leaves of my front hedge. The lonely sound was repeated from another direction. Goodness! We were waking neighbors. At least, we were waking Thunder, the German shepherd next door. I saw a light or two pop on across the street as well.

"Shh!" I hissed. "Brian, stop being a jerk and come into my porch light." For nearly seven months I'd been practicing the mantra of "conflict is good," given me by my critique group friends. No story moves along without conflict — a lot of it — and I'd best get used to diving in, rather than running away from, uncomfortable situations. Did too much of that for most of my adult life.

"I don' wanna," came the plaintive voice of Ginny's boyfriend. Hang on. That voice wasn't in the suave tones I'd been expecting. I waited and the voice came again. "You is mad. You talka too much. I scared-a-you."

Oops. I may have had the wrong picture of Ginny's boyfriend. She did say he was frightened. I simply jumped to the conclusion that he was uncomfortable meeting people who would protect Ginny from him. "Brian, I don't bite. Please come out of the bushes."

More rustling, then a small, rotund figure appeared. From my porch, and in the moonlight, it was hard to tell much, but any pre-conceived image of a flimflam man melted immediately away into the reality of a trembling boy in a too-late-for-this-time-of-year snow jacket. His fidgeting and stumbling projected that Ginny had found herself an equal match. My heart went out to the boy, and I invited him inside, this time for real.

Brian shook his head and stepped back toward the bushes.

"It's okay, Brian," I said, allowing all my softness into my tone. "I won't hurt you. Please, dear, come in."

A coyote like howling was Brian's only reply. More lights started coming on in the houses around me.

"What's going on out there?" called my across-the-street neighbor.

"It's all right, Mr. Kerns. Special needs visitor," I answered.

"Harrumph," came the response and a slammed door to boot.

"Shh! Brian, please," I stage whispered. "We don't want to disturb more neighbors."

Brian dove back into the bushes. The door behind me opened, and Ginny came onto the porch.

"Bri-Ann, you git in here. Now!" shouted Ginny. "Else I won't give you hugs."

Brian stepped into the light once more. "No Ginny. Your friend, My Daisy, is too scary mad."

I let down any pretense of authority and reached a hand toward Brian. "I'm sorry I scared you, good guy. Are you hungry? You want to find something in my house to eat?"

Bingo! Young people and hungry are two terms that should never be separated. In this, both the special community, and everyone else are the same. Brian came running up the porch stairs with an agility I wouldn't have thought possible. I followed him and Ginny back inside.

When I had both mischief-makers sitting on my couch, cookie in hand, I paced the floor and said, "Now. I need to find out more about what's been going on. It is very serious that you two are out so late, but I think we can make things right. Brian, please take off your jacket and let's get to the bottom of this."

Brian gazed uncertainly at Ginny, who nodded, and started helping him off with it. He was a handsome young man, now that I took a good look at him. Bit of a scruffy beard growth, but his soft brown hair curled around his face and ears charmingly. He didn't possess the almond-shaped eyes that earmarked Down syndrome, but developmental delays can be caused by an array of fate twists, so I wasn't surprised he looked average. Brian unzipped his jacket slowly, Ginny trying to hurry the operation along. He struggled with the sleeves for a minute and gave up, but I could see his clothes underneath. The supposedly white golf shirt Brian wore was filthy. *Someone should work with this young man on hygiene,* I thought. There were brown streaks everywhere . . .

Wait a minute!

Not brown, but rusty red. Oh, my stars! I stopped and gazed more intently at Brian's shirt. It wasn't just his shirt, but his neck and jeans were covered in . . .

"Brian, is that blood all over you?" I felt

23

my knees go weak and collapsed in a chair as the young man before me nodded and began to cry once more.

"I don't know. It's something serious, but I haven't been able to figure it out yet. Ginny said Brian called her from work. She went to find him and they came straight here."

"Why here? If they were in trouble, why didn't Ginny just bring Brian home?"

Silently, I looked over Gabe. I took my time to examine him from the top of his six-foot frame down through his angry face, the dark outfit with obvious gun bulge, the polished shoes and back up into Gabe's beautiful blue eyes.

He blushed. "I see." Gabe paced the living room much as Ginny had earlier, but at last settled on my couch and waited for me to speak.

"I didn't get much out of them while we were waiting for you. Brian said he couldn't take off his coat, but Gabe, I did get a glimpse of his shirt underneath. It was covered in blood. Brian said something about Mississippi being asleep in the bathroom."

"Mississippi? Blood? Bathroom? Makes no sense."

"Tell me about it. But someone or something being asleep with blood all over Brian seems to be a serious situation, even if we don't understand. Perhaps —"

"We need to get to the bottom of this." And that was that. Gabe jumped up off the couch, took charge, and called for the curfew breakers to come out to the living room.

When Ginny and Brian stepped into the room, he stood in front of them, a model of displeased attitude. His hands were fisted on his hips, and he tapped his foot. Then Gabe frowned again and said, "I'm not pleased that you were out so late, Ginny. You know it's not safe this time of night. No" — he held up a hand — "don't give me one of your 'but dads.' We'll talk about this later."

He turned to Brian. "And I don't know who you are, mister, to think my daughter can go traipsing around Littleton after midnight." Gabe wagged a finger in Brian's direction. Ginny and Brian looked at each other, guilt written all over their faces, then turned back to Gabe. He continued his lecture.

"Right now, Ms. Daisy says you have a problem with the Mississippi River being asleep at your work, so we'll go check it out."

Ginny rolled her eyes. "Oh Daad. Misses Sippy is not a river. Misses Sippy is a friend of Bri-Ann's. She is a nice lady. Not a river.

You are so silly."

I could see Gabe inhale deeply and admired him for the fact that he didn't let Ginny's reprimand distract him. Gabe looked over at Brian.

The young man apparently had made an attempt to clean up when he and Ginny were in my kitchen. His jacket was re-zipped, but his hands and face were clean of any signs of blood, and someone had pulled a comb through his hair. While Brian trembled under Gabe's glare, he lifted his chin and held out his hand.

"Mr. Care-filly, I Brian Hughes. I love Ginny. I sorry we are out past Ginny's bedtime, an' that you are mad. Ginny is my friend. She said we should come here. She said My Daisy would help us. Please do not be mad at us."

Gabe pulled his arms across his chest. I stepped near him and nudged his side. He glared at me then slowly reached out to shake Brian's hand.

"We'll worry about your friendship with my daughter another time. Right now, tell me about this Miss Sippy, and why you think she's sleeping in the bathroom."

Brian gulped. His jaw slackened and a tear slid down a cheek.

Gabe impatiently tapped his foot. "Well?"

I laid a hand on his arm. "Brian, dear," I tried in my old patient teacher voice. "It would help a lot if you could tell us about your trouble tonight."

"I dunno," said Brian. He looked to Ginny for help. His girlfriend nodded encouragement. Brian gulped once more and turned back to Gabe and me.

"I fink Misses Sippy is sleepin' in da baffroom. But she wouldn't waked up when I aksed her. I shaked her, but she wouldn't waked up an' she wouldn't talk a me. She looked yucky an' she was sticky an' I fink she poked herself."

"Poked herself, dear?"

Brian nodded. "Wiff a knife."

My grip on Gabe's sleeve tightened.

"Ow!" he yelped and pulled my hand off. Oops. I threw him an apologetic look before returning my attention to Ginny and Brian.

"And the bathroom is at work, Brian, or at your home?"

Ginny stepped in front of Brian to face her dad and me. "At work, work, work, My Daisy. Sometimes you as silly as my daad. Misses Sippy is sleepin' at the gro-sery store. At the store where we work. She sleepin' in the baffroom at work!" Ginny huffed a big sigh as if Gabe and I were the stupidest creatures alive.

30

I turned to Gabe. "Don't you think we should —"

"Get your coats, all of you," said Gabe, moving toward my front door. "We're heading to Gigantos."

A quick glance down showed I needed a little more than a coat. My fuzzy pink slippers peeped out from under my snuggly blue robe. The robe covered what had once been a comfortable flannel nightie, but was now a sad, saggy sack of faded blue flowers on a sea of green leaves. No, I was not quite ready for prime time or a crime scene. And the overall look was definitely not scoring high on the attract-your-police-friend, hopefully-future-lover scale.

"I need just a minute more," I whispered to Gabe. He gave me a once-over and nodded.

"We'll wait for you in the car. Hurry."

Gabe shepherded our two night owls outside and I ran to make a desperately quick attempt to look decent.

In my bedroom, Dan Block's review lay neglected on the covers, but my mind was focused on what one should wear to see a river of blood in a supermarket bathroom. I glanced at Dan's red marks and shivered.

CHAPTER 4

The parking lot around Gigantos glowed in soft, mauve-colored fluorescent lights, except for the alley between it and the roller rink next door. Those areas reached out with dark, creepy fingers of shadow and a chill ran through me. It was nice to know I had a fully armed police officer along for protection. The place was too quiet. I glanced at my watch. Nearly one, a couple of hours past the store's closing time.

Gabe tried both main doors before returning to our car. He called on his police radio, and before long, a marked Littleton police cruiser pulled into the lot.

Gabe waved to the officer inside. "Thanks for coming over, Matt. It's locked up tight out front here. I didn't see anything out of order when I scanned through the windows with my flashlight. Nothing out of place in the parking lot, as far as I can tell, either. Head to the back and check out the employee entrance."

"No problem, Lieutenant," said Matt. I recognized Matt Hawkins as one of Gabe's staff from when I met him last fall. Last fall, when murder made its way into my unsuspecting life as a romance writer. Another chill strolled down my spine. I touched the locket at my neck.

Gabe turned back to Brian, Ginny, and me. "Where's the bathroom, son?"

Brian pointed. "Right dare. Misses Sippy is in dat baffroom dare."

Gabe walked up to the window and flashed his light into the store. He shrugged his shoulders, then stilled as his light trained on some movement in the supermarket. I crept closer to see too.

Matt walked toward Gabe from within the store, Gabe's beam reflecting off the younger man's badge. Gabe directed his flashlight toward the bathroom, and Matt nodded, then walked in that direction. Brian, nearby, backed up and put his hands over his face. Ginny gaped at her friend.

A few moments later, Matt reemerged from the bathroom and into Gabe's beam of light. He looked at us with horrified eyes and shook his head.

Gabe turned to me. "Stay here, Daisy, and keep the kids in the car." I nodded and he took off at a run, talking into his walkie-talkie as he ran. He reached the corner of the store, the place of dark shadows and the alley entrance, and then turned back to me.

"Stay in the car, Daisy."

His words gave my legs motion and I bundled Ginny and Brian away. I certainly had no desire to see more. Something awful was waiting for whoever entered the bathroom of my local Gigantos supermarket, and secretly I was glad my brave Gabe had to investigate, and not me.

In the car, I turned from the front passenger seat to face Ginny and Brian.

"Hey, guys," I said. "Let's play a game."

Ginny yawned. "No fanks, My Daisy. I sleepy now." She laid her head on Brian's shoulder and closed her eyes. I wished I could sleep right then, too, but more and more police cars were arriving, with sirens blaring. Something was terribly wrong at Gigantos, and I had a creepy feeling about it.

"Brian," I said after a few moments of watching outside, "are you Ginny's boyfriend?"

He nodded in response.

"Have you been her boyfriend long?"

Another nod.

"Can you tell me about it?"

Brian shook his head this time.

"Won't you talk with me?"

"Shh," replied the young man, putting a finger to his lips. Then he risked a whisper. "My Ginny is sleepin'. Misses Sippy is sleepin'. We haveta be quiet now."

"I think, if we whisper, it will be okay," I said. "Who is Miss Sippy?"

"Misses Sippy is my friend. She lives near me, an' she takes me at work sometimes. I like Misses Sippy."

"Is Miss Sippy your girlfriend too?" I asked.

Brian thought about it for a few moments. Then he shook his head. "No. Not like my Ginny. Misses Sippy is old, like you, My Daisy. She is not a girlfriend woman. She is a old woman. But I like her."

They say the truth hurts. More hurt than I cared for. I swallowed my annoyance and tried again.

"What do you and Ginny do to be boyfriend and girlfriend?"

"We talka the cell-telephone, and we hold hands at break time, an' we smile at each other all da time. I love Ginny, an' she loves me."

"And do your mom and dad know you have a girlfriend?" Sweet though the relationship seemed to be, parental guidance was probably still an important part of Brian's and Ginny's success.

"My mom an' my dad don' live wiff me. I live by myself, an' Misses Sippy lives near me. She helps me, an' scolds me if I do bad stuff, but I have my own 'partment."

My heart constricted. How could parents desert their developmentally delayed son? I know the job is monumental, but part of becoming a parent is understanding and accepting the risks that go with it.

"Do your mom and dad visit then?"

Brian sighed. "No, dey can't. M and M says so."

More puzzles. Why couldn't Brian's parents visit their own son? And who were M and M? I smiled at the young man, who was nodding off himself. Only a little while ago I thought Brian could have been someone taking advantage of Ginny, but now? Sitting together, this young couple looked like they had been born for each other. I wondered if Brian's mom had had a difficult pregnancy. Or perhaps this young man had been born normal, only to fall victim to fate. To the outside world, he would look normal, but the minute he opened his mouth, the intellectual challenges would be obvious.

A light tap at my window made me jump.

Gabe waved me outside.

"Daisy, this is going to be a long night. You and the kids okay here? I can see about some blankets for you, but I can't break away right now."

"What happened?" The question popped out of my mouth before I could stop it.

Gabe shook his head sadly. "A woman in the bathroom was stabbed to death."

"Oh, Gabe! How awful." Visions of last fall's murder invaded my mind, and my stomach nose-dived along with them. This couldn't be happening again. Littleton was too nice a town to have such a crime wave. But Gabe was talking again.

"I have to keep Ginny's boyfriend here for questioning. He's our best sus— er — witness right now. But if you want to take Ginny home in my car —"

"No, Gabe. Brian apparently doesn't have parents we can call. I'll stay and help him through this."

Gabe looked hard at me and shook his head. "Daisy," he said on a warning note, "don't get more involved here than you need."

I looked back into the car. Ginny and Brian were softly sleeping, heads resting against each other. If I intended to help with their relationship, I'd certainly need to stay involved.

"Don't worry, Gabe. I'm simply making sure Brian has a capable friend with him."

Gabe scowled but said no more.

CHAPTER 5

Twenty minutes earlier, Gigantos's parking lot seemed rather ghostly, all dark and quiet, with the May night creeping over our restless anticipation of what Brian had seen. Now the area was lit up like high-school open house on meet-the-teachers night. A garish, bizarre feeling flowed in and around police cars, an ambulance, and other official vehicles that were parked at strategic angles, their blue and red lights creating an air of excitement for everyone but the dead body Matt had found in the main customer bathroom. Someone had cordoned off a large area with crime scene barricade tape, and officers engaged in talking with each other and back to the station in loud voices. I almost preferred the dark, quiet chill before we found the body to this manic atmosphere.

Ginny and Brian had woken, and stared around without comment. We sat at the sidelines of the drama for a couple of hours. I was sleep-deprived dizzy, as were my charges. A nice, tea-stained quilt and warm mattress pad were sounding very good to me.

Gabe broke away from directing the investigation a few times to check on Ginny and Brian, and to give me updates. During one check-in he said that the victim's license read "Cissy Melato," so I guessed that my charges had been trying to say "Ms. Cissy," not "Mississippi."

Gabe did his work and coordinated operations with a deftness and confidence that made me proud to know him. Officers approached my friend with their questions and their evidence and Gabe replied with gestures and pats on the back, even the occasional smile. I could tell that he was in the place his spirit belonged. He was a good police officer.

I only wished for a pad of paper and pen to record the comings and goings. One of my novels would definitely have a policeman for the romantic hero.

A small black Volkswagen pulled into the lot, and my happy thoughts took a dive. It was Linda Taylor, Gabe's right-hand woman.

I'd gained a grudging respect for Linda

since she joined our writing group and I'd begun to know her a little better. Her writing, like everything else about her, was efficient and clear almost all of the time. She was writing a police procedural with a hero that showed Linda's attraction to guns a hint more closely than I was comfortable knowing.

Tonight, she had come in a pair of dark, skin-tight yoga pants that showed her fantastically in-shape legs. She also wore a white, soft-looking sweater with the oversized collar only women with swan necks look good in, and a brown leather bomber jacket kept everything but the promises of cuddles locked underneath.

I was not jealous. No way.

Inevitably, Linda approached Gabe first, and started taking notes on her ever-present clipboard. I wondered what stories that clipboard could tell, what with the constant use it had.

Gabe gave Linda one of his most charming smiles, the one that contained a tad of irreverence to it, and nudged her as only the best of friends do. She threw back her head and laughed. Did she have to be so stunningly beautiful as well as being younger than me by almost two decades, a professional in Gabe's line of interest, and as brave as a lion?

I told myself again that I was not jealous, but Art came whispering in my head. "Liar." *Now, Art. Shush.* I sighed like a schoolgirl.

Suddenly, I heard a sports car wheel into the parking lot with rumbling mufflers and squealing tires. Ginny sat up from her slumbering slouch next to Brian in Gabe's back seat and cried out, "Is that Roddy?"

Interesting. I looked toward the noise and saw an old yellow Chevy Camaro squeeze into a space between two police cars. Was the driver thinking clearly? Squealing tires? Speeding into a parking lot full of police? Not good. Not good or smart at all.

A young man jumped from the vehicle. He wore a leather jacket, black, but otherwise not too dissimilar from Linda's, and had a dark expression to match. I guess there was a certain grace in the saunter he executed going up to Gabe and the other officers, who had all turned to watch him. The young man spoke and the cluster of police shifted to listen closely.

In my limited experience, when a member of the force pays too close attention to what you're saying, you're more than likely to find yourself visiting their offices for a chat. Who was this fool?

"Oooh! It *is* Roddy," cried Ginny from

the back seat. She started bouncing up and down and opened her window. "Roddy, Roddy! It's me." A big smile spread across her features.

Next to her in the back, Brian had an almost opposite reaction. He scowled and slumped down in his seat, his lower lip stuck out in an exaggerated pose of frustration.

Ginny turned to her boyfriend. "Bri-Ann, let's go see Roddy. We can tell him what is goin' on. We will know more dan he does dis time."

Brian crossed his arms and wriggled down as if trying to drill his way into the floorboards. "No. I don' like Roddy. No."

But Ginny was having none of her boyfriend's nonsense. She opened the door and practically ran to Roddy's side.

"Isn't Roddy your friend?" I asked.

Brian snorted. "I no like Roddy. He's mean a lot. He spills yucky stuff an' den I have to clean it up."

"But isn't that your job, Brian? Keeping the store clean?"

"I can clean da store, an' I do a good job. But Roddy makes big messes, an' he laughs at me, an' he calls me stupid. I no like Roddy."

I didn't think I'd like Roddy either, if what Brian said was true.

"But Roddy is your manager? Your boss?"

Brian tapped his foot, thinking for a few moments. "Yeah." He heaved a sigh and followed Ginny.

I guessed that if Ginny and Brian could leave the car for a stretch, so could I. At least they gave me a good excuse to stretch my legs and possibly hear what was going on. I followed them toward the action, both with Roddy and between Linda and Gabe. It would be good to keep an eye on That Woman and my police lieutenant.

Ginny had taken the lead. She looked at Roddy as if he were a movie star. "Hi, Roddy." She blushed and grinned at the young man, who swept a lazy gaze over her. Then he glared at Brian. I was farther back and out of his view.

Roddy worked his jaw in thought. There was something about this guy that I took an instant dislike to, even beyond Brian's obvious dislike. He reminded me of the "cool" boys at Independence High who turned out to be sadistic bullies of my special-education kids.

Roddy reached out and ran a careless finger along Ginny's soft chin line. "Hey, sweet cheeks. What are you doing here?"

Brian began to growl. Ginny giggled. I glanced over at Gabe, whose nicely tall figure began to tense.

Roddy smirked at Brian. "Down boy. I know she's your girlfriend. I was only being nice. You need to watch that temper of yours." Roddy winked at Ginny, who giggled again, and I fully wanted to growl along with Brian. Was this Roddy character baiting Ginny's boyfriend?

Gabe stepped closer. "Ginny, go to the car with Ms. Arthur." His tone of voice warned that he would broach no nonsense.

"But Daad, Roddy is my man-ger. I need to stay wiff him case he needs me."

At the word "dad" Roddy's slack posture completely transformed. He straightened up and oozed respect for Ginny from every pore. This guy should have been in the movies. Academy Award candidate for sure. I took a longer look at him.

Roddy was flawlessly dressed, though not with any extravagance. He wore a starched white shirt under his black leather jacket and sported a tie as well. His pants were pressed. Marks of leftover wars with acne sparred across his sharp-featured face, but his thick hair and light-colored eyes could make him seem handsome. In fact, he was better dressed than anyone but Gabe and Sergeant Linda. Interesting. Why would a guy look so fresh this late at night?

"Mr. McKeague? Thank you for coming. I appreciated your phone conversation and willingness to help so late at night," said Linda Taylor. "You're the night manager, correct? I have a consent to search form and some questions for you when you have a moment."

Roddy gave Linda the once-over and seemed to like what he saw.

So, Linda had telephoned the emergency number posted on Gigantos's door, and Roddy responded. Still, he looked very tidy. Could he have been anticipating a call from the police?

Ginny sure seemed to find nothing wrong in Roddy's appearance. She kept grinning at him, ignoring the scowls and frowns of her boyfriend standing next to her.

But Roddy was speaking again. "Mr. Caerphilly? Are you Ginny's dad? I should have known. The family resemblance is so strong. You must be very proud of your daughter, sir."

Puh-lease! The guy was pouring on the syrup like he had a corner on the maple tree market. Worse, Gabe seemed to be eating it up. He straightened his shoulders and put an arm around Ginny.

Linda and I caught each other's eye. We nodded in silent agreement that Roddy was a put-on. I rolled my eyes and she smiled, and then made a note on her clipboard.

Beside me, Brian huffed through his nose. Well put, I thought.

But Roddy wasn't done. "You know, Mr. Caerphilly, Ginny is the best of our special-needs employees — always on time, always happy and helpful."

Blah, blah, blah. He kept going on. I was ready to barf. Surely Gabe couldn't fall for this act. Surely he noticed the "of our special-needs people" separator. Talk about code for "not like us *real* people."

"Well," said Gabe, stretching even more across his shoulders, "Ginny and I work very hard at being responsible. And you can call me Gabe."

I couldn't look directly at Linda. She was madly scribbling away on her clipboard. How could Gabe fall for this rubbish?

Roddy gave a measured look at Brian, and then spoke once more to Gabe. "I wish I could say the same for all of our team at Gigantos." He turned again toward his employee. "Brian, Brian, Brian. What have you done?"

Brian frowned his incomprehension.

Roddy stood patronizingly over him. "You and I were the last employees at closing, remember? You were in charge of the bathrooms because I had that important office stuff to take care of — writing and all that?" He turned to Gabe. "Office shut down."

Brian growled, "You told me to clean the baffrooms again. You made me stay late to clean. I already cleaned dem, but you said go do it again. You made me leave after everbody. You left too. An' you turned off the lights on me."

"I think you have that wrong, buddy." Roddy turned more directly toward Brian. He gave another quick glimpse over his staff member. Then he let his eyes get big.

"Brian, is that *blood* on your shirt?" He said it loud enough to draw the attention of all the officers around, who turned to look at Brian. Brian wriggled with slow-dawning comprehension. He pulled his heavy winter jacket closer in an awkward attempt to hide his shirt.

"You a bad man!" shouted Brian toward Roddy.

Roddy allowed a smidgeon of a smirk to flicker across his face. "I don't think so."

Almost everyone was focused on Brian. I think they must have missed Roddy's look, but Brian didn't.

"Yes. You bad. I fink I ate you!" He lunged toward Roddy with more agility than I would have expected and got in the first punch. Roddy didn't seem at all surprised at the attack and was more than ready to pitch in.

Gabe nodded to his officers, and they swooped around to pull the two apart.

The high-pitched sound of metal against cement cut through the mayhem as Roddy and Brian were separated. Its piercing tone grabbed everyone's attention.

On the ground between Brian and Roddy, the parking lot lights from above caught on the gleaming blade of a butcher knife. A knife dotted in more blood.

We all fell silent. All except Roddy.

"Brian! What have you done now?"

CHAPTER 6

Everything at the crime scene froze in a communal moment of shock. The most important piece of evidence lay like a pirate's treasure between Roddy and Brian. I couldn't tell exactly where the knife had fallen from, why it might have appeared precisely at this moment, in this way. But as happens, the bloody knife pointed at Brian's probable guilt in the murder of the woman in the store.

Brian made a lunge toward Roddy again, this time held in check by a couple of police officers.

"You a bad man!" he shouted again. Then his arms slipped from his over-large snow jacket, and the police officers were left holding nothing more than water-repellant down sleeves between them.

Brian made his move and rushed into Roddy's ribs. With a surprised "oomph!" Roddy fell to the pavement. Brian jumped on top and pummeled his manager's face with both hands.

Roddy screamed in pain and frustration. "Get off of me, you retarded oaf! Ow! Get off!"

Brian kept going.

One officer, then two, then three ganged up to pull Brian away, but the young man wriggled and broke free again. He started toward Roddy once more, but the manager jumped up and began running. Brian flew after him.

The police gave chase to Brian, who hit one in the face and broke free once more. He showed surprising strength and agility, like perhaps he'd been in one or two fist-fights before this.

Guns emerged in officer's hands. Gabe shouted, "Stop, Brian! That's an order."

Brian kept spinning and blindly hitting at whatever was in his reach. Cars, bushes, and the like all fell victim to his temper. When my special kids got this way at school, we had to call in the police. Too big to not do damage with their fights, and too incapable to manage their anger once it flared, this was a very dangerous situation. I heard the click of guns being cocked. I sucked in air, ready to scream, my hands flying over my mouth, my spirit frozen in place.

Suddenly, a soft hoot cut through the air.

Brian stopped. Ginny whistled a small tune I hadn't heard before. He turned in her direction. Ginny's was not a song, but more a soothing sound. Quietly, she walked to Brian.

"Bri-Ann, hush now. There, there. Be nice. God loves you."

Brian stopped swinging and stared into his girlfriend's face. Ginny walked up to him. "Do you need a hug, Bri-Ann?"

Suddenly, Brian began to cry again and nodded. Ginny responded. The officers started moving in, but Gabe signaled them back. His daughter took charge and soon had Brian walking toward Gabe, the young man's once violent fists softened into a tender clasp for his Ginny's hands.

The tension in the air eased into sadness as Ginny led Brian to Linda, who handcuffed and led him away. Ginny started crying and I moved to soothe her.

Roddy came walking back, less saunter in his stride.

"You saw him," said Roddy. "He's a lunatic. Almost killed me. You going to arrest him?" Roddy's nose was bleeding and his mouth showed signs of a fat lip emerging. "I'll sign a complaint."

Somehow, I was still on Brian's side.

Ginny raised her head from my shoulder. "Roddy, Bri-Ann is right. You a bad man. My dad should 'rest you!"

Roddy glared at Ginny and huffed. She turned to Gabe. "Dad, Bri-Ann is a good guy. I love him. Please, please don' put him in jail wiff da bad guys. He is good. He jus' gets mad sometimes. Jus' like you."

Gabe pulled Ginny into a hug and spoke over her head. "Mr. McKeague, if you will go with Officer Hawkins, he'll take your statement."

As Roddy and Matt walked off, Gabe pulled Ginny away so he could lean down and talk directly to her. "Ginny Bear, I know you think you love Brian, but I'm afraid he is not a good guy for you. I think he hurt someone very badly."

"Roddy de-served it, Daad," said Ginny.

"I don't mean Roddy, Love. I mean the woman in the bathroom."

"No Daad. Bri-Ann loves Misses Sippy. Bri-Ann did not hurt her. He is a good man, my Bri-Ann."

Gabe sucked in air and rose to full stature. "Ginny. Enough. Brian is not good for you. I think he did a very bad thing and he is go-ing to jail. You will not —"

"No!" Ginny screamed the word and stomped her foot. She put her hands over her ears and screamed "no" several more times. The other officers looked away and carefully found dutiful things to do.

Linda came back. "I read him his rights, Gabe. Matt will take him in for booking, when he's done with the manager." There was a slight edge to her voice when Linda said "manager." Once again I felt like we were on the same side. Did she find Roddy as distasteful as I?

Ginny broke away from her dad and flew into my arms. "My Daisy. Bri-Ann is a good guy. Do not let my dad 'rest him. Please!"

My heart sank as I looked over Ginny's head to her dad. "Gabe."

"No, Daisy. Enough. I need to do my job. Please take Ginny home." He turned once again to his daughter. "Ginny, you go to your room and get some rest. I will tell your bosses that you're not coming in today."

This wouldn't do. I cleared my throat and caught Gabe's eye. "I'll take Ginny to my house, Gabe. She shouldn't be alone right now. No one in her place should have to be alone." Ginny and I started off, then turned. "May I borrow your keys or get a ride with one of your officers?"

Linda stepped up. "I'll take them home." Gabe thanked her and walked over to give Ginny a kiss. She pulled away.

"You a bad man too, Daad," said Ginny, but there was no energy in her charge. She walked to Linda's car ahead of us all.

Gabe ran frustrated fingers through his hair. "Sometimes I can't win with that girl."

I couldn't hold back. "Sometimes you shouldn't win. Sometimes you should listen to her."

Gabe frowned at me. "What's that supposed to mean?"

"It means that you've had it in for Brian since you met him a couple of hours ago, and you're jumping to some terribly wrong conclusions."

"So now you're going to tell me how to do my job?"

"No, but Gabe, I'd be more suspicious of that Roddy fellow than Brian in this case."

"And your evidence for this?"

"His baiting of Brian . . . his demeanor . . . oh, I'm not sure, but every feeling says this puzzle isn't being put together right."

"That's rich. Every feeling. I'll be sure to write that in my report and give it to the district attorney."

I hung my head. As completely as I felt that Brian was innocent of the murder laid out before us, the hard evidence of the blood all over him, the knife, his explosive anger, all added up to a good suspect.

Linda gave a discreet cough. "Daisy? Ginny's waiting."

I tossed one more look at Gabe, who turned on his heel and started calling out orders to his team. Back to business as usual, if you can call murder usual.

Ginny sat in the back of Linda's car, a tissue to her eyes and a blanket wrapped around her waist. I sat in the front passenger's seat.

Everything in the vehicle was orderly, quite homey. Linda had put in a waste container, a tissue holder and other items that allowed her to almost live in the car.

Ginny's blanket came from Linda's trunk where an emergency pack held power bars, water and other goodies. The woman must have been listening when local news stations did their annual "with Colorado's wild winters, keep these in your car at all times" report.

I turned my attention to my driver. "Linda, I don't want to interfere in Gabe's and your investigation, but isn't it possible that Brian is not the murderer?"

Linda kept her attention on the road ahead. "It's possible, Daisy, but not likely."

"What makes you say that so confidently?"

"This has all the markings of a crime of

56

passion. I don't have the official count, but I saw several wounds on the victim. Her head was almost — well, she was brutally maimed in other ways, too. Only close friends and relatives generally do so much damage to a body."

I pictured a knife going up and down into someone and shivered. "I would never have thought that."

"Bri-Ann did not hurt Ms. Sippy," said Ginny. "Bri-Ann is good, Linda. You have candy in your glove box?"

"Sure, honey," said Linda and nodded to me. I opened the glove box and found a small bag of peanut butter cups. I took out a couple.

"Give her the whole bag. Poor thing deserves a little comfort right now," said Linda. She turned on a blinker and lowered her voice. "Sad, but true. Love turns to blind, violent hatred a lot easier than a simple predatory kill. That's when you get this kind of mutilation." She thought a moment. "Think I should put that in my Raymond Cruz story. What do you think?"

Raymond Cruz was the name of the book Linda was writing and bringing to our critique any Tuesday night she had off. It gave me the creeps, but was a gripping tale of murder from the perspective of a serial killer. I had to drink chamomile tea every time Linda read.

"Can you make the victim Dan Block?" I said. "With all his red marks I feel like I come home with stab wounds every week."

Linda laughed. "Yeah. I never thought of it like that, but if you turned his ink to blood, that man would certainly be short a pint or two."

I hesitated a moment, then decided to trust Linda. "May I tell you a secret?"

She shifted her gaze from the road to me for a split second. "Go on."

"I don't want to be mean, but Dan makes me nervous. I'd kind of like to encourage him to leave our group. I'm frightened of the way he stares at everybody, and is always following us out to the car lot. It gives me the creeps."

"His car is in the lot too. What else is he supposed to do?"

"I don't know, Linda. Maybe be the first to leave sometimes. Maybe walk with us instead of following like a stalker."

"Careful, Daisy. You're sounding pretty prejudiced here." Her gaze returned to the job of driving.

"I'm not talking about his skin color," I said, surprised the conversation would even go in that direction. "I'm talking about the intensity of his remarks and scribbles across our pages. They seem so angry."

"Oh. I see what you mean. I wouldn't worry about it."

"But I do. As the group leader, I'd feel responsible if Dan's force turned into something more aggressive."

"Daisy, that's a huge leap. There's nothing in either Dan's demeanor or actions that would indicate he'd go physically violent. No need. He already cuts us to shreds with his words."

"Okay." I sighed. "I'm really intimidated by his remarks. He makes me feel stupid, what with his great writing and my stuff that is hardly passable."

"I'm right there with you on that one. But what can we do? Tell Dan he's too good for us? We want a more amateur writer so we can all dream of being published together?"

It was my turn to laugh.

Linda relaxed into a more thoughtful expression. "We could reverse what he does to us, in our comments to him."

"What do you mean?"

"He chops everything we write. We could tell him he needs to expand his copy."

"I see — write 'explain' everywhere he suggests or hints at a bigger feeling."

"And write it huge across his page, in red."

"That would be too obvious, Linda. Maybe in purple or green."

Linda laughed again. "I'd be scared to get on your bad side, Daisy."

From the back seat, Ginny suddenly spoke. "You jus missed My Daisy's house, Linda. Pay tension."

CHAPTER 7

Ginny fell asleep on my couch almost as soon as she lay down, but I tossed and turned in my bed for another hour or so.

The joy of menopause. Sleep, a precious commodity, eludes you even when you're exhausted.

At last, wild dreams of gleaming knife blades turning into gourmet food prep and back into knives covered in blood took over. Hmm. Sleep may be an overrated concept.

At about eight, my back door slammed open and I heard Chip McPherson call out.

"Ms. D.? Daisy, you home?" Chip, my next door neighbor, had taken to wandering in my house at will over the past several months, dropping off his German shepherd, Thunder, for puppy sitting, and gobbling up my cookies and milk. I often thought about using my door locks, but while Chip was a bit of a character, there was no harm in the young man, and I did enjoy his company. I kept reminding him to knock, but that was probably a lost cause by now.

I threw on my robe and shuffled out to the kitchen. "Shh! I have company," I said in a stage whisper.

"Oh, ho! I thought I saw that police officer of yours last night. So you're making progress. Congrats." Chip started rummaging in my fridge and pulled out an apple.

I snatched the apple from his hand. "It's not Gabe. And don't you have your own fruit at home?" He gave me an overgrown pout.

"Sorry, Ms. D. Didn't think you'd mind. A little out of sorts this morning?"

I took a deep breath. "A bit tired, Chip." I washed and handed him back the apple. "We were up until almost four this morning, and then I had a hard time getting to sleep. Ginny's in the living room."

"Ah. Babysitting again. Ms. D., you are a rare gem in these days of me, me, me."

"Yeah. I'm a real diamond in the rough." I looked down at my dowdy old robe then back at my friend and smiled.

"Even sleep deprived, you keep those puns coming." Chip grinned and shook his head. "Okay, so what's the scoop? How come you and Ginny were up so late?"

"There was a murder last night! Ginny's

boyfriend's unofficial guardian was killed at Gigantos Supermarket."

"Yeah. Heard about it over the radio this morning. Do you think this Brian guy did it?"

"No. Definitely not."

"Why not?" Chip took a bite of the apple.

"Because he has no motive. He likes Cissy Melato."

"That the vic?" Chip slung his ever-present backpack off his shoulder and leaned against my ledge.

"Vic? Victim, you mean? Yes."

"So how come the police arrested him?"

"Because he lost his temper with his creepster boss. And . . ."

"And?" Chip leaned toward me.

"And because Ginny's dad doesn't want any man around his little girl. But don't quote me on that." Chip had begun to reach in his backpack, no doubt for something to write with.

"You say some of the juiciest things, Ms. D. If you'd only let me quote you, I'd have Pulitzer material for every story."

"Thanks, but no thanks. I'm conjecturing and have no proof."

"You make a pretty darn good detective, Ms. D. If you were on the force, I'd be happier for it."

"Okay, Chip. What do you want this time?"

"Why should I want anything?" He plastered a shocked look on his face as if I were some cynical ogre.

"Because you never compliment me without wanting something in return."

"No. I don't want anything. Except maybe a good news story. I've hit a dry spell, and my editor is getting a bit antsy for me to bring in a winner." He took another bite of the apple, then turned to me once more. "But then, now that you mention it, Kitty and I were planning to go to A-Basin this weekend for a late spring ski."

Arapaho Basin, or A-Basin as the locals call it, is a great ski place. With a base elevation at over 10,000 feet, this place is not a resort for tourists, but the true Coloradan ski enthusiast's legend. Slopes often don't close there until June, and have even been known to host skiers for Independence Day, much later than most other resorts. If I were a skier, this is where I'd go. Real rough and ready without the trappings of restaurants, gift shops, and other superfluous stuff. Then again, maybe not. I liked the nachos at Keystone, the art shops in Breckinridge, and the catering to every level of skier at all the big resorts. Couldn't blame Chip and Kitty for wanting to get a few runs in during the beginning of May, though.

"And you want me to watch Thunder for you." I finished Chip's thought for him.

He smiled. "Would you? You're a great friend."

"You're just lucky I like Kitty so much. You'll be back for dinner on Sunday?"

"Wouldn't miss it."

Kitty and Chip met last fall at my house, as we wound up what I called the case of *Faith on the Rocks*. Someone had murdered Rico, a Catholic priest. Rico was also from my writing group, and the rest of us fell under suspicion by the Littleton police. That was when I re-met Gabe Caerphilly and for me, at least, the sparks began to fly.

And it was love at first sight between my reporter for the *Post* neighbor and my bartending writing group colleague as well. Kitty and Chip made one of the most adorable couples I'd seen in a long time, as they were both small in stature, but each had a large personality. Chip's shone through his skill at wheedling me into almost anything I didn't want to do, and Kitty was blunt, honest, and a fashion diva. I loved them both.

"Just leave Thunder's leash in my mailbox before you go," I said.

Chip smiled at me. "What would I do

without you, Ms. D.?"

"Probably grow up." I lightened the re-mark by offering up a dish of peanut butter to go with the Granny Smith I'd given him.

Soon, Ginny woke and joined Chip and me in the kitchen.

"You are my best friend," she cried as I put a plate of cheesy scrambled eggs and toast in front of her. I kissed Ginny's head and went to pour myself a cup of tea.

The front door bell rang. "That will be your dad," I said to Ginny as I put down my cup.

"Love to stay and hear the news from his perspective, but I gotta go, Ms. D.," said Chip. He gave me a quick peck on the cheek and headed out the back. "Say hi to your police friend for me. Make sure he keeps you out of jail." Chip chuckled at his weak joke and headed out.

At the front door, Gabe looked no worse for wear, even after staying up all night with the crime scene and murder. You could hardly tell the man had spent the last several hours walking and poking around a river of blood in a grocery store bathroom.

I smiled at this special man. "Coffee?"

"That'd be great." Gabe followed me into the kitchen and gave Ginny a big hug. "How's my Ginny Bear?"

"Daad, that was so scary last night! Your work is busy, busy!"

Gabe laughed. "Now you really know what I do for work, and you were very brave, sweetheart." Ginny leaned her head on Gabe's chest and smiled. I handed him a cup of coffee.

"How'd it go?"

"We finished processing the scene before the morning rush, and management agreed to keep the bathroom locked and taped if we agreed to let the store open for business as usual."

Ginny jumped up from a chair she'd sat in as Gabe started his cup of coffee. "Open for business? I am late! I gotta go at work."

Gabe grabbed her arm as she tried to run toward the living room. "Not today, princess. I already told your manager you will not be in today."

"Why not, Daad? The store is open. I need to work. I am very good at my work. I help ever-body to bag their groceries. I help dem to der cars."

"Not today," repeated Gabe, his tone firm. "Today you catch up on some sleep."

"But I not sleepy Daad. It's morning. I waked up."

"You will be sleepy again soon. And if you don't get back to bed, you will be more bear than Ginny. Now, go fetch your things and we'll let Ms. Daisy have her house back."

Ginny looked as if she'd like to argue, but Gabe pointed to the living room, and, with a bear-like *hmmph,* she stomped out. They made a great team. I smiled.

"Gabe, what do you think happened at Gigantos?"

He shook his head. "Looks like Ginny's friend lost his temper with the victim. The destruction to that poor woman was worse than I've ever seen before. Brian's boss said he has a problem with anger management at work. This has all the markings of a crime of passion. I just need to outline the link between Brian and Cissy Melato, then we'll send the case to court."

"But what about Ginny? She doesn't believe that Brian could do such a bad thing. She believes her boyfriend is innocent."

"No offense, Daisy, but Ginny isn't exactly what I'd call a great character witness. She loves almost everybody who walks in our door and says a kind word to her."

"I think in this case, she may be right. Brian didn't impress me as a murderer either. From what he told me, I think you might want to look more carefully at the night manager — what's his name? Roddy?"

"Roddy McKeague. He's all right. Look, Daisy, who's the policeman here?" Gabe gave me the firm tone he'd just used on Ginny. "You saw how that Brian guy reacted to his boss and how much force was needed to settle him down again."

"I saw how Ginny was able to get through to him with a small, whistled tune, and that when it was made clear to him what he was supposed to do, Brian completely co-operated."

"I know he's a part of your special community, my girl, but this Brian Hughes is our doer."

"I think you're a little biased because Brian is trying to date your daughter."

Gabe's temper flared. "Are you implying that I'm not doing my job?"

"Of course you're doing your job, Gabe. But I think Brian is a convenient first suspect. You need to look around to be sure you have the right man. Maybe look into Cissy's life a little."

Gabe calmed, his glare replaced by that professional mask I'd seen the night before. "Funny you should say that, because I'm heading over to Cissy Melato's apartment this morning after a quick nap and shower."

Ginny had wandered back into the kitchen by this point, and plopped her purse on a chair near her dad.

"Good, daad," said Ginny. "When you go to Misses Sippy's will you feed poor Queenie? She will be so sad."

Gabe and I looked at Ginny. That young woman was constantly surprising us.

"Queenie, Ginny Bear?" asked Gabe.

"Yes," said Ginny. "Queenie. She is a so cute doggie. She is Misses Sippy's doggie. Bri-Ann takes good care of Queenie, an' he walks her, an' he gives her doggie food for Misses Sippy when she is tired. She is tired lots."

Gabe put his head in his hands and began muttering. "Great. Just great. Up all night, and now I have a strange dog to deal with."

I spoke up. "Ginny, how big is Queenie?"

Ginny smiled at me. "Queenie is so cute. She is littler than me, an' she has round eyes and big ears." Then Ginny thought a moment more. "But she bites Brian sometimes, an' he says 'ow.' Den Misses Sippy scolds Queenie."

"Bites?" said Gabe. "I don't need bites." Suddenly his face brightened. He turned to me.

"Daisy. I've noticed how good you are with your neighbor's dog."

"Oh, no, Gabe . . ."

Gabe gave me that devastatingly irrever-

70

ent smile of his. "But you're so good with dogs."

"But this is your case."

"But if I go and the dog bites me, I'll have to do another report and the dog will have to be put down."

Ginny piped in. "No, no. Misses Sippy does not put down Queenie. She puts Queenie in her kennel, in da kitchen. Queenie is already down. She has little tiny legs."

Gabe kept grinning at me. I wanted both to push him out my door and to laugh and hug him at the same time. "You are a monster," I said. "Has Chip been giving you wheedling lessons?"

He smiled broader than before. "I'm a mutt monster. Pick you up in an hour? Besides. You might find a different suspect than Brian if you go with me."

Sold. "An hour. You go change and I'll see you back here then."

"Bri-Ann is not a 'spect,' " said Ginny. "Brian is a good guy. Daad, you is too silly. You let Brian out of jail, now!" She stamped her foot for emphasis.

"Ginny, let's talk about this when we get home," said Gabe. "Right now, you head out to the car. I will be right there."

"Let's go get Bri-Ann, Daad."

"We'll talk soon, Ginny Bear. Now out to the car, please." He spoke with a firmness Ginny seemed to understand better than any words. She stomped out to the living room, toward my front door.

"An hour?" asked Gabe.

"An hour. But if that creature bites me . . ."

"The dog? I'll call animal control myself." Gabe pushed out the kitchen door, and trotted down the drive toward his car and his daughter.

I looked at the mess from breakfast and wondered how I let myself get caught up in these things.

CHAPTER 8

Gabe and I walked in the wake of The Creek View Apartments manager toward Cissy Melato's place. The manager was a twenty-something dyed blonde with long legs and an excited demeanor. Gabe seemed to enjoy following her. I poked him in the ribs and he winked at me.

As soon as Amber confirmed that her apartment complex couldn't in any way be held responsible for the murder at Gigantos, she became a veritable radio station of information and enthusiasm.

"It's so hard to imagine someone you know up and dead," said Amber. "And murdered! Cissy Melato. The accountant. Who'd have guessed? I mean accountants are such dull folks. And you say Brian Hughes did it?"

Gabe wasn't saying anything, so I decided to prod. "We didn't say Brian did it, only that he was a person of interest. You knew

73

Cissy? And Brian?"

"Not well. Ms. Melato paid her rent regularly and made sure that the retarded guy did too. Guess I'll have to go collect the rent from him in the future. Not sure if I want him here, though, if he killed someone."

"We don't know that Brian killed Cissy," I said, emphasizing the word *don't.* "And he'd be called special needs or developmentally delayed, not retarded." Amber shrugged, so I went on. "Did Cissy have a lot of friends in the complex?"

Amber snorted in a young, pretty sort of way. "Ms. Melato? I don't think so. I mean everybody stays to themselves, except in summer, when we have pool parties. But Ms. Melato didn't exactly have a pool party figure, know what I mean?" Amber gave me a quick once-over and I could see her guessing my own swimsuit size wasn't quite Creek View material.

I let it pass. "A bit overweight?"

"A bit! Man, that woman was big enough to have her own mountain peak name!" Amber turned a cutsie shade of pink. "Sorry. I shouldn't have said that, but a few trips to the fitness room would have done her a world of good. Here's her apartment."

Amber reached for the door and put her

key in the lock. A yipping noise made her jump back. "Anybody warn you about that dog?" She turned to Gabe and me.

Gabe spoke for the first time. "If it's dangerous, I'll call animal control."

Amber nodded, and stepped away. "You can keep the key for a few days. And here's one for Hughes's place. We'll have the locks changed when we paint Ms. Melato's anyway. Any idea when we can get in to clear out?"

"I suggest you hold off any plans of re-renting until our investigation is done." Gabe pocketed the keys.

"No problem. Ms. Melato's paid until the end of the month. I may want to show the place, is all."

"Not until the investigation is done," Gabe repeated and handed Amber a business card. "We'll be in touch."

The apartment manager nodded and left.

Gabe turned to me and said, "Ready, Ms. Dog Watcher?"

I grimaced in reply. The yapping on the other side of the door had turned into a frantic howl. Gabe opened the door.

We walked in, me safely behind him. It took a moment for our eyes to adjust. Denver has more sun than most other places in the entire country, and today was

75

no exception. Cissy's apartment was relatively dark, brought on by closed curtains and a west-facing entrance. There was a single light on in the direction of what I assumed was the bedroom. I strained to see details.

A blur of fur darted behind the living area couch, then came charging out at us, barking and growling. I first saw huge ears, then a squat body and big, round, protuberant eyes.

"It's a Corgi, Gabe," I said and smiled. "I always liked this breed." I bent down to take a closer look. Gabe grabbed my waist and pulled me back.

"Daisy, I thought you said you've been reading up on dogs. Don't you know never to get in the face of a strange animal? Even these little guys — though this one looks a bit on the chunky side — even they will move fast and bite when you get in their space."

I looked down. The Corgi was indeed getting excited. She circled around Gabe and me, found a strategic route and zeroed in on Gabe's ankle.

"Ow!" he cried. "What was that for?"

"She's stressed, and you just made an aggressive move on me. Remember her owner is — er, was — a woman. Looks like

Queenie is a good watch dog." I smiled and reached down again. Queenie walked into my outstretched hand for a nice scratch behind those adorably large ears.

Gabe rolled down his sock and rubbed his heel. Meanwhile, Queenie raced past Gabe and me, through the front door we'd left open, and did her business in the small grass space between the apartment and the parking lot. She trotted right back inside with the air of a dog who owned the place, but she let me scratch her ears again.

I stood up and started wandering through the apartment. "We need to figure out who this Cissy Melato was."

"Stop, Daisy," said Gabe. "You're here to watch after the dog, not to investigate. In fact, you should try to kennel that mutt, and then take her to the car and wait for me there."

"What? I'm not supposed to look around with you?"

Gabe shook his head. "Evidence has to be collected carefully. I don't want your finger prints all over this crime scene."

"You tricked me! I thought you wanted my help."

"I do. With the dog."

"Not fair, Gabe. I'm good at observing crime scene details. You know that."

Gabe walked over and encircled me in a hug. His body felt warm and safe. It was quite a lovely distraction in our crime scene investigation. "Not this time, Daisy. I want you well away from this case. Last time you got involved, you were nearly killed, remember?"

I did remember, and shuddered at the vision of being chased in the woods, of the stick crashing down on me, and poor Thunder's wounds. It was much nicer to be safe in the arms of my police lieutenant.

"You're right, Gabe." I huffed a sigh. "Guess I'll look for Queenie's leash and kennel." Reluctantly, I disengaged myself from Gabe's embrace and ambled toward the light. It was a path to the kitchen. Gabe turned right, opened a curtain, and started calling out what he found.

"Fireplace not used in the living room. Bathroom's clean too. This must be a closet — oops — nope. It's an office."

I came running back. "Office? This must be a two-bedroom place."

"Back, Daisy."

"Come on, Gabe. I know better than to touch anything. I'm not a person of interest, and you invited me along."

"Don't make me regret that." Gabe looked sternly at me, but made no more effort to stop me. Queenie ran point in front of us.

We walked in. The office was, like everything else in the apartment, neat and orderly. There was a serviceable file cabinet and large desk to eat up most of the room. The chair looked well worn, but was ergonomically designed for the user. Two guest chairs sat on the opposite side of the desk.

I noticed a pile of magazines on top of the cabinet and went toward them. Gabe stopped me.

"Here," he said, digging in his pocket. "If you're going to wander, at least put these on." He handed me a pair of police-issue latex gloves.

As I donned the gloves, he continued. "If you touch anything, anything at all, put it back *exactly* as you found it."

"I've watched enough police shows to know my basics, Mr. Worry Wart." I rolled my eyes, Ginny fashion.

"We're not playing at cops and robbers, Daisy. This is the real thing. I'm already stretching the rules bringing you along for the dog."

"Why do you care so much about Queenie?"

"I don't. But Ginny would kill me if I let animal control take the thing."

I smiled. Priorities were always in place

with my Gabe. I liked that.

I wandered to the stack of magazines and carefully shifted them to glance at the titles. On top was one for the *American Society of Women Accountants,* then some on accounting principles, and at the bottom was an oversized one called *Accounting Today.*

Sandwiched between these business publications, however, were magazines more my style. "Body Shaping in Six Easy Steps" shouted at me from the cover of one. This was put right next to a "Recipe for the Cake That Will Surely Lure Him." I wondered which title captured Cissy's attention. A magazine on diabetic eating looked as though it hadn't been touched. From the variety of other magazine titles, I thought I might just find Cissy an interesting woman.

Gabe gave a shout of triumph. "Got in," he said from behind the computer screen. "I can see all her appointments."

I stepped around the desk to peek over his shoulder. "Anything interesting?"

"Looks like the usual stuff. Meeting with a Dr. Mobley at the family clinic, Martha Beeman at the ice cream shop and here, on yesterday's schedule, it simply says 'Ramona.' "

"I wonder who Ramona is," I mused.

"Hmm. And here's an entry for a Joe

Smaldone. Interesting." Gabe took a note-pad from his pocket and began scribbling.

"Interesting?"

"Yes. The Smaldone family was big in Denver a decade or two ago. Most of them ended up in federal prison or dead. I didn't know about any Joe, though. Think I'll try to print this schedule."

"Looks to me like there might be more suspects to Cissy's murder than just Brian Hughes."

Gabe snapped out of his thoughts to glower toward me. "Don't you have a dog to kennel?"

I didn't say the smart retort that came to mind, but I gave Gabe my best overly dramatic glare, turned, and left. "Queenie," I called, "let's find some treats for you."

The dog responded immediately to the word *treats*. I followed her into the kitchen, her tailless backend wagging with all its might. I'd bet Queenie was used to three square meals a day, and she hadn't eaten since last night.

After Queenie gobbled a fistful of doggie nuggets and half my hand to boot, I asked her if she wanted to go out for a quick *walkie*. She responded as if I were her best friend in the world, wriggling and whining, and racing to the apartment door. We grabbed a plastic bag from a kitchen cupboard and her leash from the ledge, then left.

When Queenie and I returned, I tried to emphasize the *kennel* word. Unlike *treat* or *walkie, kennel* put Queenie in flight mode. She ran away from the cage I'd found in the hall closet, and dove under Cissy's couch. I chased her out with a little broom prod, but her growling warned me not to use that trick more than once.

We dashed around the apartment, up on furniture, down under tables, wherever her clever mind would take her. So much for my careful not touching of anything. I gave up and sat down. "You win, Queenie. No more chase."

She came up to me, panting either with exhaustion or glee, I couldn't tell which. I reached over and scratched behind her ears. "You have anything else to show me, girl?" I smiled at the bright look on her face. It seemed as though she understood every word I said.

Gabe started yelling at the computer in the office. Apparently, he was having printer problems. His temper could be very stressful, and I was glad I wasn't in the same room with him. Queenie yapped at Gabe from afar, then turned to me. She made a half-move in the opposite direction from him and the office.

"I know, Queenie," I said. "But his bark is worse than his bite." She tilted her head and I laughed. Then Queenie ran off past the kitchen area.

I stood, glanced in the direction of the computer abuse, and decided to follow the dog instead. Queenie led me into the master bedroom.

Cissy's place was decorated in lavish Italian style with ornate frames around replicas of old masters' sketches. I recognized a Da-Vinci drawing of a woman and a Michelangelo Pieta sketch. A small cross stood on Cissy's nightstand. The walls remained a pristine white, and the furniture was dark. Queenie jumped on Cissy's floral bedspread and settled down.

Like me, Cissy had a bookshelf in her room. I couldn't resist and started peering through the titles: *Case Studies for the Modern Accountant, Systems Analysis Methods, Ethics of Accountancy.* These would surely put me to sleep fast.

On a lower shelf, among the more interesting, paperback books there was a small tome whose spine showed no title. I pulled it out. Lilies adorned its cover, along with the word "Addresses." Nice! I opened up the book to a bunch of hand-written entries. This could be very useful in Gabe's and my investigation.

"Daisy? Where are you?" called Gabe from across the apartment. "You're not moving things around, are you?"

Guiltily, I reached to put the address book back. But Gabe's checking on me was an irritation. What did he think I was, a crime scene newbie without common sense? I'd found good evidence and Gabe was acting as though I couldn't be trusted to handle it. Spite thwarted my common sense. I pulled open my purse and popped the address book inside. I'd be sure to tell him about it.

Some time.

I wandered out to the living area and met Gabe, who was holding a sheaf of papers.

"It took forever to get the calendar to print, and then the paper kept jamming," he said. His hair was tousled from his habit of running fingers through it whenever he got frustrated.

I reached up and smoothed his hair. "So I see. Do I get a copy too?"

"Why? You don't need it."

"I think I might want to help Brian by taking a peek into this whole murder business."

"No you don't, Daisy. I don't want you

involved here."

"But Gabe" — my voice took on a plaintive whine — "you're already closing the book on Brian. It's not fair. And I think you're doing this because you don't like that he's dating your daughter."

"Am not!" His tone was an explosion on my ears. I flinched, but he didn't seem to notice. "Are you accusing me of being less than professional?"

"No, but you have to admit, you're not exactly trying to see things from Brian's perspective."

"Not my job to. Look. Weren't you there last night, Daisy? Didn't you see that guy's violent temper? Did that blood pour itself all over him by accident? Get real."

Violent temper. I wondered if Gabe had any idea of his own unsteady temperament lately. For a few months, the slightest aggravation had him shouting and slamming about.

"I know it looks bad, but after meeting Brian, I can't believe he'd really hurt a friend."

"Happens all the time in police work, my girl. This Brian Hughes is a dangerous character, and I want him locked away where he can't hurt anyone."

"Especially your daughter."

"Especially anyone who might get in his way." Gabe closed the distance between us and frowned. "Why aren't you on my side about this?"

I shrugged. "Let's just call it woman's intuition."

"Put the intuition aside and look at the facts. Most murders happen among people who know each other. The murder of Cissy Melato was a crime of passion, thus done by someone she knew well. I won't go into details but Brian" — he rolled his eyes at my frown — "or whoever killed that woman — went way beyond even a passionate kill. He didn't merely stab her. The woman's head was almost completely severed. There was, to be brutally honest, a lot of gore you don't want to know about. Strangers or murderers in an opportunistic situation don't usually do that kind of damage. This took rage. Brian's kind of rage."

No use arguing. Gabe had found his trail, and like a hound dog, wasn't going to veer from it.

At our feet, Queenie began to growl again, so I walked away to fetch her kennel.

CHAPTER 9

I woke Thursday morning to a knotted set of feelings, none of them good. It probably would have been better to stay in bed, but the distinct scent of cat poo made me groan and throw off the covers with a loud huff.

Maybe it was the mediation work between my new foster dog and my old cat. Maybe it was the lack of sleep for two nights in a row as the cat and dog bugged each other incessantly. Maybe it was the idea that Littleton was suffering another murder case in less than a year. Something was extremely out of balance in this life.

Whatever the cause, I was in no mood to go through one more day of upheaval.

"Georgette, where did you make the stink? Bad girl!" I scolded thin air for a good five minutes, all the while sniffing and looking for the nasty nest of poo I knew I'd find.

And there it was, behind my living room couch. "Just you wait until I find you, you monstrous thing. I'm going to take Queenie for a quick walk, then you and I are going to sit down and have a woman to cat chat." I shoved the couch forward and hoped I sounded tough enough to let Georgette know she was not my favorite creature right then. But I knew when I found her, I'd do no more than hold my kitty and rub my face against her fuzzy forehead and pink nose. It wasn't her fault for being stressed.

"Walkies!" I shouted. Queenie leapt from her kennel in my kitchen and click-clicked on doggie claws across my wood floor. We found her leash and stepped out to the back yard. If any neighbor emerged to see what was going on, they'd just have to know I slept in a flannel nightie. So, I wasn't a Victoria's Secret model.

Queenie raced into the yard and ran to every bush and tree possible behind my chain link fence, exactly as she had done about a hundred times the day before.

I was rousted from my tired thoughts by a familiar voice. "Hey, Ms. D. Did you get a dog?"

It was Chip. He was out in his raggedy old terrycloth robe, watching Thunder perform the same doggie morning ritual as Queenie.

"Morning, Chip." I gave a half-hearted

wave across our mutual fence. "Want another dog to go with Thunder? I hear it's easier with two."

"Ha! That's a good one." Chip wandered in my direction, careful to step around any land-mine piles from Thunder. He leaned over the fence, coffee cup in hand. That coffee smelled very good, even to a tea drinker like me.

"Where'd you get the beast?" He smiled at Queenie, who decided to show off her vocal cords with a round of barking at Thunder. Thunder stuck his nose through the fence in an effort to figure out what that noisy dog was all about.

"Queenie belongs to the murder victim we found Tuesday night," I said. "Ginny didn't want to give her up to animal control, so Gabe suckered me into dog sitting until we can find her a new home. Seriously, Chip, any chance you might take her for a while? She and Georgette are not getting along."

"Sorry, Ms. D., but I haven't been producing the number of stories the *Post* wants lately, and I'm feeling the heat to go in search of newsworthy events. If I took Queenie, I'd only have to turn around and ask you to dog-sit both her and Thunder."

"What if I promised you an interview

about the murder?" I was desperate. If fifteen minutes with Chip would solve my dog issues, it was worth being a newspaperman's tattler.

"Afraid that's old news. Already got what I needed from Gabe. Like I said, sorry." Chip was a morning person, and looking sorry was the last thing his bright-eyed face showed. In my mood, I wanted to shake him. After all, how many times had I helped out with Thunder?

Thunder must have known I was thinking about him because he chose that moment to jump up against the fence and give me a lick.

"Eew, Thunder!" I cried. But I couldn't help it. That dog had long ago stolen my heart. "Good morning to you, good boy." I reached over the fence to scratch his ears. He looked at me with those loving eyes and licked the air in front of my face again. I laughed. "I love your dog," I said to Chip, who smiled his reply and pulled Thunder off the fence.

Queenie came up and started barking toward Thunder again.

"She's a bit overprotective," I said to Chip.

"Then it's just as well that you keep her." He turned and started to go. "Hope you have a great day. Cute little dog you have.

Suits you. Thunder!" He slapped his thigh to get Thunder's attention and began to walk toward his house. "C'mon, boy. We have a busy day in front of us."

I shook my head and turned to Queenie. "C'mon, your highness. We have a busy day in front of us too."

Queenie looked like every word I said was a dish of ice cream. She jumped around my ankles and we made our way inside.

In the kitchen, I poured out some dog food and called for my new pet, but she didn't come. That was unusual, unless she was chasing Georgette again. I didn't hear any meows, but thought it best to find Queenie before anything more happened.

I wandered into the living room to a soft, not-quite-right, slopping sound. The sofa out of place reminded me I had a job to do, and the sound was coming from that direction. I leaned behind the couch to see Queenie licking her lips, a happy grin on her face.

"Eew, Queenie! We don't eat cat poo!" I cried.

Queenie's overindulgent breakfast left me reeling. I threw on some jeans and a fleece shirt, stuffed the poo-eating dog in her kennel and away from my cat, grabbed my

91

purse, and fled. I needed breakfast and some quiet time alone.

Fifteen minutes later, I sat in my local bagel shop, a nice cinnamon-raisin with butter in hand. My new tablet computer sat next to me with my word processor open.

The tablet was a present I gave myself for finishing *Love Finds a Way,* my first romance novel. None of my writing group friends encouraged me to find an agent for the project, and in fact, discouraged me from sending sample chapters to editors in the romance publishing business.

With my new tablet, perhaps I'd have better luck. I started my new novel traveling to different eateries and writing whenever I felt like it. This second story was about an office manager who was an artist in her spare time. Someone stole one of her paintings, and she was going to take it out on the handsome new CEO at work. In the end . . . somehow I'd have to force those two to fall in love. This would make a great romantic comedy.

After wiping away bagel crumbs, I opened the tablet and my novel.

No words came. I tried opening a new document. Maybe a nice character sketch would help.

I began typing, but all the features were

made for a bad guy, and a little while later I realized I was describing Roddy McKeague, the night manager at Gigantos.

Thoughts of the murder flooded onto my tablet — thoughts about Roddy being such a slimo, and about Brian so seemingly lost — until his temper kicked in, that is.

Maybe Gabe was right. Maybe Brian's temper was fierce enough to kill someone. Maybe Ginny wasn't safe with him. And what about the Smaldone man Gabe found so interesting in Cissy's calendar? Who was on Cissy's calendar for her last appointment? I strained to remember. To me, there were too many loose ends in this murder. Sometimes I wished I had Gabe's convictions.

Gabe assumed Brian killed Cissy. I assumed Brian did not. Somewhere between us, Gabe and I lost perspective on the subject. I needed to find out more. If Brian was innocent, he could lose his freedom for a long, long time, and Ginny would lose her boyfriend, forever.

Not good.

I finished my breakfast and decided to revisit the crime scene, Gigantos. Maybe I could get a clue there. Besides, I needed some cat food and doggie biscuits. I jumped into my Versa and headed to the store.

CHAPTER 10

In the daytime, Gigantos was like most any supermarket. It sat as the anchor store in a small shopping center near Carpenter and Platte Canyon Roads.

I walked into a bright, cheery, don't-you-want-to-buy atmosphere. Produce to the left; canned goods down most aisles; meat, dairy, and deli stations lined the walls; and a pharmacy sat in the right corner. If ever we got stuck in one of Colorado's famous blizzards, this was the place I'd want to be. It had everything a person would need to survive, including a candy counter about two miles long right in front of the pharmacy and diabetic snacks.

I wasn't quite sure where to begin, didn't know what I was looking for. How do you go up to total strangers and ask if they knew the murder victim or who the murderer might be?

Lost in thought, I jumped when someone

called my name. Turning, I saw an old friend from my teaching days at Independence High.

"Connie?" I said, and my spirits lifted. "Connie Allessi! How great to see you again. I didn't realize you worked here."

"Daisy Arthur. You look super." Connie gave me a hug and smiled. "I'm glad to see you too. Yep. Got transferred when they closed the Gigantos over on Broadway. What brings you here? I thought you shopped at King Soopers."

"Normally do." I only hesitated for a split second before deciding to be straightforward with Connie. She had aged a bit since we worked together to place special-needs high-school kids in jobs with Gigantos. Her hair was still the chocolate brown I'd always been familiar with, but there was a hint that maybe the color was helped along with tinting now. At the corners of Connie's large brown eyes, the laugh lines were turning into crows' feet, and dark circles seemed to have found a home under those expressive eyes.

"I'm here about the murder the other night."

Connie's pretty face clouded. "Oh. That. I would never have thought such a horrid thing would actually improve business.

We've had a bunch of gawkers and thrill seekers in since word got out. Just look." She pointed in the direction of the women's bathroom at the front.

Someone was taking pictures of the police-taped bathroom door with his cell phone. A woman stood posing for the camera making what I assumed was a hammed up version of a dead person. It was ridiculous.

I turned back to my friend.

"It's awful," I said and shook my head. "I understand that one of your developmentally delayed employees, Brian Hughes, was arrested in connection with the killing."

Connie gave a contemptuous huff. "As if."

"You don't think Brian did it?"

"Brian? No way." She shook her head and exhaled deeply. "All right, he has a bad temper. But murder? His spirit is too gentle. If his temper were really a danger, I wouldn't have had him as an employee. I think the cops wanted a convenient way to close their case."

I hoped my face didn't show how much I agreed with Connie. "But I understand he was acquainted with Cissy Melato, the victim."

"So? I was acquainted with her too. Does that make me a murder suspect?"

"No. But you weren't around when the

body was discovered."

"How did you know? Daisy, how exactly are you involved with all of this? No. Wait." Connie laid a hand on my arm and gave a glance around the store. "I'm due for a break anyway, and this isn't a good place to talk. Let's go outside."

She stepped to the service desk and let a staff member know she was on break time. We left.

Gigantos employees had a bench, still in sight of the store, but far enough away to be able to smoke in peace. Connie and I grabbed seats on the bench, no one else being around this time of the day. We watched cars pull in and out of the lot before talking.

Connie looked at me, her face all earnestness. "Okay, Daisy. Now. How are you so much in the know about this murder?"

"I'm a friend of Ginny Caerphilly."

"Ah, I see. And Ginny's dad is with the Littleton police. He told you about this?"

"Actually, Ginny, Brian, Gabe, and I were there when the body was found."

"Wow." She inhaled from her cigarette and thought a moment. "Then you must know more than I do. Is my store safe, do you think? Is Brian all right? How is Ginny? Her dad's called in for her the past couple of days."

"I think your store is fine. Ginny and Brian are too. Though to be honest, I haven't seen Brian since they arrested him. Does he have family or friends that you know of?"

Connie shook her head. "Cissy was his only real friend that I ever saw. She was great. Acted as his advocate sometimes. I understand they were neighbors. Poor Brian."

"What do you mean?"

"He's one of the ones that fell through the cracks in the system. I don't know who will look after him, now that Cissy's gone. I still can't believe it."

"Can you tell me about Cissy? I never met her."

Connie smiled. "I didn't know her very well, you understand, but I liked her a lot. She was this rotund woman who seemed all feisty and mean, but I could tell she was a marshmallow inside."

"Do tell." I leaned in closer.

Connie looked for her details across the parking lot. "Let me see. Cissy was one of those few patrons who would bring back items past their expire date, show us a receipt with the same item dated only a day before and demand a double replacement. Yet, whenever we'd do a canned food drive, she would bring in bags and bags of goods for weeks straight."

"Sounds like a pain."

Connie shrugged. "We were used to her. She didn't mean any harm." Connie lit another cigarette and inhaled deeply. "Then, about a year ago, she started bringing Brian to work on any rainy or snow days. When I asked Brian about it, he said 'Ms. Cissy says we treat neighbors neighborly.' He told me about walking her dog and how she made him dinner sometimes. Seems they had a good relationship."

"Did you talk with Cissy much?"

"We'd share hellos and good-byes mostly." Connie smiled. "Grocery business doesn't allow a lot of chit-chat time, you know that. Anyway, Cissy was a bit overweight and had a sweet tooth like you wouldn't believe. I made sure to stock a lot of canned Glub-jammen, precisely for her. She was one of the few people to buy it."

"Glubjammen?"

"It's an Asian dessert. Gigantos is always looking for the next great grocery item fad to stock. And Cissy would tell me that all Indian food was healthier than the stuff we Americans eat on a normal basis. I don't

99

think she even glanced at the ingredients. Those Glubjammen things are nothing more than soggy donut holes in a Karo syrup sauce. Far too rich for my liking."

I laughed at the just-bit-a-lemon look Connie gave.

"So, an overweight woman who eats Asian sweets in the hopes of staying healthy?"

Connie joined me in the laughter. "Worse than that. Lately, she shared with me that she was trying to become a vegetarian in order to lose some pounds."

"How overweight was she?"

"I'm no expert, Daisy, but I'd have to guess she was a good hundred and fifty."

"Hundred and fifty isn't such a huge weight," I said, guiltily thinking about my own groaning scales.

"Not a hundred and fifty total, Daisy. She was a hundred and fifty pounds overweight. I'd have to guess Cissy was closer to three hundred pounds. And she was only my height, five four."

I motioned a whistle. "Now I really see what you mean."

"But I think her heart, at least where Brian was concerned, was equally large."

"What do you mean?"

"Last year sometime in March or April — 'tax season' Cissy called it — she came storming into the store. She demanded to see Roddy McKeague. He's our night manager. I heard her shout about stealing candy from babies, and something like watching Brian's paychecks from then on, so he wouldn't be ripped off again. That's when she started giving Brian rides to work as well."

"I met Roddy," I said without bothering to hide my contempt. "Didn't give me a good first impression."

Connie let her eyes dart around the parking lot, as if looking for the bogeyman or something. "Hush, Daisy. Even out here I gotta be careful."

"What do you mean?" I looked around. It was still the same parking lot with people coming and going into the strip center's stores.

"The grocery business is very competitive. We measure profits in pennies, not dollars. And even unimpressive people like Roddy gain power by tattling on other employees for unofficial giveaways and evidence of poor attitude. I think Roddy has high level friends he reports to."

"What about you and Brian? Do you not have friends in high places?"

Connie's shoulders slumped. "No. I don't know what I did, but I'm getting called on the carpet more and more. Somehow, Roddy's night work is making my team look like slouches. I don't know how he does it. Luckily, my shifts are still meeting sales quotas or I'd be axed."

"Ouch! And you think Roddy's behind all this?"

"I can't say. Wish I knew." She shook her head sadly, then looked around again and leaned toward me. "But I've said too much already. Even this bench has ears," she said, and got up as if we'd been sitting on a hot burner.

I rose and followed her. I clutched her arm and swung her around to face me. "Connie. You look like you've seen a ghost. Is there more to this Roddy? Dangerous maybe? Should I tell Gabe Caerphilly about him?"

"Shh! No!" Connie gulped and scoped out the parking lot again. Her glance rested on a handsome man in a business suit who was walking purposefully into Gigantos. "God, I gotta go." She made to break away.

"Wait, Connie. Tell me about Roddy. Is he the one making you so nervous?"

She shook her head and leaned in toward me again. She dropped her voice to almost a whisper. "Roddy is an arrogant little twerp. A real bully. I would have gotten rid of him long ago. But" — she looked back over her shoulder toward the store — "but he has very powerful, nasty friends. Be careful, Daisy. Leave Roddy alone."

Then Connie fled, leaving me more chilled than this bright Colorado spring day would normally warrant.

Suddenly, Art came to mind. I grabbed my locket and held onto my memories. Art whispered in my head, "Be careful, Daisy. Business can be pretty cut-throat at times."

CHAPTER 11

"I founded your doorbell," said Ginny as she marched across my threshold, passed by me, and settled into my living room.

"Hello to you too, Ginny," I said, closing my front door behind her. "What can I do for you? Does your dad know you're out and about?"

Ginny gave a shrug. "My daad is bein' a bad boy." She stomped her foot.

It was unusual to see Ginny in anything but a Gigantos golf shirt and the uniform burgundy colored pants. Today she looked more adult than I'd ever seen her, with her gold hair combed meticulously, and dark blue skirt suit to replace the grocery store uniform. Only her sneakers and over abundance of blue eye shadow above her almond shaped eyes disrupted the impression of a woman on a business mission.

"You look very serious today."

"I am. I am so serious, an' I am worried,

104

an' I want to see my boyfriend. I want to see Bri-Ann."

"Ginny, Brian is in jail."

"I know that, silly. But yesterday my daad was on the phone with Ms. Sergeant Linda Taylor, an' he said he talked to Bri-Ann, but Bri-Ann didn't say anything. If my daad can see Bri-Ann, I can too."

"I don't know, Ginny. Your dad doesn't want you visiting Brian."

"I don' care!" Ginny stamped her foot again. "My daad is bein' silly. Bri-Ann is a good guy. I love him an' I want to see him."

Made sense to me. Ginny had a right to choose her own friends, even if this one might end up in jail for a good long time. It would also be good for me to see Brian. There didn't seem to be any other adults in his life who might advocate for him.

"Let's check on visiting hours and rules." I led Ginny toward my office and computer to look them up.

At the jail, Ginny and I passed quickly through security, having left our purses in the car. Ginny only kept a stuffed bear with her, something she hoped to give to Brian. The bear was x-rayed and we passed through.

As we were led down a hall toward the

visitors' room we ran into Gabe, who was leaving at the same time.

"What are you two doing here?" He frowned at seeing us. Ginny folded her arms across her teddy bear and turned toward the wall. Gabe's voice dropped to a soft caress. "Still not talking to me, Ginny Bear?"

Ginny shook her head and refused to look at her dad.

"We came to visit Brian," I said.

"I thought I asked you" — he frowned — "both of you, to stay out of this case."

"You may have, Gabe. But neither Ginny nor I agreed that staying away from Brian was a good thing."

Gabe ran his fingers through his hair. "Daisy —"

"Gabe." I wasn't going to let him intimidate me. "Prison rules give Ginny and me under an hour to visit, so if you'll excuse us . . ."

"Wait." Gabe sighed. "I just came from seeing Brian. He won't talk. You're not going to get anything from him."

My turn to frown. "We aren't here to *get* anything. We're here to *give* him some support."

Gabe blew out a breath. "I see." He shrugged. "But if you can convince him to talk with me about what happened, it would

106

be helping him as much as me."

Ginny turned back toward her dad. "You want Bri-Ann in jail, Daad. It would not help my Bri-Ann to talk a you."

Gabe stared at his daughter, then turned to me. "Maybe I could listen while you and Brian talk? If he says something that could help his case, I could follow up on it."

"Go 'way, Daad. You a bad man. You 'rested my Bri-Ann. Go 'way."

I shrugged. "This is mostly Ginny's visit, Gabe." I didn't mention that he hadn't exactly shared information he'd taken off Cissy Melato's computer when we went to her apartment. I didn't mention that he had been bullying Ginny and me to keep out of "his" case since we found the body together a few nights earlier. And I definitely didn't mention that Ginny and Brian came to me for help, not him. I didn't mention those things, but they affected my own attitude about helping Gabe.

Gabe ran fingers through his hair again in frustration. "All right, you win," he said. I had the feeling as he glared at me that Ginny and I might have won the battle, but the war concerning Brian's freedom was far from over.

I turned to Gabe's daughter. "Let's go, Ginny. We don't have much time left to visit

Brian."

The visitors' room of the county jail was stark, almost cafeteria-like, with large cinder-block walls painted an antiseptic white, folding tables, and plastic benches. Guards wandered as close as possible without infringing on the privacy rights of the prisoners.

Brian was escorted in, wearing chains and an orange jumpsuit. His brown hair was matted, and his eyes were swollen, presumably from crying, but when he saw Ginny and me, he broke out in a wide grin and shuffled over as fast as his restraints and guard would allow.

"Ginny! Ginny, I love you. You camed to visit me. You are a good girl."

"Bri-Ann, you look awful," said Ginny. She whipped a comb out of her pocket and immediately went to care for Brian's hair.

The nearest guard stepped forward. "Hands off, Miss. Felony One criminals are not to have personal contact with visitors."

Ginny whirled on the guard. "Stop yellin' at us. Bri-Ann has messy hair. I comb his hair for him. He's a good guy."

The guard looked over Ginny and Brian, and then turned to me. "It's the rules, Ms. She has to keep her hands off."

"Officer," I said with as much sweetness as I could muster, "Ginny is Littleton police lieutenant Gabriel Caerphilly's daughter. I'm a special-needs teacher from Independence High. I think Ginny is truly intending only to comb Brian's hair."

I name-dropped and left off the retired part of my job description to add a little weight. Then I thought of something else. "You may listen to our conversation if you'd like."

The guard swept a glance around then nodded to us. "Two minutes with the hair. Be quick about it." Ginny went to work and had Brian appearing much better before the guard got back into our vicinity.

Brian sat across from us and smiled at Ginny. There was a short screen, like a ping-pong net, between the two or they would have held hands.

I leaned next to Ginny, so that Brian would have to see me too. "Brian, can I ask you some questions? Questions about what happened to Ms. Cissy?"

Brian's smile faded. Slowly, he turned toward me. "I sorry, My Daisy. I do not like a talk about Misses Sippy. She sleepin' in da baffroom and I got put in jail."

"Yes, Brian, I know. Are you okay in jail?"

"Yeah. They give me food an' they talk a

me lots. They gaveded me new clothes." He looked down. "Do you like my new clothes, Ginny?"

Ginny nodded. "You have orange. Now you look like a orange. I could gobble you." She laughed at her joke and Brian joined her.

Then he became serious again. He wriggled in his seat and his restraints jingled. "I do not like these handcuffs. I want to go home. I want to see Misses Sippy and Queenie and I want to go for a walk wiff you, Ginny. Pah."

I tried to stay calm, but it was hard to see this confused young man sitting before me. "Brian, do your mom and dad live near here? Would you like me to call them for you?"

"My mom an' my dad hadded 'nother car accident. They are in heaven. Mary Margaret said so."

"Another car accident? Mary Margaret?"

Brian nodded. "Like when I was a baby. M an' M is my sister. But she lives in Texas wiff Kyle. She loves Kyle. But Kyle doesn't wanna be wiff me. So I live by myself. An' my neighbor is Misses Sippy. An' M an' M calls me ever Saturday at nine o'clock if I am not workin'."

"Brian. Ms. Cissy is in heaven now too." I

said it as matter-of-factly as possible. Brian and Ginny stared at me.

Ginny moved first. "Is Brian in jail 'cause Misses Sippy is in heaven?"

"I'm afraid so."

"I no like heaven," said Brian. "People go there an' they forget, an' they don' come home no more. Why did Misses Sippy have to go to heaven?"

"She went to heaven, dear, when someone put a knife in her tummy."

Brian nodded. "The knife was really sharp. Misses Sippy wasn't careful wiff da knife an' she gotted poked."

"Brian" — goodness, I didn't want to ask this — "Brian, did *you* poke Misses Sippy?"

"No, My Daisy. Misses Sippy poked herself. I took da knife away."

"If Ginny and I listen very carefully, will you tell us what happened?"

"I do not like to fink about what I saw." Brian rubbed his eyes. No wonder they were sore. He was probably trying to rub out the memories.

"The floor was all sticky an' messy an' red. It smelled worse dan da meat cut room. The red was on the walls too. I started to clean up da mess.

"Den I saw two feet sticking out from the toilet room. I saw da shoes. I saw Misses

Sippy's shoes. 'Misses Sippy?' I said. 'Can I come in?' She did not answer, but da door was not closed all the way, so I pushed it open."

Brian stopped to rub his eyes again.

I leaned as close as the visitor screen would allow. "You're doing a good job, Brian. I know it's scary to remember, but this is important. What else did you see?"

Brian looked at Ginny. "I want to go home, Ginny Bear. I wanna go home." He started crying.

Ginny started crying too. "I want to take you home, Bri-Ann. You a good guy. But you is in jail."

"Please, Brian," I said. "Please tell me what you saw in the bathroom."

The guard was looking in our direction. He would not let us stay much longer, I was sure of it. I grabbed two tissues from my pocket and waved them so the guard could see. He nodded and I handed them to Ginny and Brian.

Brian blew his nose and handed me back the tissue. "There was red stuff everwhere," he said. "It was on da walls. It was on da toilet. It was on Misses Sippy. She was layin' on da floor, an' her head was on its side. Her eyes did not move. I called her and I said, 'You cannot sleep here,' but she would

112

not waked up. I took da knife out of her so she wouldn't hurt when she waked up."

So it truly was Brian who held the knife the night he was arrested. "Then what happened, Brian?"

Brian squeezed his eyes shut to concentrate. "I ranned outta da baffroom, but the store lights was off. Roddy musta forgot I was still cleaning da baffrooms. I ran outta da store. I used my cell telephone an' I called Ginny."

Ginny looked earnestly at me. "I tol' Bri-Ann to take a bus to your house. I tol' him what bus number, and I got him from the stop. Then we camed to your house, My Daisy."

I believed them. In my heart, I knew Brian didn't commit this murder. The problem was, how were we to convince Gabe and, more importantly, a judge and jury?

The guard came over. "Time's up, Mr. Hughes," he said and helped Brian to his feet.

"I want to go home!" cried Brian. "I don' like jail no more." He began to struggle.

"Be nice, Bri-Ann," said Ginny. "Be nice and calm. My Daisy will find a way for you to come home soon. Den I will hug you and kiss you. I love you." She gave Brian the teddy bear. "Here. You hold my teddy bear

113

and you will be oh-kay."

Brian calmed immediately. Ginny's magic worked again.

"I love you, Ginny," said Brian, and then he was gone.

Ginny sighed. It was the saddest sound I had ever heard from my friend. It was the sound she made when she told me that her mom had left and her dad was so sad. That was ten years ago, when she was a freshman at Independence. I put my arm around Ginny and we walked out.

On the steps as we left, I heard a woman arguing with one of the guards. What a sad place a jail is.

"What do you mean, Mr. Hughes has had all the visitors allowed for today? I'm his court-appointed lawyer, and I found out about this case only about an hour ago. I need to see him, *now.*"

Mr. Hughes? Brian?

I looked more closely at the woman. She was young, dressed in a brown pants suit and had papers trying to escape her grasp. The briefcase at her side was open and more clutter seemed to be popping out from it like popcorn.

The guard at the door remained firm. "Visitor hours are coming to an end, and you're not on the list of approved visitors yet anyway. We're open tomorrow, too. Come back then. He'll still be here."

"Great," snapped the woman. "There goes another Saturday off. I'll remember this" — she leaned in to read the guard's tag — "Stubbins."

Stubbins smiled at her. "I'm sure you will. Have a nice day." He turned on his heel and walked back inside.

The lawyer put down her briefcase and began shoving her extra papers into it. She muttered about getting stuck with loser cases, late assignments, and damned guards.

I leaned over to Ginny. "Can you wait here a minute, Ginny? I want to meet that woman."

"Okay, My Daisy," said Ginny. "But hurry. I need to go to da baffroom."

"Okay, sweet girl." I winked at her and stepped over to the young woman, who looked like she finally had her papers in order.

"Excuse me," I said, "but I couldn't help over hearing you. Are you, by chance, Brian Hughes's lawyer?"

"Yes," she said on a scowl. "Who are you?"

I explained Ginny's and my relationship to Brian, and that Ginny's dad was the arresting officer in this case.

"I'm Heather Dunlap." She offered her

hand and the shake was much firmer than I would have expected. I winced.

"Sorry," she said. "Been practicing my handshake so I don't come across as wimpy."

"How long have you been practicing law?" I asked.

She bit her lip, weighing whether to tell me the truth, no doubt. "Long enough."

"Right out of school, then." I didn't make it a question.

"Depends what you mean by 'right out of school.' " Then she smiled. "Okay. I'm a newbie. That's why they gave me this case. Said it was open and shut. Mr. Hughes knifed Ms. Melato, plain and simple."

"Not so simple. Developmentally delayed people need special care. They're at a disadvantage in our court system as is. You have to be more involved than just open and shut."

"No. All I have to do is make sure he looks decent at his trial and try to get life for him."

"Get life? That's not acceptable."

"As a special-needs man, Mr. Hughes may not have had a premeditated plan to mutilate the body so badly. Getting him life should be pretty easy."

"Wait! Open and shut? No question he did this? You're his lawyer. You're supposed to defend him."

"And I will. Like I said, I'll get him life." She began fidgeting with her briefcase and papers again.

"Life? And the alternative?" I couldn't believe Ms. Dunlap could be so casual about Brian's future. Maybe she didn't know how young he was.

She turned on my tone of voice and stared at me a full minute. "Colorado has the death penalty for such heinous crimes, Ms. Arthur. Mr. Hughes will be lucky if I get him life."

My stomach dropped. I glanced over at Ginny, who smiled and waved at me. She was hopping up and down. She needed a bathroom. Now I did too.

Chapter 12

The computer screen glared at me with a blankness I couldn't ignore. My novel about the office manager/part-time artist had hit a wall.

"Ruth," I said to the screen, "show yourself. Who are you? Why do you love that man? He's a slob. You're nice and neat. He's dominating. You need your space. Are you really in love or only in lust with this guy?"

I sat in silence for a couple more minutes, but then Georgette came dashing into my office and heaved her bulk to my desktop by way of the empty guest chair. She turned and arched as much as a lazy old cat can toward the empty space flowing through my office door, until Queenie came trotting in.

Georgette hissed. Queenie barked in a that's-not-fair accusatory way. Whoever made up the expression *fighting like cats and dogs* was right on target as far as I was concerned.

I rubbed my face and scolded my charges. "Will you two leave me in peace for five minutes? I'm trying to write here!"

Georgette dashed off, Queenie on her trail. Soon there was a crashing sound in the kitchen.

I rolled my eyes and blew out a breath before going to see what the latest disaster could be.

In the kitchen, Georgette had managed to knock my plate of freshly baked oatmeal cookies onto the floor. Apparently, Queenie thought this was a good thing as she grabbed a cookie and ran to her kennel. Georgette was attempting to continue her aerial attack by pushing a saltshaker toward the edge of the counter.

"No you don't, Ms. Spoiled Brat," I said, and scooped her up off the ledge. I dumped her plump body in the direction of the mudroom and her litter box, and then turned to clean up the mess.

After four long days and three sleepless nights steeped in murder, my nerves were on edge. I needed to get out of the house and calm down. But it wasn't anywhere near mealtime and I didn't much feel like shopping when anything I bought was likely to come under attack from my pets.

While I was picking up the cookie and

broken plate mess, I heard Thunder bark next door. He must have found another squirrel running along the top of his fence. Poor Thunder. Such a good dog, compared to Queenie. He probably needed a walk.

That gave me an idea. I put the dustpan away and found my phone to call my dog-walking friend, Sam.

Sam and I met at the park behind Aspen Grove when Thunder was still less than a year old. He and his golden retriever, Rocky, taught me about dogs and their care, and we four often took walks together. Sam encouraged me to buy a pass to Chatfield State Park. It was worth every penny, as the park had over seventy acres of off-leash area that let Thunder roam and sniff at will, and I got plenty of exercise walking the paths.

"You bringing the Corgi?" asked Sam.

I loved his slight western twang. It made me feel like I was in a John Wayne western. "I don't think so, Sam."

"Might wear her out a bit, you know."

"You're right, of course, but I don't think I can handle two dogs today. Think I'll stick with Thunder this time."

"Your call. See you at Chatfield."

Thunder tumbled out of my car and strained at the leash until we were safely behind the fence at the off-leash dog park. In less than five minutes, he had finished his poo business and was barking and hopping back at the gate. A white pick-up drove into the lot and Sam got out, Rocky in a perfect heel, as usual, at Sam's side. Inwardly I laughed at the notion that the first time we'd met I thought Sam was just an old geezer. Today, he had his usual plaid flannel jacket thrown over cargo pants, but I could see that he walked with the energy of a much younger man, and his white hair was still thicker than a lot of those twenty years his junior. Thicker, even, than Gabe's.

Thunder wagged his tail profusely.

I laughed. "Thunder misses Rocky, I think."

Sam smiled and came in with his dog. The click of the leash being unsnapped from Rocky's collar must have been some sort of starting gun, as the two dogs took off at a run. I couldn't help staring at their graceful gallops, paws hardly touching the ground. It was like watching the world's fastest ballet.

"They sure are beautiful," I said to Sam. He smiled.

We walked for about fifteen minutes in silence, and then I couldn't stand any more.

"Sam, you seem to have something on

your mind."

"Sorry, Daisy. Only the stuff of life, I suppose."

"Are you okay?"

"Me? Couldn't be better." He smiled, but the grin faded as quickly as it came.

"Hello. Sam? Friend here. What's going on?"

Sam gazed for a long moment after the dogs. They had stopped and were sniffing at the weeds together. A strange dog came up and Thunder barked at it. That was odd. Thunder liked all other dogs. The intruder backed away, then trotted off to find its master.

As Thunder returned to his friend, I noticed Rocky had acquired a slight hobble.

"Looks like Rocky might have a thorn there, Sam." I started walking toward the two dogs.

"Stop, Daisy. It's okay." Sam's voice was quiet, resigned.

"Sam?" I looked at my friend. Over the months we'd been walking dogs together, I came to see the warmth in his personality, and the lines etched on his face were nothing more than memories of the laughter we often shared. I don't know how I could ever have thought of Sam as old. Sure, he had bushy eyebrows, but the warmth and sparkle of his brown eyes beneath said there was plenty of life left in my friend.

I looked harder at Sam. "Please, tell me what's wrong."

Sam dug his hands deep into his pockets and looked down. "Took Rocky to the vet this morning. He's been off his food a bit, and hobbling like a much older dog than he is. Had to confirm what I've suspected for a while."

"And?"

"Cancer. Inoperable."

The spring air took on a sudden chill for me. I stared at Sam, bereft of words. My chest heaved, but I couldn't breathe. "How long?" I whispered.

"I've seen this kind of thing before. Dogs can go very quickly when they start showing signs." His eyes watered, and suddenly Sam looked small and frail for all his height over me, and his rugged persona.

I grabbed him in a big hug. I wished with all my heart for some miracle. A misdiagnosis. A recovery as sudden and complete as a summer thunderstorm gone by.

Tears welled in my own eyes. "Oh, Sam. I'm so very sorry!"

Sam hugged me back. I felt the rocking of his shoulders against my face and looked up. Tears flowed down his cheeks. He tried to pull away, but I put a hand to the side of his cheek, brushed a tear away with my thumb. He was so warm.

Sam stilled, holding me in his gaze. The wind picked up and blew my hair, but I hardly noticed as I stood in the middle of Chatfield's open range, hugging and being hugged by my friend.

Sam drew his face closer to mine, hesitated a heartbeat, and then kissed me. I closed my eyes and kissed him back. His lips were gentle, surprisingly soft at first, and then the urgency of his grief and the excitement of the moment took over.

I swam in the luxury of a man's embrace, the scent of his aftershave, the warmth of his body. I hadn't felt this kind of willingness to surrender to the moment since —

Gabe!

Goodness, what was I thinking?

I pulled back from Sam, and at that moment Thunder jumped on us, knocking us to the ground. Rocky sat nearby, a silly dog grin on his face. Thunder growled at us.

"Down, boy," said Sam. He rolled over, then stood and helped me up. Thunder sat and put a paw on Sam's thigh.

Sam chuckled. "You're right, Thunder, ol' boy. I forgot myself."

He turned to me. "Looks like you have a

good chaperone." He smiled again.

"Darn it." I grinned and gazed playfully at Sam before remembering I was Gabriel Caerphilly's girlfriend — almost girlfriend, almost lover. Hmm.

I had stopped blushing when menopause stole my hormones, but every feeling was still there, right under the surface of my skin. Sam and I stood, and looked about the park awkwardly for a few moments.

He cleared his throat. "We'd best be going, Rocky and me." He leaned down and clipped the leash on his dog. "Heel." Sam walked away.

I didn't follow. Just when I least wanted to, I had to think.

Think Caerphilly.

CHAPTER 13

Chip gave me the obligatory peck on a cheek as he and Kitty made their way in my back door. Kitty stopped to give me a hug.

"I love our Sunday Chinese food nights," she said with enthusiasm.

This evening my pixie-sized friend was a radiant vision of teal and gold, with a hand-painted t-shirt and dark pants. She had a gold spring sweater casually draped over her delicate shoulders, and, with her large hoop earrings, the outfit was dazzling.

"Kitty, you look gorgeous, as always," I said. "If you ever give up your bartending, I think the fashion industry could use your panache."

Kitty giggled and Chip came back to put an arm possessively around his girlfriend. As they smiled at me, I felt a wash of contentment flow through my heart. In a crazy world, Chip and Kitty made a good, old-fashioned heaven-inspired match.

"Did you order, Ms. D.?" said Chip. "I'm starving."

I laughed. "When aren't you starving, my friend? And yes, delivery is on the way."

We wandered into the living room and sat. I had replaced Art's old man-chair with a soft new rocker, and sat in that as Kitty and Chip found places on my sofa.

"So what game do we play tonight?" asked Kitty.

"How about Boggle?" I answered, reaching for a box from the stack of games I had brought out earlier.

"I love that game," said Chip. "You ladies better watch out. I'm a wizard at words."

Kitty took up the challenge. "You forget you have two writers to play against." She waggled a finger at him.

"I think I can handle you two. After all, I'm the published newspaper man here." He wiggled his eyebrows in a teasing response.

I rolled my eyes. "Let's put our words where our cubes are."

We pulled out the contents of the game — pads of paper for tracking words, timer, pencils, and the cubes of letters.

Chip shook the box of wooden blocks. The rumbling sound of game pieces echoed around the room with Chip's enthusiastic shaking.

Queenie came running and barking from the kitchen. She yapped at Chip and nipped his ankle.

"Ow! Ms. D., you need to train this mutt!"

"Sorry, Chip." I leaned over to grab Queenie, but she shied away. Chip moved in at the same time and our elbows bumped each other.

Kitty shouted, "Watch out!" a split second too late. Chip's hand flew up and dropped the Boggle container. Letter blocks flew out in all directions.

With the rattle that only sixteen cubes falling over furniture and a wood floor can make, our quiet game became the starting gun for mayhem. Queenie went into a yapping frenzy. Georgette dashed into the room as fast as her feline heft would allow, took a look, and made a swipe at the dog. Sodas spilt, papers got soaked, and there was instant mess everywhere.

Kitty ran toward the kitchen. "I'll get a cloth."

"I'll get the dog out of here," I replied. "If Queenie goes, I think Georgette will follow." I ran after my charge and put her in her kennel in the kitchen. Georgette had disappeared, presumably to my room and under my bed.

"I have the game pieces," said Chip, scrambling on hands and knees for the blocks under the coffee table.

The doorbell rang. Dinner. I stepped through the dining room and grabbed my purse as I went to pay for the food.

When I returned, both Chip and Kitty were kneeling on the floor.

"Searching for something, or are we inventing a new game here?" I asked.

"Chip's lost one of the cubes," said Kitty.

"Aw, Chip, couldn't you find a better way to throw the game?" I said. "Is it near the window?"

"Very funny, Ms. D. Your new dog is at the heart of this fiasco."

"I'll put our sweet and sour in the oven until we're ready to eat." Life with Chip was never dull, that was for sure.

In the kitchen, I stood up from putting the cartons of food in the oven, and saw Queenie hunched over, wheezing and making regurgitating sounds from her round little belly. My goodness! I'd never seen her look so stressed. What should I do? I thought of Chip. He had more dog experience than me.

"Chip!" I called. "Chip, I think Queenie's got something wrong with her. Help!"

Chip and Kitty came running. Queenie

kept heaving and gasping.

"Sounds like she's got something stuck," said Chip. "Not much you can do but pry open her jaws and fish it out."

"Eew. Really?" I said. "Won't it come out by itself?"

"She sounds pretty bad," said Kitty.

"I'll hold her for you, Ms. D.," said Chip, "but you have to pry her mouth and get out whatever she's swallowed."

"Okay, but wait a minute." I opened a drawer and pulled out my rubber gloves. With rubber gloves, I could touch anything. Just in case, I grabbed a spoon.

Queenie frantically wriggled in Chip's arms.

"Hurry," he said. "She's too stressed. Could hurt herself. No, no. You can't use the spoon to open her mouth. Here." He handed Queenie to Kitty, who held the dog with calm but firm arms. Then he put one hand around the top of Queenie's muzzle and used his other hand to push the front of her mouth and lower jaw open.

I stood there, rubber gloved but useless.

Chip dug his hand down Queenie's throat and pulled out a small object. Kitty put the dog down. Queenie promptly vomited on the floor and hobbled off to her kennel. "Good dog," said Kitty, but she backed away and crinkled her nose at the slop.

"At least I know how to clean up here," I said, reaching into a cupboard for the large box of baking soda. I sprinkled a generous amount of the powder over Queenie's vomit and turned to Chip. "What did she eat?"

He held up half of a game block. "Apparently, she likes wooden cubes in her diet."

"No," I said. "The remains of that cube show a definite *W. W* is for Woof. I think she likes to eat her own words."

Chip and Kitty groaned.

I cleaned the doggie mess while Kitty and Chip set the table for dinner. As we sat down to our pork ribs and sweet and sour chicken, Kitty said, "By the way, Daisy, I might not make it to Tuesday's critique."

"Darn! I was going to ask you to lead the session for me. I'm attending a funeral earlier in the day and think I might not be focused on our work."

"Funeral?" Both Chip and Kitty said it together. Chip took over from there.

"Someone close to you die, old girl? I'm sorry to hear that. Can we help?"

"Not someone close to me, Chip. It's Cissy Melato's funeral. Queenie's caregiver."

"But you never met her," said Kitty. "Why

would you go to her funeral?"

I shrugged and looked down.

"What was that?" said Chip, leaning toward me. "You're looking for something there? Did you say *suspects*?"

"Oh, no, Daisy," said Kitty. She shook her head, and her hoop earrings waved about her shoulders. "You're not playing at detective again, are you? You know you got in over your head last time."

"Ginny's boyfriend is in trouble," I said and looked at each of my young friends. "Gabe's railroaded the poor guy into the role of a villain. Even arrested him."

"So?" Chip joined Kitty in shaking his head, and then took a bite of rib.

"So, I think Gabe's fingering Brian because this young man is in love with Ginny. I think that's blocking Gabe's ability to be fair."

Kitty wiped her mouth. "What evidence does he have against Brian?"

I told my friends what I knew.

"It sounds bad," said Chip.

"Blood on the knife that fell from Brian's sleeve —" joined in Kitty. Then they pelted me ping-pong fashion with thoughts.

"Blood all over his shirt —" said Chip.

"Bad tempers make for good suspects —" said Kitty.

"Crime of passion —"

"Means and opportunity, for sure."

I jumped in. "But no real motive. Ginny told me Brian and Cissy never fought."

"Never fought that she knows of," said Chip. "Pass the water, will you?"

"I think you should stick with your romance writing, Daisy," said Kitty, handing the pitcher to Chip. "This really sounds like an open and shut case. I'm sure everything will work out fine in the end."

"And if it doesn't?" I asked. "If Brian is convicted, he could end up in jail for the rest of his life. He's your age. Maybe younger. Could you handle being in jail for the rest of your life?"

"That's not likely to happen," said Chip. "They'll take into consideration that Brian is a special-needs guy."

"If they do, he might get life. If they don't, Brian could get the death penalty."

"That's awful!" said Kitty. "What can we do?"

I looked hard at my friend. "We can solve this crime and make sure Brian is *not* convicted. I'm going to that funeral and plan to watch my suspects. At least see if there are any new suspects there. That's why I need you to step in for me Tuesday."

"Daisy, I wish I could. I promised my

mom to help with a political caucus Tuesday evening." Kitty looked down in concentration, then her head snapped up and she beamed at me. "I know! You could ask Dan Block to step in for you."

"Dan Block!" I didn't mean to let his name slip out with such obvious revulsion.

"You don't like Dan?" said Kitty.

"No." I shook my head, ashamed at myself. "He gives me the creeps. He's too — too — perfect. Know what I mean?"

"That sounds weak, Daisy," said Kitty.

"What is it?" said Chip. "Why exactly don't you like this Dan guy?"

I hung my head. "He makes me feel like I'm starting all over as a writer. A real newbie. I thought I was making progress, and now he comes along with his slash marks on my papers and his constant harping on trimming words, and I want to scream. Dan is harder on me than even Eleanor Rapp was when I first started."

"He is difficult," said Kitty, "but I'm learning so much from him." She turned to Chip. "Dan joined us at the beginning of the year. He writes like Ernest Hemmingway, and I think has had a couple of short stories published. He's also quite handsome and really nice."

Chip raised his eyebrows. "I didn't need

to hear that last part, miss flirty pixie."

Kitty giggled. "Have to keep you on your toes. Can't be taking me for granted. But Dan has to be six five if he's an inch. I like my men more eye to eye level. You're the one I want."

She looked at Chip with such a burning gaze that I knew dinner and our Sunday night party would end soon. Then I would make a list of suspects from Cissy's address book and from what I could remember of her calendar. I wished Gabe had let me have a longer look at that.

CHAPTER 14

Monday morning I woke with a sense of purpose. Brian had spent the weekend in jail, and if I didn't step in, he was likely to remain there. Ginny would lose her boyfriend, Brian his freedom, and Gabe would lose the close relationship he had with Ginny. So very much was at stake. But what could I do?

In my creative writing, I started a spiral notebook for each of my big writing projects. Read about how to do that in my growing collection of writers' books. Perhaps this strategy would work for helping on the Cissy Melato murder investigation. Grabbing a new notebook, I wrote "The Case of the Sliced Vegetarian" across the front. Connie had said Cissy was a vegetarian, and that sounded more interesting than "The Case of the Knifed CPA."

If this situation were a novel, I would begin the first page with a list of potential characters. As today I was working on solving a crime, I decided to start with a list of suspects and persons of interest, or POIs, in my notes.

I thought about the crime scene. Whose face came to mind?

Brian's.

Brian was the one who looked most like a suspect, acted most uncontrollably, and knew the victim. My heart sank as I wrote his name down: POI — Brian Hughes.

I wanted to scratch that name right out, but Gabe was convinced that Brian murdered Cissy, so I couldn't act on blind faith alone that Ginny's friend didn't.

The next name was easy — Roddy McKeague.

That guy really irked me. It felt good to write his name in block capitals. Sometimes writing by hand as opposed to typing on my computer felt as satisfying as dining at an all-you-can-eat buffet.

Now, what did Kitty always rattle on about in writing her romantic mysteries — *means, motive, and opportunity*? I'd have to investigate that with my list of suspects — my list with only two names on it.

There had to be more suspects. What would Gabe do if he didn't think Brian killed Cissy?

He would start with finding out about the victim's life. He'd go to Cissy's house to see whom else she knew. Of course! I turned to another page and jotted down "Cissy Melato" and what little I'd learned about her.

Gabe might have put Brian in jail, but he was a good cop. He did go to Cissy's. How could I have been so foolish as to think he wouldn't properly investigate?

Filled with happiness about my special police officer, I picked up the phone and dialed his office. On the third ring, a woman picked up the phone. She had the breathless response of someone who was in the midst of a good laugh.

"Lieutenant Caerphilly's office, Sergeant Taylor speaking."

Why could I never stop feeling like That Woman was trouble for me? She was a nice enough person. She wrote stories that were as amateur as my own. She wasn't perfect.

But when working, I knew Linda was as much in her element as Gabe. Maybe they seemed like such a matched set, my jealous antennae naturally jumped into overdrive.

"Hi, Linda. Daisy here." Enthusiasm eluded me. "Is Gabe free?"

The laughter died from Linda's voice. "Hi, Daisy. I'll check."

A moment later Gabe was on the line.

"Hello, Daisy." Gabe's voice held a melodic baritone level, which thrilled and calmed me all at once. Even if he read the telephone directory to me, I would be enthralled with every syllable. I waited for more, but Gabe was in the office and would be all business.

"Oh! Sorry," I said, shaking myself out of the drug-like trance Gabe's voice sent me into. "Gabe, I was thinking about you and wondered if you'd like to go to lunch together?"

There was a pause, just long enough for me to wonder if Linda were listening in on this conversation. Suddenly, I felt like I shouldn't have called.

"Sorry, Daisy," said Gabe. "I have a lot on my plate today. Probably working through lunch."

"I understand." I couldn't help the disappointment that crept into my voice.

"But I'll still see you Wednesday for dinner, right?" he said.

"Right." I smiled.

"Was there something you wanted that can't wait till then?"

"No. Simply wanted to say I think you're a great police officer, and I believe in you."

Another awkward silence, then, "Thanks. Gotta go."

Gabe hung up without waiting for me to finish. When he cut me off like that, I felt like I'd been stabbed with an icicle. It dug to the bone, and melted so no one else would see the hurt.

I remembered Art was sometimes abrupt when I called him at the office, but somehow we always ended our conversations with proper good-byes. I reminded myself that no two people are exactly alike, and more and more, people hung up on each other without the old fashioned, time-wasting good-bye nonsense.

I heaved a sigh and looked down. At my feet sat Queenie, with one of my slippers in her mouth. "Monster!" I cried, and she jumped back out of reach.

I couldn't help it. Her back end was wagging mightily. She was inviting me to play. I laughed and said I would get her, and then spent a couple of minutes chasing her around my house.

If Gabe had seen me, he probably wouldn't have been impressed, but Gabe wasn't there, and I was having fun. After wearing ourselves out completely, which took all of two minutes, I slumped on my couch. Queenie jumped up beside me. She dropped the slipper into my lap. Its pink fur was matted with dog slime and looked like an overly slobbery, but much loved, Easter bunny. Eww. I picked the slipper up with one finger and a thumb tip and quietly dropped it out of sight so that Queenie could snuggle into my lap for a nice chat.

I scratched behind my dog's ears. "So, woman to woman — er — woman to dog, Queenie, what do you think I should do about Gabe? Do you think he loves me?"

Queenie sat staring at me with her glossy round eyes as if to say, "Not sure what you mean, but go on."

So I did. I told her how Gabe and I had been dating off and on — mostly off — since last fall and that, while I still thrilled to his kisses, we really hadn't become serious in our relationship. I said that sometimes he made me feel like there was no one else in the world for him, but then, like an older version of Chip, he'd ask me for a favor instead of for a commitment.

Queenie blew out her breath as only a dog can do. She let her head flop on my lap, so I stroked her shoulders and went on a while more.

"You know what I think is worst, Queenie? I think Gabe doesn't respect my life skills. I mean, maybe I haven't been published, but I do write. And I am getting better. And I'm a good detective, with all the mysteries

I read, even if I'm not a police officer, or even a private eye —" I stopped mid-thought.

"Wait a minute. Private eye! I can be a sleuth and too busy for lunch as well. Queenie, where did I put Cissy's address book? I'll bet it has more suspects than Brian and that creepster, Roddy. I can go figure things out this morning. Bet I'll solve this murder before Gabe gets out of the office."

That thought made me smile and I puffed up my chest. Queenie yapped and jumped back. I found my purse and rifled through to the address book — the book Gabe didn't know about. I grabbed my spiral with "Sliced Vegetarian" written across it and sat with both it and the address book at my kitchen table.

Queenie wandered off in search, no doubt, of interrupting Georgette's beauty sleep.

I flipped to a fresh sheet of paper and wrote across the top: *What Were Cissy's Last Appointments?*

I squeezed my eyes shut in concentration. What had Gabe said at Cissy's? What did I see on her computer screen?

There had been a single name typed in for Tuesday night, the night Cissy died. What was that name? Regina? Rosalyn? No.

I flipped through the address book. No luck. I'd have to remember that name. I wrote an R on the appointment page, and searched my brain for other appointments.

I remembered Gabe saying someone was interesting. Last name the same as a mob family in Denver. Started with an "S." I flipped through Cissy's address book again.

Smaldone! That was the name. Joe Smaldone. I wrote down his contact information, and dove back into Cissy's address book.

I didn't find much there, but Cissy had been organized enough to indicate "client" from "friend/family" with appropriate "c's" and "f's" after the names. Interesting, Joe Smaldone had both a "c" and an "f." *Client and friend? Was he perhaps a secret lover? Very interesting.*

No doubt about it. I, Daisy Arthur, was a good detective, and I'd solve this case in no time. Ha!

I found a Dr. Mobley and R.J. with the "f" indicator erased and drawn in a couple of times over, then crossed out. Interesting. I'd have to remember that. I also remembered at least Dr. Mobley had been on the appointment list. It was time to do some interviewing.

■ ■ ■ ■

The doctor's office had a waiting room filled with the usual array of people and worn-out magazines. The patients leaned in toward each other, only to start coughing and wheezing. I tried to control the shiver that went through me. Too many germs here for my comfort. Would it be impolite to dig a hanky out of my purse and cover my nose?

A woman with apathetic efficiency written in every move she made greeted me. She hardly looked up from her reception desk as she shoved a clipboard in my direction.

"Insurance?" said the receptionist.

"I'm not here for an appointment."

The woman looked up. Had I discombobulated her routine? She gazed over the rim of her reading glasses and raised an accusatory eyebrow. "Oh?"

"I'd like to talk with Dr. Mobley" — I looked around the waiting room — "if he has a moment between patients."

"Dr. Mobley is very busy, Ms. . . . ?"

"Arthur. Daisy Arthur."

"Ms. Arthur. May I tell him what this is about?"

"One of his patients. Cissy Melato."

The receptionist gave me a funny look.

"Really? I thought he just spoke with — never mind. I'll see if he has more time."

She got up and walked behind a sign that said, "Good Health Starts With Good Care. Eat Well." It had pictures of fruits and vegetables arranged in a wreath around the border, as if by looking at the picture I wouldn't be inspired to jump up and go out to grab a steak for lunch.

Ten minutes later, the doctor came out. He was a young man with premature grey appearing at his temples, a pleasant but not overly attractive face, and an expression that said I'd better not be wasting his time.

"Ms. Arthur." The doctor reached out to shake hands. "I'm Peter Mobley. Anita said you have more questions about Cissy Melato?"

More questions? Had either Linda or Gabe beaten me to this witness? Apparently, the doctor was assuming I worked with the police. Should I tell him otherwise?

"Thank you for breaking into your day once more," I said. Why bother the doctor with unnecessary details? "Yes. I've only a few items to ask about."

We walked into the examination area. Several nurses worked at a large workstation encircled by small examination rooms for the orderly flow of patients. Dr. Mobley

145

stepped over to one of the nurses and let her know he was running a couple of minutes late. The comment was for my benefit, as the nurse looked towards me.

The doctor and I stepped to a counter-lined corner a little out of the way.

"Welcome to my office." He smiled apologetically. "When I was in med school, they said things had changed since my dad's days."

I returned his smile. "One thing remains. Doctors really do care for their patients. Looks like you work hard around here."

"I do work hard. And I care. But with the number of patients I have to see every day, I'm afraid I won't be much help in your investigation. I had Ms. Melato's records pulled when I spoke with your colleague on the phone earlier." The doctor flipped open a brown folder. "I was going to review this after work tonight. There isn't more on her chart than I told him. Patient was a fifty-eight-year-old woman, obese, borderline diabetic with potential heart problems."

"So, Ms. Melato would have had to come in often to visit? Maybe took medicines for her cholesterol?"

The doctor shook his head, still flipping through Cissy's chart. A small note card fell from the file. He bent to pick it up, then smiled.

"Ah," he said. "Now I remember. Cissy. Of course."

I smiled back at him once more.

"This helps me remember." He showed me the note card. It was a standard thank-you, the kind I used to receive on teacher appreciation day.

Inside the note said, "You trim my fat, I'll trim your balance sheet expenses. Your favorite CPA, Cissy Melato."

I looked at the doctor.

"Cissy was trying to get our business. Said she wanted some of the money back we supposedly stole from her with all of her visits." He smiled again and shook his head. "She was quite a character. I'll miss her."

"Can you tell me more about her?"

"She was very bright, except where it came to her weight control. With the weight, she said she was going to become a vegetarian, but her definition and diet were nothing like what healthy vegetarians eat."

I remembered seeing bags of potato chips and boxes of cookies in Cissy's cupboards as I searched for Queenie's dog food. The doctor continued.

"She could see at a glance where a small adjustment would save us a lot of expense, but make the same kind of adjustments to save her own health? It was a real block for her. Personally, I think she was in denial about her weight problem."

"How heavy was she?"

"Says here one hundred and sixty-five over what is considered healthy. And growing." He looked at his notes once more, as if by doing so, he could recall the patient better.

"Is there anything else you can tell me?" I asked.

"Your colleague said Cissy was murdered. I'm not a police officer, but if this were my case, I'd look at business associates and clients. These days, more businesses are run by the balance sheet and not by the service provided. If Cissy found something wrong in any accounting — and knowing her, she would have — Cissy would pounce on the error and not give up until it was resolved. Not afraid of confrontation. Except, of course, with her eating habits."

"Thank you, Dr. Mobley. You've been a big help."

We shook hands and I left. I needed to think things over. Cissy was a borderline diabetic with diet issues. She'd befriended Brian — perhaps because of his work around food? She had several contacts marked with "c" in her address book. I thought that "c" indicated "clients." Dr. Mobley and my memory of Art said business could be cut-throat. Had someone interpreted that phrase literally? And all this talk with Dr. Mobley about food and diet made me hungry. Perhaps Gabe was too busy for lunch, but I certainly wasn't. I could sense my "Sliced Vegetarian" notebook filling up over a good meal. Now, where to eat?

CHAPTER 15

I grabbed a bite at Alexio's Greek Food, a little place on Main Street where the local business folk and serious shoppers ate. Gabe and I were regulars there. Two brothers ran the place and flirted outrageously with all the women.

"Allo, Dahling," said the brother with the neat goatee and dark, penetrating stare. "What can I get for you today?"

The cheeky side of me played in my brain. I wondered what that man would say if I took him seriously and responded, "Hello, Lover, I'll take one of you smooshed into a snug round pita with a little tzatziki sauce on the side." Probably scare the heck out of him.

Instead, I glanced up to the chalkboard menu and ordered a gyro with lemonade. Not too cheeky, but it got the job done. I was no more likely to make an impression on the Greek brothers than on Dr. Mobley, who would have to pull out more than a file to recall me, if I'd been his patient.

I grabbed a seat in one of the corner tables and whipped out my spiral to jot down impressions from my chat with the doctor. Then I started to plan out my next suspect interview.

Tables at Alexio's were pushed strategically close together, remarkably like the cafés in Europe. These round-topped stands soaked up all the Littleton gossip with the discretion of a monk. Sitting here, I could learn all sorts of interesting personal news.

". . . So I told him he could just take his Porsche and drive off into the sunset for all I cared" ". . . We can move this copy to the left column to make more room for the logo down there" ". . . Did you see the sale on at Sugar Rush? I'll have to go to Yoga twice this week for sure . . ."

In a way, the chatter felt like a shower of civilization washing over my thoughts. I wasn't noticed, and life rushed on about me. Private and yet a part of it all, I was comfortable.

Then I thought of Brian. The gossip around me seemed shallow and self-centered. Didn't anybody know or care about the injustice of that boy-man being

151

held in jail for something he probably didn't do?

I jotted a question at the top of a fresh page: *Who is Brian Hughes and how do I know he didn't kill Cissy Melato?* Then I began to dump any ideas that came to mind.

Thoughts flooded out onto my paper, but mostly they were questions rather than statements. Why did I feel so strongly Brian didn't kill that woman in the store? Why was an overweight vegetarian and CPA killed in a grocery store bathroom? Who would name their kid "Cissy?"

I glanced up from my writing to see a couple at the counter ordering lunch. She was a pretty woman in a dark jacket that seemed to make her chocolate brown eyes gleam as she smiled up at the six-foot man with the fun-loving grin on his face.

My stomach roller-coastered to the floor along with my pen.

Gabe! With Linda Taylor!

For goodness sake, I hoped they didn't see me. I dove for my pen. It rolled farther away than I could easily reach.

When I looked up again, Gabe and Linda had taken their tray of lunch and were headed out the door towards the café tables outside. His hand was gently resting at the small of her back. Whew! They didn't see me. I shouldn't be here. I shouldn't —

Hang on. Why shouldn't I have seen them? Why shouldn't I be here? Just because I had invited Gabe to lunch and he was "too busy to eat" — at least with me — did that mean I couldn't eat?

Gabe and Linda grabbed a table on the sidewalk. I could see them, but obviously they didn't see me. They were engaged in a serious conversation, poring over papers, heads close together. Gabe's arm was draped over Linda's chair. If I were Georgette, I would be arching my back about now. If I were Queenie, Linda Taylor's ankles would be in shreds. If I were Thunder, those two's lunches would be history and their stupid papers would be flying down Main Street.

I huffed and wished I hadn't seen them at all. A ball of fire dropped down into my stomach and I swallowed.

I thought I'd been building a relationship with Gabe, but he looked like he was building one with That Woman.

Wait a minute. I didn't need to be embarrassed about seeing those two together. I wasn't the one who lied about not having time for lunch. Eleanor and Kitty from writing group were always pushing me to put more conflict in my writing. Here was a perfect opportunity to try that conflict out in real life.

The goatee guy stepped up and stood over me. "Are you all right, pretty lady?" He looked at me with real concern. Probably had something to do with the tears spilling down my hot cheeks. I tried a smile, but could feel it fall as flat as the pita bread.

"Yeah," I said. "I'm fine. Choked on my soda, is all."

The man stared at me with those pools of Godiva, then glanced out the window to where Gabe and Linda sat. He stooped and picked up something from the floor.

"Your pen." He put the object in my hand and left his own fingers on top of mine for a moment before squeezing little enough, but to let me know he understood. I guessed that working at Alexio's you'd see it all. Fresh tears threatened to spill over. My chest squeezed my soul.

"Is there perhaps a back door, Mr. . . . ?"

"Pete. I'm Alexio's brother. Alas, no escape. We have a back door, but only for employees and deliveries." He looked outside again. "Life is full of challenges we must face, no? Or you can wait here. They will be gone soon. Theirs is usually an eat-and-run kind of lunch." He smiled and I felt my face flush again. No hot flash, only a once-anonymous woman embarrassed to have Pete know her heart had been wounded.

"Thanks, Pete. I'll be fine." I gave him a watery smile. He nodded and went back to work.

Gabe and Linda ate with lightning speed, and before long he was bringing their tray of refuse back into the restaurant to throw away.

I wanted to hide behind my *Writing Magic* magazine, but I stood up. Pete was in the back. No one seemed to notice the tall, handsome, plain-clothes cop dumping his leftovers. Gabe stood at the door a few moments looking around. His gaze fell on me. I lifted my chin and glared at him.

"Daisy!" At least he had the decency to flush. He stepped toward me. I grabbed my lunch remains, purse, and writing materials. Impressive what a little anger will make a woman capable of carrying.

"Too busy for lunch, Gabe? I can see that."

"Daisy, it isn't what you think. Linda and I were —"

"Gabe. One thing you and I always seemed to have was honesty between us. Please don't make excuses now and stop that one good thing."

"You're blowing this out of proportion, my girl."

"And you're making way too many excuses for this to be any innocent situation. And I don't think I'm your girl."

"Daisy let me explain. At dinner. Shit — I can't do dinner tonight. How 'bout our Wednesday date? I can explain."

His eyes read "honest, I can," but my heart wasn't in the mood for any honest explanations.

"I have to go," I said and pushed past him. The restaurant had become quieter than I'd ever heard it. More fodder for the squished-together table gossip.

Outside, Linda and I had a moment to register on each other's radar. I glared at her and said nothing. Then I turned and walked in the opposite direction.

Conflict, my eye. Conflict wasn't at all what the writing group cracked it up to be. Kitty and Eleanor could keep their conflicts. I was ready to throw up.

A light spring rain drizzled down on me as I reached my car. At least the sky matched my mood. Funny, most days were so sunny that I never even noticed the Denver skies, but then something would sweep in off the Rockies and everything changed.

Today was that kind of day.

I shoved the key in my car door, opened it, and slumped in. I pitched my purse into the passenger seat and rested my head against the steering wheel, allowing my tears to fall.

I'm not sure how long I sat, but eventually my breathing slowed and I rolled up into a proper sitting position. The solid brick back wall of a store stared at me through my windshield.

Art's voice whispered in my head. *He's not me, you know. I'm like that brick wall — steady, solid, reliable. He's like the storm coming in. You really want that storm?*

Did I want the storm? Great question, Art. Gabe's beautiful face swam before my imagination. I saw his smile and those periwinkle eyes that matched the cloud colors rolling in. I remembered the tenderness and patience he showed Ginny. I also remembered our phone call and how he cut me off. I remembered his flash flood–like tempers. He was so different from Art.

Art was right. There were no mysteries with my dead husband. He was firm and boring, but I could count on him to do the little things right, when he was still alive. He finished conversations, and while he was often disappointed in my less-than-thought-out actions, he didn't yell at me. Gabe yelled. Art was quiet. Two very different men. How could my heart belong to both?

Then I remembered kissing Sam.

I kissed Sam.

What if Gabe had seen that? Next to lunch with Linda, that kiss was way over the line for someone in a relationship with someone else. All so confusing. My head hurt.

I sighed and glanced over at my passenger seat. My purse lay there with its contents half splayed across the tan leather of my seat. I leaned over to push things back into place.

Cissy Melato's address book lay under some coupons. Should have given that book to Gabe and not used it to play at detective. Brian's life was on the line. How could I have thought I could do a better job than Gabe? Correction. Gabe and Linda.

Another huff of Rocky Mountain air escaped my lungs.

The address book lay open to the "S" page. Joe Smaldone's contact information stared me right in the face. Maybe I would do something with it later. After a nice warm shower and a nap.

The brick wall before me started to talk again. Not Art this time, but Brian. "My Daisy. I took da knife away. I want to go home now." I saw his pathetic face screwed up and ready to cry.

Then I remembered what Connie Alessi told me. *Roddy is an arrogant little twerp, but he has powerful friends. Be careful.* Could she have been talking about Joe Smaldone? Gabe said Joe Smaldone was possibly part of a powerful mob family.

I was in a foul enough mood to give as good as I got today. Maybe a visit to this Joe Smaldone guy would be better than that shower and nap. I rubbed dry my eyes, shoved the keys into my ignition, and took off.

CHAPTER 16

The drive south on Santa Fe gave me time to think. Joe Smaldone. Maybe the mob wasn't gone from Denver. Maybe Cissy was involved with some sort of gangster business. An accountant could easily find herself in trouble that way. Rather than guessing, I wanted to hear this from Smaldone himself. What was up with his "c *and* f" relationship?

In my mind, old James Cagney movies wound themselves around my questions, and Eliot Ness of the FBI (in other words, me) would unwind the knot and be a hero once again. Pretty cool stuff.

What I really wanted was a good old-fashioned confession from this Joe guy. Whoever he was.

I pulled into a gravel driveway that my GPS assured was the right address. The Smaldone house sat on several acres of open land in Louviers. Its massive modern stone architecture made a daunting impression. Rocky mountain foothills towered above, but I could see for miles on all other sides of the property. This mansion seemed out of place, jutting up as it did in the middle of nowhere. I drove through a private gate and parked in the circular drive.

A man in a conservative suit with white shirt and dark tie met me before I had a chance to step out of my car. He also hid his stare behind dark glasses, even though the clouds were still pregnant with rain.

"Appointment?" said the man.

"No. Are you Mr. Smaldone?"

He snorted a laugh. "No appointment, no seeing the boss."

I gulped. This really was a *Godfather* movie remake. "But I want to ask him a couple of questions about Cissy Melato." I stepped from my car to face the man. I would not allow myself to be intimidated by this behemoth of a guy. Heck, I had just stood up to Gabe Caerphilly — I could stand up to him . . . maybe.

"She don't live here. Go 'way." The man's face solidified. I couldn't tell if he was staring at me behind those glasses.

I cleared my throat. "You do know it's not sunny?"

"Who are you?" he barked. But the stone-faced man turned his gaze to the sky, and slipped down his lenses for a moment.

"My name is Daisy Arthur. I'm a friend of . . ." Whom should I say I was a friend of? A friend of the police might not get me past this guard guy. A friend of Cissy's? I never met her.

Exactly who was I to barge in on a total stranger like Joe Smaldone and ask questions about a dead woman who was his vendor and possibly his friend? How was he more connected to this case than the hundred or so other names in Cissy's address book?

"I'm a friend of Brian Hughes, Cissy's special-needs neighbor." When in doubt, go for the truth.

"What's so special 'bout his needs? I never heard of da guy." Stone Face placed his hands on his hips and barged into my personal space.

"No. I mean *special needs* is a term for those with intellectual challenges." I backed up a foot in order to breathe better, but something about the man's speech patterns caught my attention. Even his movements, while powerful, seemed a bit awkward.

"You mean he's got questions, too?" asked Stone Face. "Don't we all?"

"No!" I almost shouted at the guy's ob-

162

tuseness. Was this oaf playing me? Then I thought about his possible capabilities or lack thereof, and tried again. "Brian is a bit slow . . ."

"Oh! You mean a re-tard." The light bulbs seemed to come on, as Stone Face nodded his head.

Instantly, I was in special-education mode. I softened my voice. "We normally say *special needs* or *developmentally delayed.*"

Stone Face shrugged and toed the gravel at his feet. "Sugar coating for re-tard."

I shook my head. Not enough hours in the day for this conversation. "At any rate, may I go in and visit with Joe — er — with the boss?"

Stone Face's head snapped back up. "Wait here," he said. "I'll see if you's okay."

When I didn't move, he nodded toward my car and I climbed back in. For good measure, I locked my doors. All the bravery born of my bad mood was dissipating fast. The unnerving man disappeared into his mansion.

A few minutes later, Stone Face came back and, with as few words as possible, escorted me into the house. I tried to gauge his level of intelligence. High functioning, for sure, but not quite to the hundred IQ points that would make him average.

Had I been more comfortable, I'd have liked to explore both my escort and the villa more closely. Smaldone's home was magnificent in a Baroque-Italian kind of way. As we walked past the living room, I caught a glimpse of the brilliant view provided by two-story high windows. Whatever else, this Joe Smaldone knew how to live large.

Stone Face walked me back through Joe's home. For some reason, my escort reminded me of Thunder. Probably had something to do with the fact that he kept turning to make sure I was following. All that the guy needed was to hang out his tongue and I'd be scratching him behind the ears. I wondered if he could be as goofy as Thunder, too. I smiled at him on one of his turns, and his gangster image slipped enough for him to return the favor.

We entered a room that was more cave-like than Art's home office had ever been. The papered walls were a deep, forest green, with bookshelves that seemed to push out everywhere there weren't windows. A massive, dark wood desk with carved panels grew out of the center of the floor as if it had been there since the beginning of time. The guest chairs, covered in rust-colored leather, were much larger than the service-able duet I'd seen in Cissy's home office.

"Wait here," said Stone Face, then he disappeared.

I wandered to the windows. Outside a vineyard stretched a good distance away. Although May was too early to see any growth, I could imagine that in the summer, the orchard would bring its owner a lot of pleasure and hours of work.

I turned attention back indoors.

A good detective would make best use of this opportunity by snooping around. What exactly that detective would be looking for was beyond me, but as I was playing at the role, I should at least browse and try to remember all that occupied this room. I might find a link to Cissy's murder here.

The bookshelves were filled with winemaking and farmers' guides, some restaurant and catering textbooks, and some books whose titles seemed to be in Italian. Would books in Italian be enough to connect Mr. Smaldone to the mob? Had I seen any Italian books in Cissy's condo?

I saw a painting in a corner and went to examine that. It was a picture of Jesus, beautifully done, but when I looked for the signature, there was none.

A man's voice close behind made me jump. "My Uncle Clyde painted that."

I swirled around to look into the strikingly

handsome face and glacier blue eyes of the man I guessed was Joe Smaldone. He wore an expression that mixed annoyance and amusement.

"Your uncle Clyde is very talented," I said backing away.

"He painted that when he was in jail."

I didn't know whether to say *cool,* as in it was cool that Uncle Clyde used his jail time to expand his talents, or *sorry,* because no one likes to think of a relative in jail. I chose the ever neutral, "Oh, interesting."

Joe strolled over to his desk and pulled open the lid of a wooden box. From inside he retrieved a cigar and promptly lit up. That explained the musky smell of the place.

He blew smoke from his cigar in my direction and I did the best I could not to swat at it. This was, after all, Joe's home and not mine. I couldn't help but give a little cough. He smiled a slow, lazy grin and I felt like the proverbial mouse under the cat's paw.

"You know my uncle, then," he said.

"He's a talented artist," I replied and gazed back toward the painting.

"Ha!" The sound was like a sudden burst of thunder that made me jump, but the smile that crinkled the edges of his eyes was genuine. "Artist. That's good. Where'd you meet Uncle Clyde?"

How had I given the impression I knew his uncle? This interview was not going the way I'd imagined it would. "We shared an art class a year or so ago?" I guessed with more bravado than my voice betrayed.

Joe watched his own hand snub out his hardly used cigar. He took his time rolling the hot end of the thing into the large marble ashtray on his desktop, before returning his icy gaze to me. He strolled over, invading my comfort zone. I wondered if this was standard operating procedure for gangsters. It worked on me, and I was uncomfortable again. The man towered over me so I had to tilt my head back to see his face.

Goodness, Joe Smaldone was trouble. I could feel the heat from his body and my breath caught on the scent of cigar and aftershave. I could hear Art's most urgent voice, *Get the heck out of there, Daisy.* I gulped.

Joe seemed to sense his advantage. He leaned over me and brushed a stray curl of hair from my ear. Then he whispered, "Uncle Clyde died in nineteen ninety-eight."

Oh, interesting wouldn't do for a response, so I shortened it to a more serviceable, "Oh."

Quick as lightning Joe spun away from me and turned back, piercing me with a stare full of icy anger and a finger pointed in my face like a gun.

"Who the hell are you and what do you want? Are you some snoopy gossip columnist? When are you reporters going to leave me and my family in peace?"

I bit my lip. "My name's Daisy Arthur. I'm not a reporter. I'm a friend of a friend, and I'm here to ask you about Cissy Melato."

"Why?"

"Because you were apparently Cissy's client, and possibly her friend. And my friend, Brian, is in jail, charged with her murder." Oops. That wasn't exactly keeping my card hand close to the chest. What would Jimmy Cagney do with me?

However, my outburst put a damper on Joe's righteous wrath. He sank into one of his guest chairs and nodded for me to occupy the other. His full mouth turned down as he stared at me for a lingering minute.

Finally, Joe said, "Why the hell should I help you? I want that scumbag to pay for what he did."

"Thing is, I don't believe Brian did — kill Cissy, that is."

Joe's head tilted back. He was giving me

more room to hang myself. "Go on." As if I hadn't already made a muddle of this investigation.

I did go on. I told Joe about meeting Brian, how he was a special-needs man, how I suspected that he was in the wrong place at the wrong time, even how he was Ginny's boyfriend.

"So you think he's being framed." Joe phrased succinctly what my subconscious brain had been toying with for a couple of days.

"I guess so," I said. It took a moment to sink in, and then I smiled. "Thanks, Joe. You're absolutely right. He's being framed. Now all I have to do is figure out who would want to do that to Brian."

"Or more precisely, who would want to kill my cousin, and why."

"Your *cousin*? Cissy Melato is a *family* member, not just *friend*?"

"Cousin through marriage." He shrugged.

"Joe, I am so sorry! I can't imagine your pain." I reached over and touched his arm. "No one should have to deal with a loved one murdered."

"Cissy was a special woman." He nodded. "Did you ever know her?"

"I never met her, but from what I can tell, she had a huge heart." She had to. Not many people befriend those with developmental delays. I suspected she cared for Brian like a son, and that indeed would be special.

"That she did."

"But I think she was pretty tough, too. I think she helped Brian get fair pay at work."

"Sounds like something Cissy would do. One time there was a kid from the community college class she taught who was being ripped off by his bosses at the restaurant he worked for. She not only showed this accounting major kid how to find evidence that his pay was being docked unnecessarily, but went in with him and was able to show the scums how she could have the health department shut them down permanently, if they didn't clean up their act."

"Impressive. And dangerous."

"Don't you know it. When I set up my business, I had Cissy come in and give me a clean bill-of-financial-health regularly."

"Sounds like you and Cissy had a special relationship."

"Yeah," Joe smiled at his memories, then seemed to shake himself. "But I'm talking too much. How'd you do that?"

"Do what?"

"Get me to say more than I wanted."

I shrugged. "Joe. I'm pretending to be an

investigator. I just ask questions, though. I don't have an agenda."

"Keep pretending, and you'll find my Cissy's killer." He thought for a moment and smiled at another memory, no doubt. "All the same, I loved her. She was an intelligent woman who did my accounting. Made my taxes sparkle for the IRS man, and never asked too many questions." He stared pointedly at me and I swallowed.

Joe smiled again, leaned back, and relit his cigar. "You should have seen ol' Cis in her younger years. Bright, fun-loving, and with a figure to make Raquel Welsh jealous. *Bella!*" He paused on the memory, and then sighed. "A few too many gelatos after the divorce from Ralphie."

"Cissy was divorced?" There could be another suspect. *R* from the address book, maybe. Wasn't Cissy's last appointment with someone starting with an *R*? Hmm. Brian would get out of jail, if only I could get Gabe to look in other directions for his killer. "Would Ralphie have any grudges left? Could he — ?"

"Naw. Ralphie's kind of a goofball. Never really grew up. Cissy left him when his gambling budget grew too big for her income to cover. And that was years ago."

"I see." Darn! Scratch Ralphie from the

suspect list. I was stumped. "Why do you think anyone would want to kill Cissy, Joe?"

"I don't know, but when I find the stupid lowlife . . ." He jabbed his cigar into his ashtray, this time with enough force to completely pulverize it. The rage on his face wasn't quelled in his glance back my way, and my hand flew to the safety of the locket I wore. Art, you're right. I need to be out of here.

I stood up. "I can see I've upset you. Sorry. I'd better go."

Joe curled his lip in a contemptuous sneer but escorted me back to my car like a gentleman. When I was safe inside my vehicle he said, "Look. I like you. You're smart, and I can see you're trying to help find my cousin's killer. But nice ladies like you shouldn't be trying to do detective work. Could be dangerous."

"Somebody has to do this, Joe. Brian shouldn't be in jail, and Cissy, by the sounds of it, deserves closure at the very least."

Joe nodded, giving me a measured look. "I see. Okay, so if you're planning to go through with this, maybe you should come to the funeral tomorrow. Give you a chance to see who pays Cissy respects, and maybe you can observe who needs further investigation."

I didn't say I'd already intended to do just that. "What a great idea, Joe. Thanks. You'd make a pretty good detective yourself."

"I am. And I'll be there to watch over things too."

The way he said it, with that simmering threat in his voice, gave me the chills. I said *ciao* and drove home with the heater on in my car.

CHAPTER 17

I had always thought of funerals as taking place in the rain, but for Cissy's, the sun shone brightly.

The priest of Most Holy Saints church, Father Wright, gave a stirring eulogy before we all left for a graveside prayer in the Littleton Cemetery.

The graveyard was a place of traditional headstones dating back to the Civil War, and sweeping hills that overlooked the railroad tracks carrying commuters from our small town to Denver about eight miles away. Wind chime decorations at various gravesides blew and sang in the breezes so that relatives of those whose final resting place was there had some mystical interaction with the dead.

I had heard that 1873's Colorado cannibal, Alferd Packer, reposed there, but I'd never seen his grave. Made me think though. At a cemetery, all that the stones gave for information was a birth date and a death date. No judgments here of good or bad souls. All were equal in God's eyes.

There were about thirty people gathered around Cissy's freshly dug grave. I recognized Joe Smaldone in one of the chairs reserved for family. Next to him was a woman covered in black, with a traditional funeral veil hiding her face. On the other side sat Stone Face. Although his glasses were still in place, I could see tears running down his cheeks. The other two family chairs were empty. Stone Face had called Joe "boss," but he sat in a family chair. Interesting.

An average looking man, perhaps a few years older than me, reached down from his position behind the woman in black and squeezed her shoulder. She stretched up and patted his hand.

Then, rooted a pace or two away, stood Roddy McKeague. He, too, wore sunglasses, but I suspected his were in place more because of the sun than any cover for grief. He didn't know Cissy. Why was he here? Thanks, Joe, for the tip to watch who came to pay respects — and the notion of Brian being framed. Hmm.

Next to Roddy stood a good-looking man. He seemed familiar, but I couldn't quite place him. At one point, the man nudged Roddy, and the young manager covered his smirk with a cough.

I let my eyes wander the crowd more. I saw Toni Piccolo from my writing group. She wore her customary black polka-dot dress and little make-up. I wondered if anyone would dare to dress her differently when it came time for her own funeral, then immediately shook myself. Not nice, Daisy.

I hadn't realized that Toni knew Cissy, but then, other than sending out the weekly email invitation to the critique group, I hadn't contacted anyone but Kitty for a chat. I'd been wrapped up in Cissy's murder and foster care for her dog.

A voice hissed in my ear. "What are you doing here?" I jumped and spun around to see Gabe glaring down at me.

"I'm paying my respects," I whispered back. "Now hush. Father Wright is praying." I resisted asking about Linda Taylor's whereabouts.

We mumbled through the Catholic version of the Lord's Prayer before Gabe turned to me again. The time gave me a chance to think. Why was I here? Why should I speak with Gabe at all?

He didn't want me involved, so I couldn't say I was looking for new suspects. I turned

176

to him and whispered in my best if-you-really-must-know cool voice. "I'm representing Queenie. Didn't think it would be appropriate for her to come in person — er — dog-hood. She is filled with grief but wanted me to give her respects."

Gabe's blazing look melted into a grin, but he still shook his head. "I've told you to stay out of this, Daisy. Do I need to put you under house arrest each time I'm on a new case?"

"Ooh, promises." I smiled, batted my eyes, and held my hands out as if for handcuffs.

"Look. About yesterday, about lunch —"

Someone turned and shushed us. Yes. Yesterday's lunch with Linda, not me, and not a problem for Gabe's overfull plate. Maybe it was a good thing the shusher was there.

Father Wright's voice rose in the wind. "In the name of the Father, and of the Son . . ."

I turned to Gabe again. "Think I'll wander over and offer my condolences to the family."

"No, no you don't." He put a hand on my arm. "The last person I want you to meet is Joe Smaldone. I'll go. You can ask me about it later."

I bit my lip and decided discretion was

the better part of valor in this case. The fact that I'd already met Joe could cause another ruffle in Gabe's and my already strained relations.

The funeral group was dispersing. I watched Gabe walk up to the grieving family. At one point, Joe Smaldone stared across at me, so I shrugged my shoulders and fingered a small wave. He turned his attention back to Gabe. Would he let on that we'd talked? If he did, I was sure to hear about it from my police lieutenant.

Toni Piccolo tapped my arm. "I didn't know you knew my friend," she said.

"Hi, Toni. To be honest, I didn't, but found myself involved —"

"Please, Daisy, no. You're almost as bad at solving crimes as you are at" — she stopped herself for a beat — "never mind."

"Were you going to say *writing*? I'm bad at writing?"

"You're getting better all the time," said Toni. "And you're a very good critique group leader. Stick with the writing. It's safer for you."

"What do you mean?"

"Nothing more than that when you were involved with finding Rico's killer, you almost got murdered yourself." She pursed her lips and nodded. I was being chastised in the most polite fashion.

"But I did find the killer."

"You lucked onto the killer." The prim look was replaced by the all-knowing-and-judging-mother-look that I sincerely wished I could master. "And you were lucky your police lieutenant over there came to save you."

We both looked toward Gabe, who had moved on to talking with Roddy and the man with him.

"Toni, have you any idea who that man is with Gabe?"

"Which man? Never mind. I don't know either, though the older one sure is a looker."

"Toni!"

"What? I'm married, true, but the blinders came off years ago." She shrugged.

"Where is your husband now? Did he join you today?" I'd never met Toni's husband in the entire time we'd been going to critiques together.

"Prince Charming? He's watching the grandkids for me. He didn't know Cissy either. I wonder how that good-looking man knew her. Cissy never mentioned any Adonis acquaintances. He's a bit young for me, though. More your age."

"Probably young for me too." We stood in

a communal gawking pose just the same. After a hard hour at the funeral, it was good to have a happy thought or two. And Gabe and this man provided all that, even if Gabe was in my official doghouse.

The stranger wasn't drop-dead gorgeous, but there was an air about him that would attract a lot of women. What was it that shouted out success about this guy? He stood taller than either Gabe or Roddy, but not by much, and left a hand in his expensive-looking suit pocket, feet nicely stretched to show a confidence few can fake. The thought *man's man* dashed through my brain as I tried to place the guy's face. Something in my brain was at conflict with the image before me.

Father Wright walked over to Toni and me. His white hair glowed in the sun, and I thought about his belief that people were angels.

"Hello, Daisy. Peace be with you."

"Hello, Father." I had a sensation of home as the priest enveloped me in a gentle hug. He had become something of a friend over the past few months, and I felt safe and always better for being in this angel's company.

Angel. Messenger. Maybe Father Wright could tell me something to help find out who killed Cissy.

"Father, did you know Cissy well?"

"Unfortunately, no. If it weren't for her cousin, Joe, over there" — he looked toward Joe Smaldone — "I probably wouldn't have conducted this funeral. Ms. Melato wasn't a parishioner of Most Holy Saints. The Church still officially frowns on divorcees, so she probably attended mass only on special occasions, if then."

I glanced over at Toni, who seemed to be edging away. I reached for her arm. "Oh! Father Wright, I forgot. You may not know my friend, Toni Piccolo."

Toni pinched her lips, but levitated a hand in Father Wright's direction. He held it and smiled into her tense face. "Let me guess," said the father. "You have a history with the Catholic church."

Toni paled and nodded. Father Wright turned toward me. "Daisy, the minute I saw you, I knew you would pose a delightful challenge." He winked at me with his keen eyes. "Thank you."

Then the good priest gathered Toni's hand in his arm the way gentlemen used to do in society and started walking away with her. "You have been hurt by the Church, and no one has spoken to you about it."

"How did you know?" said Toni. "I don't

tell many people about it." She gazed up at him in child-like wonder and Father John patted her hand.

"My job is to be sensitive, listen, and help heal where I can. Now tell me what happened — long ago — I think?"

"Yes." Toni, always prepared, pulled a tissue from her purse, patted her eye, and let the priest lead her to a quieter corner of the cemetery.

I watched them go, and then returned my attention toward Gabe. He was still with Roddy and the handsome stranger. Gabe reached out and the stranger shook his hand. The man's other hand slid from his pocket to grab Gabe's upper arm. It was a guy gesture that could be interpreted as a manly hug. This stranger obviously liked Gabe. I wasn't sure why that made me uncomfortable.

I slipped away from the crowd. It had been too long since I visited my Rose and Art's graves.

Rose's small, heart-shaped stone was almost lost in the shadow of her dad's more traditional rectangle. When we lost our Rosie, Art and I purchased the two spaces next to her for our final resting places. Art had handled everything, including the granite design that now only needed my birth and death information to complete the Arthur family set.

I had stopped putting flowers on their graves quite a while ago. When I visited and spoke to them, neither Rose nor Art tended to reply. When I prayed, there was the emptiness and finality of silence in return. Killing a plant only to mark a grave seemed superfluous.

I missed my family, but I didn't cry anymore. With Father John's help, I had come to accept their deaths more and more, and I knew it was important to let their spirits move on. I still loved them, but our existences were on different planes, so I only called to Art when I was stressed.

A few minutes later, Gabe found me again. I smelled his aftershave right before he laid a hand on my shoulder. "Am I interrupting?" His voice was as soft as the graveyard wind chimes.

I gazed at him a long moment. "No. Just visiting here." I bent and plucked a dandelion from Art's grave, then stood again, next to this not-quite-my-friend, but ever so lovely man. I couldn't blame Linda for pursuing a closer relationship with him. "How'd your conversations go? Did you find anything interesting about the case?"

He smiled. "I'm going to change your

name from Daisy to bulldog. Had good conversations with both the Smaldone family and the grocery guys."

"Smaldone family? Grocery guys? Then the man with Roddy . . . ?"

"Name's Keith. Keith Johnson. He's the regional manager with Gigantos. Very sharp. I liked him."

"And he liked you."

"How could you tell?"

"It was in his body language mostly. That, and the length of time you spent together. Did you get more of an impression of Roddy?"

"Not much. Why?"

"Gabe, that Roddy makes me shiver, he's so creepy. Why was he even at the funeral? Do you think he might have framed Brian?"

"Don't be silly, Daisy. Gigantos wanted to send some representatives because Cissy died in their store. Wouldn't have been good public relations to be a no-show. Roddy and Keith were those representatives."

We had walked to my car by this time, and Gabe opened the door for me.

"See you tomorrow night?" said Gabe.

I took my time answering. It still stung that he would tell me he was too busy to eat out and then be off with Linda Taylor. I was looking forward to straightening that out once and for all.

Gabe ran frustrated fingers through his hair. "Daisy, I said I was sorry."

I put a hand on his chest. "Wouldn't miss it." Then I stepped into my car.

Gabe pushed the lock on the door handle and stepped back to close the door for me. I watched him walk back toward his car. His stroll was so good looking.

Good looking. Why did that thought give me pause? What was I forgetting? There was something about it — Roddy? Gigantos? I wanted to stop him and ask more questions, but Gabe drove off.

CHAPTER 18

Tuesday evenings were my reprieves from an otherwise endless string of days with little responsibility and less activity. With ten pages of writing due each week, I had deadlines and a reason to get moving every day. Retirement had its challenges, and boredom was one of those.

Even solving murders didn't totally eat up my day. A small voice in my head told me I was still only playing at being a sleuth and also playing at this writing career of mine. One day I'd have to get serious about these things. If I didn't take myself seriously, who else would?

I took off the black dress I'd worn to Cissy's funeral as soon as I got home. Never liked the way I looked in black, so to help my spirits before group meeting time, I put on a pretty pink sweatshirt with flowers appliquéd about the neck and a pair of clean, stonewashed jeans. This softer and cozier look was much more comfortable. A quick splash of Vanilla Rush *eau de toilette* and I was set to go.

Two hours early. I sighed.

I *could* take Queenie out into the back yard again. It would only be the fortieth time or so today. I *could* bake cookies and work toward expanding my waistline to match Cissy's.

Poor Cissy! Who would murder an overweight accountant with a misguided vegetarian bent? What could she have done to incite in someone the rage involved in her killing? Would Brian have a reason to kill her, make a big mess in the bathroom at work, and then go find Ginny to help him take care of it all?

That complex a scenario didn't fit with the simple way adults with developmental delays operate. I couldn't think of a motive for him. But if not Brian, who? Would Roddy, a store manager, kill a customer — kill her with rage? Nope. He was creepy but there was no motive there, either.

I needed most definitely to be thinking about the funeral and who was there. Who was the woman in the family chair, next to Stone Face? Who was the man leaning over her? Who was that Keith Johnson guy? If he and Roddy McKeague were such good friends, I already disliked him — handsome or not.

After thinking more about the morning events, I settled into reading a little Georgette Heyer. Soon, my own Georgette snuggled into my lap and Queenie lay next to us on the couch. I opened *The Nonesuch,* read a couple of chapters, and fell asleep.

Some time later, I sensed I was being watched and stretched while opening my eyes. I rolled over and saw Queenie staring at me from beside the couch. She gave a little yip and jumped. I couldn't help but smile.

Georgette rolled over and snapped out of her beauty rest pose when she realized Queenie had woken. Immediately, the cat's tail twitched fitfully as she mewed. She executed a playful swat at the dog's nose. Queenie sneezed and shook her head, then dove in to lick Georgette's face.

And they were off. Georgette hadn't had so much exercise in years. I laughed and raised my arm to check my watch.

My goodness! It was five forty-five, and no one in my house had eaten dinner. Group started in fifteen minutes and, although the drive to the library took a mere seven minutes, I'd have to rush to get the pets fed, take the dog out for a pee, and get me ready to boot. I flew around the house as fast as Georgette being chased by Queenie. I wondered how Cissy had kept up with her dog.

Out of breath, I managed to trudge into the library at three minutes past six. Looked like a good, full, group meeting. Kitty was there in an outfit of pearlescent lavender and green.

"I thought you were busy tonight," I threw at her as I set my things down.

She shrugged. "Mom got a last-minute replacement for me. I wasn't enthusiastic enough for handing out flyers to more than this group." She handed me a brochure titled "Dangerous Groceries? Get the Facts!" Kitty's mom must be some kind of political junkie. I spotted Toni, who hadn't changed her black with polka-dot print, and Linda Taylor sat with a neat stack of papers. She must have been the first to arrive, as she was the only one ready to read her manuscript.

And there was Dan Block.

He sat between Kitty and Toni, large hands locked behind his head in a pose that said he owned the world, or at least this writing group. His almost black eyes wandered lazily in my direction. I gave an inward sigh and tried to think more positive thoughts about the guy.

"Our fearless leader is precisely what we need," said Eleanor from her spot near Linda and the lobby door into the main reading room. "Daisy, we have a question for you."

I tried to smile even though Eleanor calling me "fearless leader" ignited a desire to run. "Something wrong?"

Kitty piped up. "Not really, Daisy. It's only that some of us are thinking of entering the writing contest that goes on at the big conference in September. We want to work with synopses and agent pitches for a while instead of the usual ten novel pages."

Dan sat up straighter, his height swallowing up our small alcove space. "Not entering the writing contest," he said. "Don't know about synopsis writing. Want to keep focused on my novel."

"So you see the dilemma," said Toni. "To write or not to write the contest synopsis for this group's review."

"I can't enter the contest," said Eleanor. "It's only open to *un*published writers, and you know I don't fit that category." She actually flung her ash-blond hair over her shoulder. Eleanor was lucky I'd become better acquainted with the big heart she kept so well hidden most of the time.

I held my breath for a moment. Although Dan, Eleanor, and I were of the same mind, I just couldn't see myself agreeing with them to the exclusion of the others. Okay, and to be honest, I didn't want to agree with a snobby published writer and a guy who was always so confident he intimidated and irritated me no end.

"I think" — I bit my lower lip — "we should compromise. My knee-jerk reaction to this idea is that this is a novel writing group, not a novel sales team. But the contest is being sponsored by Rocky Mountain Fiction Writers, our own parent group. So, if Kitty and Toni want to use their time for synopsis critiques, Eleanor and Dan will have to learn what synopsis writing entails, to be able to review. Then, when it's the others' turn, we'll switch gears, so to speak."

Everyone started talking at once. We debated the logistics of switching gears, the purpose of a novel-writer's critique group, even where we chose to meet. Things were getting out of hand.

Then Dan spoke with his deep, voice-of-authority bass tone. I thought even James Earl Jones couldn't match that depth.

"I joined this group to get critiqued on

my novel. Don't want to learn about synopses, short stories, or magazine articles." He crossed his arms in a way that put an exclamation point to his words, leaned back, and nodded his head in a so-there fashion.

"Enough." I stood up to address the group. "We are running out of our critique time. I'll make a decision." As Dan leaned forward I put my hand up to stop any further discussion. "No more, Dan. You've said enough. I'll give my decision at next week's meeting."

Linda Taylor spoke up. "One last suggestion you could think about until then?"

I sucked in my breath. We didn't need to go on any more, and I sure didn't want to listen to anything That Woman said, but she had remained quiet the whole time, taking notes on the discussion. I pinched my lips to avoid projecting my latest I-detest-you thoughts. "Go ahead, Linda."

"I suggest taking the number of people here, divide it into the minutes we have, and that's it. If you write some new kind of writing, your critiques will not be as good, but you'll have the same amount of time spent on your work as everyone else. It's a compromise, but a win-win."

If I hadn't seen Linda and Gabe at lunch together, I could have hugged her in thanks.

Instead, I gave her a grateful grin.

"Linda's right," I said. "Novel writers will still get the critiques they want and will stretch their abilities by learning about synopses. Synopsis writers will have a chance to practice their new skills before submitting their work to the contest. I think one of the best things about being writers is that we are constantly learning. We stretch our minds by trying new things, reading new styles. This is a great way to grow." Taking myself seriously was a good thing. I nodded my head.

"Don't want to," said Dan. "Not a lot of time for writing as is. Don't want something new."

I snapped. "Then you can go into the main part of the library when we critique someone with a synopsis and follow their signs that read, 'Be quiet!' "

I didn't think I'd raised my voice much, but instantly the library lobby felt as though it had been struck by lightning. Everyone stared at me. I sat down. I was a serious writer. Yes, I was.

Kitty cleared her throat. "Linda, I think you were first. Want to hand out your pages?"

Linda read her work and the rest of the evening went relatively smoothly. Dan's critiques were as incisive as they were harsh. I relished the thought of being able to openly disagree with him sometime.

Dan's scribbles on my work seemed even bolder than normal. I decided they would go directly into my trash bin as soon as I got home. No need to read his mean-spirited review — even if it was insightful. Maybe I'd even rip his critique up. Maybe light it on fire before stuffing it in the old circular file. So there, Mr. *Trim, trim, trim.*

As the meeting broke up, Linda and I found ourselves walking together toward our cars.

"Nice work on the meeting tonight," said Linda. "I can see why you were asked to be the group leader."

"Thanks. But you were the one with the best suggestion on how to handle these synopses."

"You kept the discussion going so I had a chance to sit back and see where everyone was heading."

"Good job." I sighed. "I don't know how to handle that Dan Block though. He's so all-or-nothing in his thinking."

"Telling him to shut up was a good start."

"I didn't mean to be so rude. It just popped out."

"At the best moment," said Linda. "Look,

Daisy. The important thing is, this was your first big conflict since taking over the leadership of the group. It was nice to see that you could handle it and not let the noise intimidate you."

"Thanks, Linda."

"By the way. About lunch with Gabe —"

"No need to explain. You're partners is all, right?"

"Yes. But still. I told you once I'd always have Gabe's back for him. We really were only having lunch. Sorry about the confusion. If I'd known you had a date —"

"We didn't. I called to ask, and he'd already made plans with you. I can understand that." What I couldn't understand was why Gabe had lied to me and said he was not having lunch at all.

"You're amazing," said Linda. "If Gabe were my boyfriend, I'd be jealous as hell if he stood me up for another woman — partner or no."

I wanted to say *you have no idea,* but stuck with a noncommittal, "These things happen. Besides, if you two are working on Cissy Melato's murder, then you must have at least a few doubts about Brian Hughes's guilt."

"I do. Gabe doesn't. He's really stuck on pinning this on the kid. Not sure why."

"I think he's stuck on keeping Brian away from Ginny."

Linda laughed. "You're probably right. He's very protective of his daughter."

"A bit too."

"What do you mean?"

"Ginny is grown up, whether Gabe wants that to happen or not. She seems to have real and deep feelings for Brian. I'm not sure why, but Gabe is unprepared to let his little girl go."

"She's all he's got, Daisy."

"Then he needs to get something more in his life, and let Ginny have her own life back."

"You're right, of course. You're remarkable with your perceptions about people."

"Thanks, Linda. You make me feel great." My smile faded. "Only wish I could handle being with Dan Block."

Linda looked around as if to make sure no one was there. "After you and I talked last week, I did a background check on our friend. He's fine. No arrests, no outstanding warrant, a good work record from what I could see."

I felt my eyes bulge. "Background check? On a group member?"

She shrugged. "You were the one who said this guy makes you nervous. And, to be hon-

196

est, your instincts about people give me the jitters. You seem to be able to tell good and evil apart as keenly as sniffer dogs can find illegal drugs."

"Thanks. I think." We'd reached our cars and both smiled. "And thanks for the reassurance about Dan. I'll have to noodle about this more."

She nodded and we waved our good-byes.

Back at home, Georgette and Queenie had settled for the night, but jumped up at my return. I gave them each a ten o'clock midnight snack and wandered back to my bedroom.

Once in pajamas, I grabbed my spiral notebook that had become more of a personal journal than a record of story ideas. The journaling helped sort more issues than I had originally thought.

"Dan Block" I wrote, "Is a Good Man." I had to rethink this guy. No arrests, no warrants, a good work record . . . If only I could see him as the brilliant writer others saw, and not the mean, nasty monster I thought of when Dan came to mind.

As my words flowed over the journal pages, I remembered our first meeting. Dan came into the library looking like an educated football superstar. His large, dark

hand enveloped my own when we introduced ourselves, and his firm handshake
was enough to crush my bones. I thought
he was trying to intimidate me, but looking
back, I remembered the others in my group
winced too. Maybe he didn't know his own
strength. Some people don't realize it when
they go over the top with their actions.

But then, he didn't wait even a week or
two to jump into the writing work, but came
the first time with ten pages to read and his
ever-present red pen with which to critique
others. Perhaps he came from one of those
schools or families where corrections were
all done with red pens. It happens.

Then there was his writing work — terse,
powerful words that flowed with ease across
the page. Everyone was enthralled. Maybe I
was jealous of his comfort in writing.

Maybe the bad guy here was really me.

Doggone it! I had enough on my mind
with the slow progress of my novel and the
murder to solve. Did I have to inflict guilt
on myself over Dan too?

I sat up. Art was fond of saying *Temper,
temper, Daisy. Never let the sun set on your
anger.* Great, Art. What happens when
anger jumps up and bites you in the butt
after the sun has already set?

I threw off the quilt and got out of bed.

Of course Art was right. I stomped off to my computer admonishing myself to think nice thoughts, think nice thoughts — about Dan.

I zipped off an email to apologize for any rudeness he may have felt from me, then flicked over to the Internet to catch up on today's news.

Almost as soon as I sent my message, I received a ding to tell me I had mail. I clicked back to my mailbox only to see a reply had arrived from Dan. Wow. Had he known I would be writing?

The email read: "Thanks. Should use 'me' instead of 'I' in sentence two. Delete sentence three — superfluous. Want to talk? Meet me at Hershberg's Gym, Friday, 8:00. See you then. DB."

He corrected my email? Well, I could be as word stingy and quick as he. I replied. "Eight o'clock, Friday it is — DA." I hit the "send" button before realizing what I'd done.

Hershberg's Gym?

I never exercised. Exercise should be a four-letter word as far as I was concerned. What had I done now?

CHAPTER 19

Wednesday seeped into evening. I readied my outfit with care, and felt more edgy about this date with Gabe than ever before. Sure, he acted nicely at the funeral, but we hadn't exactly resolved that little *tête-à-tête* with Linda versus lunching with Daisy issue. I detested conflict, yet was offended even more that he presumed this lunch of theirs was no big deal.

My jealousy made me feel so small. In an effort to be a better person, I stuffed Cissy Melato's address book into my purse. Tonight would be a good time to give this evidence to Gabe. He might need it after all. I pictured giving it to him, and the wiser side of me showed him being upset that I hadn't returned it earlier. Did I really need another fight? Inwardly, I sighed.

Maybe things would be different. Maybe we'd have a great time, and, when I handed him the book, he'd tell me "good work" for finding it in the first place. Maybe.

My doorbell rang and I admonished the pets to be good before grabbing my purse and keys.

Gabe stood in my doorway looking like an angel as the setting sun's rays seeped around his broad shoulders. I squinted at him, and tried to smile at the same time. Probably not the best effect. Memories of my old students being asked to smile for the camera dashed forward in my brain. Their goofy, over-exaggerated smiles still warmed my heart, but the image of me doing the same wasn't so appealing. I slipped out the door and stepped ahead of Gabe down my porch stairs.

"What's your hurry?" Gabe turned to follow. "Don't you want to give Georgette and that dog a thousand kisses before you go?"

I knew he was teasing. I wasn't in the mood. Linda's image haunted my thoughts. "They'll be fine." I marched on.

He shrugged, followed my progress, and opened his car door for me. The Dodge Charger was warm and comfortable. Gabe must have turned up the heater on his way over to my house, so our late spring chill wouldn't reach into my bones. Check off another item on the good-guy list. Gabe was almost always thoughtful. But tonight that thoughtfulness made me feel trapped. How could he know me so intimately? I wouldn't have come up with such a welcome detail in dealing with him.

He didn't look at me as he drove. His habit was to pay attention to operating his car and the road ahead. Never mind. I liked his profile and knew he used all of his peripheral senses to pay attention to me.

"Where are we going?" I asked.

A grin spread across his handsome features. "You'll know when we get there."

My stomach nose-dived. "I really dislike when you do this, Gabe. I never know if I'm dressed appropriately."

"You always dress fine, Ms. fashion plate," he teased.

Tonight, I had chosen a Brooks Brothers cream-colored sweater set my sister, Camellia, had sent for my birthday. It matched my burgundy trousers, and some soft, black suede loafers. I thought the effect was nice, but Gabe didn't mention my looks when he picked me up.

He, of course, was gorgeous, in a navy suit with blue and white dress shirt and the dark red tie I'd given him last Christmas.

Hang on! I hadn't seen Gabe dressed so formally — other than for Cissy's funeral — in a long time. Panic hit.

"I'm not very fond of surprises, my friend. We're not going someplace fancy, are we?" Suddenly, wearing trousers didn't seem such a good idea.

I looked out the window. Businesses along Broadway flew south as we headed up into Englewood. We'd almost reached Hampden and the city's business district. My every instinct was to jump from the car and run home to change quickly.

"I'm only taking you someplace nice," he replied, that grin still hovering.

"What is *nice*? Are we talking *nice* like a chain steakhouse nice, or are we talking someplace where I won't fit in? You know I'm not great with silver-service stuff."

"Calm down." The grin disappeared and a muscle in Gabe's jaw started wiggling, but then he took a deep breath. "Don't worry, Daisy. You'll be fine. Almost nothing in Colorado is that fancy."

"And where exactly is this — this nice place?" My fingers itched to give quotations around the word.

"Here." He swung the Charger into a parking spot on Austin Street, in front of a trendy but pricy restaurant I'd heard of. It was an Italian eatery I'd seen in *5280 Magazine*. Gabe turned off the car and smiled fully at me. "Shall we?" He was obviously proud of his restaurant choice.

All I could think of was how much it would cost, and how inappropriate a simple unmatched pants outfit was. I swallowed and tried my own grimace in return. Those school photographers must have been hiding in nearby bushes, giggling over the face I made.

We stepped through the stone-framed main door and into a world of adobe-colored modernism, where the maître-d greeted us with a graceful welcome and did we have reservations? At least she wore an unmatched black pants suit, so I breathed a little easier.

Busts of what I assumed were Italian noblemen adorned the earthy-brown and gold walls and nooks. A man at the piano in the bar played a jazzy style of music I didn't recognize.

And the noise!

I guess the lack of floor or table coverings meant there was nothing to absorb the chatter among restaurant patrons, so between them, the piano, and the clatter of dishes, I could hardly hear our waiter give a description of tonight's special in his thick Italian accent. I think he said his name was Alonso or Udolpho, and the special had some beef in it, but that was all I could distinguish. I suspected Alonso was putting on his accent, so instead of asking for clarification, I turned to the menu.

My eyes popped. I could eat for a week on the price of one entree. Okay, so it would be a week of peanut butter and jelly, but still. These prices were way outside of a good restaurant dinner for me.

I looked over at Gabe. He didn't seem nervous about the menu prices at all. Maybe he didn't see them.

I cleared my throat. "It would be okay if we chose to leave." My mind raced through the contents of my purse hoping for hidden dollars, just in case. It skipped over the address book.

Gabe reached across the table and gazed intently at me. Immediately I was awash in the stare that seemed to glow like Rocky Mountain blue birds in this low light.

"Don't you like what you see?" asked Gabe.

"Yes, yes, I do," I replied, then realized he was talking about the menu. "Oh! I mean, the food looks good, but the prices —"

"Are nothing for you to worry about tonight. I asked *you* out, remember? My treat." He smiled again.

"Are you sure?"

"Yes." The word seemed to hiss across the

table. Then Gabe took a deep breath and tried again with me. "Look, Daisy. We don't eat this way every week so enjoy the meal experience, will you?" The words were nice, but the tone seemed more like a command than an invitation.

I smiled a silent response. Okay, Gabe. Be a big spender. I could get used to this. This dinner wouldn't cost as much as if we ate at Denver's Brown Palace after all.

We ordered drinks and an appetizer of calamari. I looked around again. A patron walked by in fashionably torn blue jeans and a scruffy tank top. She strode with a confidence I couldn't fake if my life depended on it. Okay, so at least I looked good in my pants outfit. I sat a smidgeon taller and grinned again at Gabe.

"So why such a fancy meal?" I asked.

"You know how we missed that home-made special dinner you cooked a month or so ago?"

"I remember. You had to go out on an investigation. You missed my leg of lamb." Leg of lamb had been a favorite of Art's, and I made it on just about all my special occasions. A month earlier would have been six months of having Gabe back in my life. He had been called away on an emergency, and rain-checked the meal. And the candles, the music, the fully cleaned and prepared house — including bedroom. I sighed.

"Thought I'd make up a little with a nice meal back to you."

How sweet. I looked at my handsome lieutenant and developed a new hunger that had nothing to do with food. I forgot completely about being mad at him over missing lunch with me.

"A toast," I said, raising my glass of wine. Gabe mimicked the gesture and waited.

Now that I was a writer, it should have been a simple task to say a few words. But the twinkle in Gabe's eye caught me off guard. He was playing with me. My mind went blank.

"To uh . . ." *Great, Daisy. That was eloquent.* Gabe leaned in. His aftershave swam in my senses and all I could think was, "To gorgeous men in the service of our city."

Gabe laughed outright. "How 'bout simply, 'to us?' "

"Right. To us. Partners in crime and in more."

The smallest of frowns dug its way into Gabe's forehead.

"To us," he replied and drank.

"Something wrong, partner?" I asked.

"Daisy. I like you. I like you a lot. But we're not partners. We're good friends."

"What's the difference?"

"I have a partner —" As if on cue, his phone went off.

I didn't hear it, so it must have been on vibrate. But Gabe picked it up and the soft look on his face told me exactly who was texting him.

"Linda?" I asked with no real attempt to hide my annoyance.

"Hmm? Oh! Yes. Excuse me, Daisy, I have to get this." He stood and stepped away to return his call.

Grr! Linda had to be interrupting on purpose. Impeccable timing. As Gabe's police partner she seemed to know where he was constantly. And her chat with me last night, what did she say? *If Gabe were my boyfriend, I'd be jealous as hell if he stood me up for another woman —*

If Gabe were my boyfriend . . .

I have a partner . . .

Time to make it very clear to both Gabe and Linda that he was taken. Almost.

Gabe returned, grin still painted firmly on his face. "That was Linda. Had a couple of items for the case, but sends her regards."

"How kind that she would interrupt my special dinner with you to send her regards." Sometimes That Woman's efficiency was enough to drive me nuts. "Look, Gabe.

208

About Linda —"

Our waiter came up. "Your salad, *Senora*," he said. Really? Alonso also had impeccable timing. Impeccably *bad* timing. I waited while he placed a bowl of greens in front of me, proceeded to churn fresh pepper over the dish, and then left. I drummed my fingers on the tabletop.

Gabe looked at me with a blank expression. "About Linda? Something wrong?"

"Yes, Gabe. Linda. I think —"

"Salad, *Senor*?" Alonso had slipped back with another dish, this one for Gabe. Couldn't he have brought both together? A tingly feeling of annoyance crept up my spine, but I waited in silence while Alonso finished his salad routine with Gabe.

The music from the bar started up again, and with it the volume in the restaurant area. Gabe leaned in to hear what I had to say.

I tried shouting above the noise. "Does Linda have to be a part of everything we do?"

"What? You want the beef stew? I didn't see that dish." Gabe flipped open his menu.

"No! Linda. Everything we do. She's involved."

"Yes. Linda. She's terrific, isn't she?"

"Not from where I sit."

"What?"

I huffed. "Spinach. I said I'll have the shrimp and spinach."

Gabe smiled. For an observant police officer he could be pretty dense sometimes. I heaved an inward sigh. Communication was never a strong point of mine, and this restaurant noise was making it nearly impossible.

Alonso came back and we ordered our main course. Interesting how the waiter seemed to know exactly when the piano playing would stop and the noise die down. He tried to talk me into some dish I didn't want. It was all I could do to get my order in and wish him away. Gabe's terse to-the-point talking got the job done. But the short piano break didn't give me much chance. I dove in with the thing most on my mind.

"Gabe, about Monday, about that lunch."

Gabe's face turned immediately serious. "Yes?" He said the word with caution, and I knew I was skating on thin ice.

"I know we didn't have a date or anything, but you told me you were not going to —"

"Pardon, *Senora,*" the ever-hovering Alonso broke in. "I am so sorry to say there is no more of the *Spaghetti ai Gamberoni Piccanti.* May I offer you something else?" He handed me back the menu. Bad news, bad timing. I was beginning to lose my appetite. I opened the menu with a huff.

Gabe leaned over my way to share my view of the menu.

"How about *Ravioli con Gamberoni?*" I asked.

"*Senora,* no. I apologize. We have run out of shrimp. Perhaps something else?"

I wasn't feeling like eating much at all anymore.

I turned to my date. "Gabe, maybe we could simply go now?"

"Come on, Daisy. It's all right. Why don't you try the *Filetto al Marsala* instead?"

"Veal? But I couldn't. I'd never knowingly eat a baby cow. How cruel."

Gabe rolled his eyes. "Give it a try, Daisy. The calf has already sacrificed itself. You wouldn't want to waste that, would you?" At least he didn't run fingers through his hair.

My stomach churned and I slapped the menu closed. "What he said," I snapped at the waiter. "Only, make it quick, will you?"

"Very good, *Senora,*" said Alonso as he retrieved my menu. Professionally stiff, there was no smile as he projected what a cranky patron I'd become. Bad me. I so wanted to go home.

"Daisy," said Gabe, "don't you feel well?

It's not like you to be rude to wait-staff."

"I'm not feeling good at all, Gabe. I don't care for surprises that leave me feeling so discombobulated, I can't hear half of what you're saying, and I don't believe in eating veal. I've seen the documentaries about how those poor creatures live."

"Come on, my girl," Gabe coaxed. A rigidity in his voice said my layer of ice was getting thinner all the time. "This is a great evening out, and we need to make the most of it."

I sighed. "You're right. Let's talk about something else." I looked around, but nothing immediately came to mind. Then I realized that while I couldn't talk about Linda, I could talk about Cissy Melato. "How's the case coming?" I started to reach into my purse, which lay on the floor under my chair. Time to hand Gabe this present of the address book.

"Please. Not now," he muttered, frowning at me. I sat back up without the book in hand.

"What? What cow?" I replied. There were certain advantages to not being able to hear each other properly. Note to self, when things get tough, pretend you can't hear properly. So many possibilities.

Gabe shook his head at me. "You know I

212

don't like to talk about work, especially when we're out for a meal together."

"So what do you and Linda talk about when you're out for a meal together?" With sarcasm in my heart, I fluttered my eyelids at him. Gabe blushed and glared at me.

"That's different."

"Why?"

"Daisy, I'm here with you. This is our celebration of a good friendship. I know you didn't like seeing Linda at Alexio's, but what's done is done. I want this to be a special night. A good night. Can you drop the inquisition?"

"It's rather hard to do, when the inquisition keeps calling and interrupting us."

"Linda's calls are important work. Low blow, Daisy."

"How important? Did Linda really give you information that couldn't wait until the morning?"

Gabe blushed again. "Look. I have to be free to do my work any time of the day or night. I thought we'd been over this." His voice lifted above the noise of the room, and a tension grew in the air.

Alonso magically appeared again, and rattled on about the delicious food he was putting in front of us. I glared at Gabe the whole time, as we waited in silence while the waiter finished and disappeared.

The minute Alonso went away, I started in on Gabe. "I just don't think Linda needs to be attached to you the way she is."

"She's not attached to me."

"Oh, yeah? Where is your cell phone now? Seriously, how often do you get calls from anyone but Linda or Ginny?"

Gabe took a sip of his wine before answering. His nostrils flared. "I don't want to discuss this, Daisy. I work with Linda. I need to take her calls. There is often important evidence to discuss."

"So what evidence did she have to talk to you about a few minutes ago?" Okay, so I was being stupidly jealous. Gabe and I needed to settle this once and for all.

"That's police work, Daisy. You know I can't discuss it with you."

"Boloney!" Right as I shouted the word, the piano playing stopped, so my outburst could be heard by everyone in the small eating area. Heads turned our way. I bit my lip. Alonso magically appeared again.

"Is everything all right? Do you not like your meal?" He smiled over-broadly at us, but his glance was shifting around the room nervously. I wanted to smack him for being as professional and efficient as Linda.

Gabe snapped at the waiter. "Leave us

214

alone!" He was losing it fast. I couldn't blame him, but still. Gabe needed to stay cool with strangers.

I nodded to Alonso. "We're fine, and the food is delicious. But we'd like a little privacy please."

Alonso nodded and walked away. The piano started up again.

Gabe tucked into his dinner. I felt boxed in. We couldn't talk about the Linda lunch, as we were already close to an argument there. We couldn't talk about work, or Gabe would be more upset. We couldn't talk about Ginny because that would only lead us to talking about work because of her link to Brian, and back to Linda and work. Talk about a conundrum!

I tried to keep the sarcasm from my voice as I asked Gabe, "How do you like your meal?" *Calf-killer.* Gabe had ordered the veal too. He smiled at last. All I could think of were baby cows with big blue eyes. Make that brown eyes. I took a bite of my meal. It was delicious, but I really had no heart for it.

"I love this!" Gabe grinned. He sure enjoyed his food. I wondered how he managed to stay so trim with his obvious gourmet appetite.

My police lieutenant rattled on about the

sauce, the tenderness of the meat, and the great combination of food choices, even the presentation. Alonso kept punctuating our meal with offers of refreshers on my water, an extra something to drink for Gabe, a dropped napkin picked up. He seemed to appear at all the wrong moments, moments when Gabe and I were glaring at each other in disagreement, or when one or the other of us raised a voice above the noise of the other restaurant patrons. My fingers itched to reach out and swat the waiter.

Finally, Gabe said, "Daisy, you've hardly eaten anything. Don't you like the meal?" It seemed as though my liking the meal was hugely important, so I smiled and said, "Let's box it up. You can have it for lunch tomorrow — unless you're too busy to eat again."

"Zip it, Daisy!" Gabe shouted. He smashed his hand on the tabletop to punctuate his words. Gabe's hand grazed his plate, which accidentally sent his fork full of gravy-covered calf flying across the room.

"You zip it, Gabe! I offered you my leftovers for goodness sakes. A leftover lunch is all." I threw my napkin down. It fell to the floor. The hovering Alonso came into view. "Go away, already!" I hollered at Alonso. The waiter recoiled and dashed toward the kitchen. Some person looking as mad as I felt stood up at another table.

"You implied —" Gabe jumped to his feet, a blush on both cheeks growing.

"You stood me up for another woman!" I rose too. People stopped and stared at the two of us. Gabe towered over me by a good ten inches. I made up the difference by wagging a finger in his face.

"My partner!" he exclaimed.

"My a—"

The angry man from the other table strode over. "You!" He was a big guy, taller than Gabe, and he hovered over our table, glaring at my lieutenant. "You threw a bunch of food at my wife and me!"

I looked over to see the woman in the scruffy outfit dabbing at her ugly top. Must have been the fork Gabe launched. "No worries," I said. "I'm sure the gravy will enhance her outfit tremendously. Too bad it couldn't be used to patch her raggedy jeans."

"What?" Both men turned toward me. Gabe actually stood slack-jawed. The big stranger made a lightning quick grab for Gabe's collar and smashed something into my guy's face. It was a roll with olive oil dripping from it.

Gabe stepped back from the blow, but

tumbled off balance into a tray of food Alonso had set down for another table. As Gabe spun and stepped away from that mess, he landed in the lap of another man, who'd been trying to eat a bowl of soup at another close table. The soup flew through the air and spilled on the man's date. She screamed.

Across from the screaming woman, another accidentally elbowed her date when she went to cover her ears. That resulted in him tilting backwards into someone else who spilled more food, and a chain reaction was in full swing.

Some young man stood up and shouted "food fight!" as if we were in a school cafeteria, and all chaos broke loose.

I dove for cover behind a potted plant, and watched as World War III began.

Plates crashed on the cement floor and shattered. Food flew through the air, people shoved each other, and the shouting escalated. The room seemed to erupt in a mass of hungry patrons pushing and heaving themselves and food in every direction.

The immaculate Alonso and other wait staff kept trying to break up fights, but only ended up the worse for wear. Their white shirts turned red and brown, depending on the sauce spilled on them. Their lovely long hair ended up with pasta strings in it.

The piano player tried performing more calming tunes, louder and louder, but to no avail. Someone stomped over to him and smashed the keyboard cover down, narrowly missing the guy's fingers.

Sounds bounced off the unmuffled walls, and I thought wickedly I hadn't had so much fun since I left teaching.

Finally, the hostess appeared and blew a police whistle. Everyone froze. The place went still, deathly quiet. A last plate rolled on the floor and its sound echoed a censorious tone.

Patrons openly stared at Gabe and me. He straightened his tie and grabbed my hand. His cheeks were as hot as mine felt.

"I have called the police," said the hostess to Gabe. She looked very regal with her calm, clean demeanor. "They will escort you out."

My goodness.

CHAPTER 20

My head pounded. Some dinner. Most of
my few bites of veal still roiled in my
stomach, soured by Gabe's and my embarrassing display. Gabe had hardly said a word
as we drove home and when I got out of his
car, his tires squealed as he drove off.

I looked at my watch. Only eight. An
evening spent reviewing my guilt wasn't
exactly what I'd pictured today. I still
couldn't believe we'd been asked to leave
the restaurant. This had never happened to
me before. But envisioning the man who
lost his toupee in the skirmish was enough
to make me giggle. Even Gabe smiled when
I told him about it on the ride home.

Still, Art would not have let things go so
far in a disagreement. He'd always reach a
certain level of anger, and then say to me,
"Daisy, we're obviously at an impasse. We'll
revisit this subject when we've both had a
chance to cool down. I abhor this, but I still

love you." And that was that. Gabe's tempers were getting more and more severe. It had to be more than me or Ginny or even Brian, for that matter. Maybe I was imagining things. But Gabe was so different from Art.

Art and I rarely left an argument overnight. Though, to be honest, Art's refusal to fight was often as difficult to handle as Gabe's much more frequent angry outbursts. Still, life with Art had been predictable and calm, if a little dull.

Art, how I miss you! Why do I have to feel so all-alone?

And then it hit me.

I didn't have to be so alone. If Gabe was being a poop, I could find friends elsewhere. I thought about Sam, our dog-park times, and that silly kiss. Hmm. Wouldn't mind kissing him some more. I wasn't *married* to Gabe, after all.

In fact, I'd sometimes wondered what Gabe's and my relationship was really about. More often than not, he invited me over to be a companion for Ginny while he and That Woman were out on police business. Never thought of Littleton as the Mecca of crime that Gabe's job seemed to indicate.

Yes. Meeting Sam would be a good idea. I

speed-dialed Sam's number. He picked up on the fourth ring.

"Sam! Glad I caught you."

"Hullo, Daisy. I'll be heading to bed soon. This important?"

Odd. There was an empty edge to Sam's voice tonight. And going to bed at eight-fifteen? Even *I* didn't practice that farmer-like routine. Would've thought he'd be happy to hear from me.

Please, Daisy, don't be rejected again.

"I won't keep you long. It's only that I had a rough night and was hoping we could meet at Chatfield in the morning. You and I could take the dogs for a nice walk. I'll bring both Thunder and Queenie."

There was a small hitch in Sam's voice. "I can't make it."

"Oh?" I *was* being rejected again. Had some sort of guy radio network blasted out that Daisy was a *persona non grata*? Had I been branded a shrew? Would no one want to be with me ever again after my fighting-restaurant-fiasco?

My heart sank. "Gosh, Sam, I thought a crisp spring morning walk would be good for us. To be honest, I need a nice vent with a good friend like you."

"Let me guess. Gabe?"

I nodded into the phone and sniffed.

"No, Daisy. I'm not going to be there. And after what happened the last time, I don't think I'm the right guy to talk to about your boyfriend problems."

He was right, of course. But I'd come to think of Sam as the best guy pal in my life. We shared so much in common. I loved trading puns with him. Maybe he just needed a different tactic from me.

I tried to shove as much playfulness in my voice as possible. "You mean you don't want to kiss and tell? Very disweet of you. And I'll never talk either. But surely Rocky would like a little fresh —"

"Rocky's dead!" Sam's voice blasted through my earphone. Silence whooshed right after and grabbed my heart. I couldn't have heard right.

Sam's voice raged on through ragged edges. "Damn it, woman! My dog died today. *You* need a shoulder to cry on? I told you no!" There was a small click and the line went dead.

My chest clenched uncomfortably. Rocky was dead? My goodness! And all I had been thinking about was how miserable I was over a tiff with Gabe. How selfish of me.

Poor Rocky. Poor Sam.

I redialed Sam's phone, but the call went right to voice mail. I hung up and sighed.

What would Art say?

Daisy, you have some thinking to do before getting involved with either Gabe or Sam. Think.

So I thought. I thought while I changed into my pajamas, I thought while I had a cup of herbal tea, and then another. I thought through cookies and final doggie potty for Queenie.

How could I be so needy when my friend had just lost his dog? When Brian was in jail? When Ginny and Gabe were at odds? My unfortunate friends! Where was the quiet, comfy Littleton life I knew so well?

I went into Art's office and woke my computer. I'd start with an apology to Sam. The blank screen of an incomplete email stared at me. *Okay, Daisy-girl, you're supposed to be a writer. Now write!*

I poured my sympathy into Sam's note, let the sadness flow through and into my writing. Tears rolled as I tried to offer some favorite Rocky memories — like when he and Thunder went for a swim in the fish ponds at Chatfield and shook all over Sam and me. How we'd laughed! I remembered that Rocky stayed in a heel at Sam's side, only breaking for a forgotten tennis ball dropped by some other dog. I remembered Rocky looking out with those beautiful brown eyes that seemed to say "I love you" to the whole world, but particularly shone for Sam.

I finished the note and sent it off, then had another cup of tea, hoping I'd hear from Sam before I went to bed. No such luck. He must have gone to sleep like he'd said.

I went to bed too, but lay awake. There was so much unsettled in my life, I couldn't rest. Gabe and me, Sam and Rocky, and through it all, Cissy, her killer, and Brian wove in and out of my thoughts.

Sleep in middle age is a precious thing. Our bodies seem afraid to slumber the whole night through. Perhaps our subconscious knows that we are turning the corner into old age, even death, and our fear is that if we slept through the night, we might never wake up. Time is so short for all of us. Especially short for Cissy.

Better to have these uncomfortable puzzles to work on than to lie awake admonishing myself to go to sleep. Thank goodness for writing.

I rolled over, turned on the light, and grabbed a journal. I didn't need men. I had a mystery to solve. And I *would* solve the mystery of who killed Cissy. Brian depended on me for that. Now, who would want to kill a pretend vegetarian and accountant, and why?

CHAPTER 21

The red digits on my clock read ten-twenty. Journaling hadn't helped. My non-existent dinner churned in my stomach. I was hungry, doggone it! I wanted more than outbursts from Gabe and grief from Sam to chew on.

I needed . . . I needed . . . What?

Cissy's picture came to mind. On any given night she probably went to bed, much as I did. Maybe she wore flannel nighties too. Maybe she read from those mind-numbing accounting books for a while. Maybe had a snack to help her through the more boring parts. Probably something sweet to reward herself. That was it! Snack. I needed some nice, "vegetarian," ice cream!

I jumped out of bed, dressed in sweats with a pretty pink and yellow top and charged out the door. Queenie and Georgette would have to babysit themselves without my good-byes. My trusty Versa

227

warmed instantly as I drove down Main Street towards Gigantos.

The supermarket loomed in my windshield, with fifteen minutes to spare before closing. *Food, food, junk food.*

The thought looped in a wolf-like refrain through my brain. Perhaps that was how people came up with the idea of werewolves in the first place — being hungry enough to gnaw the gizzards out of your best friend, especially when the hunger was tinged with guilty anger.

I stomped over to the freezer section, found a helpless container of mint chocolate-chip ice cream and dumped it in my cart. I grabbed a box of Fudgesicles to boot. Not enough. I paced to the snack aisle in search of potato chips and butter cookies. Even though I glared at every person in view, I was feeling better, just imagining the food orgy I was about to rip into.

Then I saw him, and my blood lust ran cold.

Roddy McKeague.

The jerk was in the produce section. Asparagus sprouted from a display nearby, and I noticed a sign about specials on the first radishes of the season. Somehow Roddy's hawkish frame suited the produce section — kind of like a crow in a cornfield. He looked as sinister as I felt, so I watched with a predatory stare. My breath came in pants of desire — desire to beat something to a pulp. I didn't care if my instincts about Roddy were accurate or not. My need to protect Brian and Ginny, coupled with my foul mood, made Roddy a perfect target for my rotten attitude.

This late at night produce started looking a bit picked-over, so I watched as Roddy shuffled fruits and vegetables around in an obvious effort to make the shelves more presentable. He didn't notice me.

I paced quietly, stalking the guy. And then he shoved some poor man with a Gigantos uniform on. The man had been clearing old produce into cardboard boxes, but apparently not quickly enough for the night manager. The man looked frightened and upset, yet let Roddy continue to push and stuff fingers in his face. I wanted to get closer, to hear what was going on. If only I could pin something illegal on Roddy — something like assault. Perhaps it would make Gabe take a stronger interest in him as Cissy's potential killer, instead of poor Brian.

A growl grew deep within my chest. The victim must be a stock boy. Only this boy looked to be almost as old as the wilted lettuce Roddy shoved under his nose. If I'd been that man, I would have shoved the lettuce up the fool's behind, then quit.

Of course, it was easy to think brave thoughts when I had my protective hoard of junk food, my bad mood, and my sense of indignation about me. And I didn't need to worry about keeping a job. Art had provided well for me. Who did the stock boy have watching his back? He could be just another Brian. Roddy was his manager, and probably had a right to demand a lot from the guy he was obviously harassing.

At almost eleven o'clock, there weren't many other patrons to be found, so maybe Roddy could get away with more than a normal amount of bullying. Was that the kind of thing he did to Brian when no one was looking? Would this kind of harassment be why Brian lit into Roddy that night? The night he was arrested, with Cissy Melato bleeding a Mississippi River's worth of blood? Did Roddy know precisely how to push Brian's buttons? I needed to know more about this guy. I really ought to stalk — er — follow him as closely as I could.

A voice whined out over the store speaker and I jumped. "Attention Gigantos shoppers. The time now is ten fifty. Our store will be closing in ten minutes. Please make your final selections. We will open again tomorrow at six a.m. Thank you for shopping the Gigantos way, where we take pride in treating you like royalty."

Guess Speaker Voice didn't see the way Roddy was treating the stock man. More like a royal pain. In fact, I'd bet Roddy got away with even more rubbish, as he was without checkout-area witnesses. How much more, I wondered. And to whom?

I was ready to walk up and tell the jerk off when another man joined Roddy. It was the handsome guy from the funeral. What did Gabe say his name was? Handsome and Roddy began talking in earnest, and the stock boy slinked away. Handsome picked up another head of lettuce and started peeling leaves off. He pointed to other lettuce, wrapped in plastic from the next bin over, but, seeming to sense my presence, looked up. Our eyes met across the department floor.

For a moment Handsome simply stared. Did he recognize me? My wolfish mood started to creep away. Why did I find so many men attractive? Wasn't I too old for the thoughts that barged in on my brain unbidden? Was menopause another word for re-adolescent?

I turned, pretending to find the shelf behind me fascinating and hoping Handsome — what was his name? — had only stared at me because he was lost in thought. I glanced back over my shoulder to see both grocery men watching me. Suddenly, I felt more lamb than wolf, and quickly turned my attention to my shopping cart. Roddy might be a gnat in wolf's clothing, but the evilness in his glare unhinged me. A chill ran down my spine. I whirled the cart around ready to rush my junk food treasures to the checkout, as the intercom voice had commanded.

Too late. After only one or two steps, a strong hand stopped me from pushing my cart forward.

"You're Brian's friend, aren't you?" said Roddy, a sneer painted across his dark features. "Why are you here so late at night, Brian's friend?"

I gulped but tried to brave it out. "I came in for a snack. Why do you ask?"

"We close soon. It's not safe, even in Littleton, to be out so late at night."

Was that a threat? Another shiver ran through me. My hand flew to Art's locket at my neck.

"Well," I drawled, wishing Roddy would take his hand from my cart, "how late I shop is not your concern. You don't close for another five minutes. And the parking lot is completely lit. Now if you don't mind . . ."

I tried to push my cart free from Roddy's grasp. He held fast. Goodness, I not only loathed this man, but I was disgusted about the way my hands were shaking. My breath came in ragged gasps.

"Nosey old ladies like you and that friend of Brian's need to learn to bake your cookies at home when it's late at night. You oughtta be safe in bed, not out where you could get hurt." He leered over me and I realized too late how intimidating Roddy could be.

"Enough!" I shouted. I don't know if it was my crummy evening, the men in my life acting like such control-freaks, or purely that I bought into my conflict-is-good writer's thought process. I dug into my purse for my cell phone. "If you're trying to threaten me, I'll — I'll call nine-one-one."

The smell of expensive aftershave crept into my nostrils. I sensed the warmth of another person behind me. At Independence High, I had the habit of tuning in to students 360 degrees. Even my non-verbal pupils couldn't easily take me by surprise. I whirled.

The second man stood behind me. He was

even handsomer up close. I jumped. Hadn't he been halfway across the produce section a few seconds ago? How did he get here so fast? Why hadn't I heard him approach?

Handsome's face held large, round, brown eyes and an expression that said, I'm-really-a-nice-guy-with-a-sad-past-and-wish-you-could-know-me-better look. Very Russell Crow.

Yet, I was uncomfortable. Maybe it was because I'd only seen him with Roddy. Bad circle of friend.

"Something wrong here, ma'am?" he said, then smiled. It was a quick flick of his lips into a beautiful curve and small blink. If I hadn't so strongly connected him to Roddy and some feeling of bad, I could have swooned into that Russell Crow charming set of muscular arms right there.

I could almost sense Art's eyes rolling, even from the grave. Almost hear him saying *not again, Daisy*.

Almost.

"No. Just finishing my shopping." I glared at Roddy, who looked like he wanted to say more. Instead he let go of my cart and slithered away. I turned to look at the man with the too-good-to-be-true face. "Thanks." Then I nodded at Roddy's retreating figure. "I'm not sure why Gigantos would keep someone like that Roddy-guy on staff. He's disgusting."

"Roddy's one of our younger managers," said my Russell Crow guy. "I've been assigned to help him refine his customer and management skills." There came that devastating smile again, and I felt my own lips curve in response.

"You must have your hands full."

"You have no idea." He laughed and the sound made my evening. "My name's Johnson. Keith Johnson. Regional manager for Gigantos." He put out his hand, and I shook it with every fiber responding to the guy's animal magnetism. Eat your heart out, Gabe and Linda. So much for my werewolf attitude. Yes, this was the Keith of the funeral.

"Daisy." I fluttered. "Daisy Arthur."

"Roddy's right about one thing, Daisy. It is very late for a pretty woman like you to be out on her own. How 'bout I help you out to your car after you've checked out?"

If I could blush, my cheeks would've been absolute fire engines. Gabe was forgotten. Sam didn't exist. Nothing mattered but the absolutely electrical excitement of looking into Keith's face. De-licious! It reminded me of someone — someone dangerous, but I couldn't put my finger on the thought.

Must be my leftover werewolf and unsatisfied need for junk food.

I checked out, embarrassed to have Keith see my super indulgence. It was almost like sharing my underwear drawer. Very inappropriate.

Keith winked at me. "Rough night?" He nodded toward my treasures.

"You have no idea," I parroted, then remembered I was tired of controlling men. "But I can handle it."

"Looks like you can." He shrugged, then grabbed my bags and walked me out into the night.

At my car, Keith helped me put my groceries in the trunk. He was a perfect gentleman. We chatted about how May evenings in Colorado are superb, with enough coolness to sleep comfortably, but warm enough to want to leave a window open. We talked about the grocery business, romance writing, dogs, and even my love of puns. Almost every car in the lot disappeared as employees left the now-closed supermarket. Keith even laughed when I said how walking me to the car was very *gallon* of him, and I'd *milk* the opportunity as much as possible. He held my hand as I stepped into my car. Then Keith leaned in toward me. His aftershave made me want to swoon.

"Roddy's right," Keith whispered. I leaned toward him to hear better. "Late nights, even in Littleton, can be dangerous. So can conversations between strangers." His breath was warm against my cheek. What did he mean *conversations could be dangerous*? I turned to thank him and smiled. Then he moved closer and kissed me.

I was so shocked! My goodness! What would Art think? What would Gabe say? My eyes flew open.

Keith smiled and stepped back. "Sorry, Daisy. I forgot myself. You're the dangerous one tonight, my dear. You've stolen my heart." Then he winked at me and shut me into my car.

Wow! For a cheesy line, it worked. Really.

As I drove off, I checked for Keith in my rearview, but he was gone. And as quickly as that, the magic of the moment disappeared. I decided I could play with that Keith guy, but he wasn't someone I'd want around for long. Not sure why. A chill ran down my spine. Must be these cool Colorado evenings.

CHAPTER 22

Wow. Two dinners out in one week. Even though I tingled with embarrassment every time I thought of the Italian place with Gabe, tonight was sure to be less stressful. I was sharing dinner with two good friends. Kitty and Chip had lit up my life since I joined the Hugs 'N' Kisses — now The wRite Stuff — writing group, and I enjoyed sharing all sorts of events with them.

Chip had stopped by with Thunder earlier in the day, and invited me out to the South Platte Bar and Grill. Very casual Mexican food and a fun atmosphere of bikers, college professors, and families all mixed together in the patchwork that was Littleton. With spring weather poking its summer promises in every day or two, and daylight savings in place, we decided to sit on the back deck overlooking the parking lot and the greenbelt that hid the Platte River a couple hundred yards away.

The deck was crowded to the point of overflowing, even though it was a huge place with four spacious eating areas on as many different levels. Chip scouted out a table under a yellow and white, beer logo–decorated umbrella. We squished past a table full of guys in t-shirts and leather vests, and snuggled into place.

Chip had maneuvered himself to sit as close as possible to Kitty, who didn't seem to mind a bit. Tonight, my pixie friend was dazzling in a gold-colored tunic over pink and red stretch pants and cowboy boots. She wore delicate gold hoop earrings that framed a face positively glowing in the happiness of Chip's company. Seven months ago, when they met, I thought Chip was going to do his usual I'll-write-a-story-about-you stuff with Kitty and the affair would end within a couple of weeks.

But Kitty was made of sterner stuff, and soon Chip was acting with a protective maturity I had never seen in my young neighbor before. While Christmas had been spent separately, New Year's, Valentine's, and Easter were all decorated with my happy couple dropping in for visits and focusing only on each other. I smiled at the thought.

"So what's the occasion, you two?" I

raised my glass of lemonade to them.

Chip leaned over to Kitty and whispered. She giggled and nodded her head.

"What?" I asked.

Chip cleared his throat. "I *propose* a toast." He lifted a beer mug to the occasion. "To good friends, warm spring evenings, and my special love." With that he pushed his mug toward Kitty.

"Chip! You goofball," said Kitty. "Don't drag it out."

"Drag what out?" I asked.

Kitty burst into another laugh. "Daisy, Chip and I are going to get married!"

I felt my jaw drop. It was the biggest surprise, and yet so totally predictable, that I felt my whole heart leap for joy. "My goodness! You two lean over here and give me a hug. I can't believe this. Yes, I can. Oh, I don't know what to say. Congratulations!"

We all stood to lean over the table between us for a group hug.

"Congratulations!" shouted several tables of people around us. Chip, ever the pistol, grabbed Kitty in a big kiss that met with more cheers and whistles from the crowd before we sat down again.

Kitty pulled out her left hand to show me her ring. As with everything else about her, the engagement ring was unique and sparkling in multiple colors of semi-precious stones.

"I didn't want one of those fake diamonds," said Chip, "and we didn't want to go for the expense of a real one, so Kitty helped me pick this ring out."

"It's perfect. Wait! Let me get my phone out and take a picture!"

Kitty happily cuddled with her hero, and I snapped away.

Soon we were enjoying nachos and Buffalo wings, with music and casual conversations flowing all around us. Kitty and Chip told me all about their plans to be married on Halloween. Kitty's mom had insisted that they wait at least a year, which was October, so having a dress-up themed wedding seemed like a fun thing to do.

I thought back to the day Kitty and Chip met. I had just solved the case of who killed father Rico Sanchez, though, to be honest, Gabe had a lot to do with that. I simply happened to meet up with the murderer at the wrong moment. Anyway, Chip came over at the same time as Kitty while we wrapped things up. I was very glad that the two hadn't met during the upheaval surrounding Rico's death. It was almost as if Chip and Kitty were meant to be together and offer all our community new hope. I smiled.

Chip piped up. "Daisy ol' girl. You're awfully quiet tonight. Are you okay?"

"I was just remembering when you two met." I winked at Chip, but then sighed.

"So what's wrong?" asked Kitty.

"Thinking about last fall, I also remember that Ginny had a boyfriend her dad didn't even know about. Maybe she let Gabe forget he was around. Maybe Ginny didn't want Gabe to know about Brian because her instincts told her that Gabe would give the boy a hard time." I pushed some sauce around my plate with a buffalo wing. "I would never have guessed he'd go so far as to make Brian a prime suspect in a murder case, though."

Kitty piped up. "He wouldn't do that to hurt Ginny. Maybe Brian *is* the bad guy, Daisy. Don't you think that's possible?"

"If you saw Brian, you wouldn't believe so. Brian probably operates at a seven- or eight-year-old maturity level. He's sweet to the bone. I don't think he'd be capable of planning a murder, of lying in wait for Cissy and then attacking her. But, like Gabe, he has a bad temper."

Chip looked calmer than I'd ever seen him before. Being engaged suited him. "Bad enough temper to kill someone, Daisy?"

"I don't think so. And from what I understand, even a bad temper wouldn't account for the damage done to poor Cissy Melato. The police are keeping the details to themselves, but I was there that night. I saw how the murder upset the officers investigating the scene."

Kitty leaned across the table and put her glowing left hand on my own. "How can we help?" she asked, already telepathically including Chip in her plans.

"I'm not sure. There is so little to go on. And the only evidence I have that the police don't is Cissy's address book."

Kitty started and leaned back, eyebrows flying to her hairline. "You kept evidence away from Gabe? Away from the police? Don't you know that's obstruction of justice?"

I bit my lip. "I've been meaning to give it to him, but there doesn't ever seem to be a good time for it." I rubbed my head and sighed again. "Gabe and I — You see, we're having a couple of problems right now." Then, like the spring rains, I poured out all my issues with Gabe, the murder, and life in general.

Two lemonades, a turkey club wrap, and several tortilla chips later, I let up on my verbal downpour.

Chip rubbed his chin. "Wow," he said. "You sure know how to step in it, Daisy."

I glared at him and Kitty poked him in the ribs. Looked like she had a little more work to do on perfecting her knight in shining armor. Chip shrugged. "So. You have Brian, his boss, Roddy, and Joe Smaldone for suspects. Anybody else?"

"I don't know who the woman at the funeral was, or the man standing behind her. I assume she was a relative of Cissy's, and he might also be someone to investigate. If the woman is a close relative, she'd have to be a suspect. Standard procedure you know."

"If it were me, I'd check out that Joe Smaldone a little more," said Chip. "I don't believe for an instant that the mob in Denver is out of business. Wherever there are laws, there are guys willing to break 'em to make a profit."

"But Joe didn't seem at all the type to commit murder. He's very nice, Chip."

"Nice? Nice, Daisy? Do you know anything about the Smaldone family?"

"Not really. I've heard they smuggled booze during prohibition."

"Not only," said Chip. "Those boys were smooth as a fresh blanket of snow, but underneath hard, cold, and dangerous. They had rocks for souls and knives always at the ready."

"C'mon, Chip. Really? Or have you been watching too many gangster movies lately?"

"No exaggeration." Chip took a sip of his beer.

Some biker dude leaned over from another table. "Better watch how you talk about the Smaldones. Word is the Rockies wouldn't be half so high if it weren't for all the bodies that mob family buried in 'em."

"Thanks," I said and scooched closer to Kitty and Chip.

Kitty piped in. "This Joe guy sounds like somebody you want to stay clear of, especially as he's living right around here. At the bar where I work, the police are always saying Santa Fe remains a route for drug smuggling and other nefarious goings-on."

"Yep," said Chip, "I'd lay a bet Smaldone is your guy. Does Gabe know about him?"

"Yes. And he seems aware of the Smaldone family already."

"Good," said Kitty. She wiped her fingers and mouth of Mexican leftovers. "Let Gabe check out the Smaldones, Daisy. I want you around to be our writing group leader for some time to come."

I smiled at Kitty then turned back to

Chip. "You don't think the murderer might be Roddy?"

Chip shook his head, buffalo wing snuggled in his cheek. He swallowed. "Guy's a jerk by the sounds of it, but a small fry. I'll look into him too, if you want, but with a murder this horrendous, Smaldone has to be a link to it all. You said he was a relative of the vic?"

"Of Cissy? Yes. Cousin I think. And her client too."

"That settles it. Smaldone's your guy. But you want to stay clear of the riff-raff, Daisy. They can be dangerous. Very dangerous."

I thought of Joe Smaldone, the house he lived in, the way he acted at the funeral. Riff-raff wouldn't at all be the word that came to my mind for him.

Kitty shivered right then. "Honey, can I borrow your jacket? It feels like some rain is ready to start."

Chip smiled at his fiancée and wrapped his jacket close about her. Goodness, they made such an adorable couple. We paid the bill and left.

CHAPTER 23

Hershberg's Gym. What a great way to spend a Friday night.

Not.

At least the place wouldn't be too crowded, I suspected. I mean, Friday night was date night as far as I knew. Who would go on a date to a gym? I walked in with extra clothes stuffed in an old backpack. The receptionist, who looked like a Barbie doll on steroids, smiled at me out of her deeply tanned face. Was that real or the spray-on stuff I'd heard of?

"Welcome to Hershberg's. Do you have a member pass?" said Barbie.

"No. I'm meeting someone here." Why would a gym issue member passes? Who would actually want one of those things? I mean, eew.

"Sorry, but without an escort or pass, I can't let you in."

"I'm here to meet a member. Can you tell

me if Dan Block's arrived?"

"No, I can't say. Privacy issues you know, but if you'll wait here, I'll call over the intercom. If he comes to the desk, you're in."

I could hardly contain my excitement. I could be let into a torture chamber of glistening metal contraptions to be met by a guy I had a hard time tolerating, and then I could pinch, poke, and sweat my way to a weekend full of aspirins for my aches. Why, oh why, had I agreed to this meeting?

"Daisy!" Dan's voice accompanied his wide smile and toned body shimmering in a slight layer of perspiration. Arms I had often suspected of being muscular actually bulged with healthiness. Goodness. I knew Dan was in shape, but *wow*.

"Hullo, Dan." I tried to smile back, but the idea of working out with a guy who had a Superman build was quite daunting.

"Didn't think you'd show." Dan opened the locked barrier, and turned his smile to Super Barbie. "She's with me, Becca."

Becca's eyebrows rose a bit, but she displayed ultimate professionalism and handed me a guest pass. "Women's lockers are to the right. Keys are in the free lockers."

I went in.

Twenty minutes later, Dan had me on one of those stationary treadmill thingies, and I was actually enjoying myself.

"You're doing great," said Dan from his treadmill next to me. "Gotta say, I'm impressed."

"Thanks," I managed to squeeze out between desperate gasps for air. My feet swelled, and my shoes became too tight; my tummy ached, but overall, I guessed I could handle this.

"Want a break?" asked Dan.

I tried to play it cool, shrugging my shoulders. Didn't want him to think I was a wimp, quitting at the first opportunity. "If you want to," I said.

He lightly stepped off his machine.

Thank you, Good Spirits! I didn't think he was the least bit winded, even though his settings were much harder than mine.

"Thought we'd talk a bit about writing." Dan reached into his gym bag and pulled out some papers. "Let's go to the juice bar. I'll buy you a power shake."

Oh, my stars, would the thrills never end? If Art could see me now. *Daisy,* he'd say, *I'm proud of you. Now if you would just lose another ten pounds . . .* Sometimes I think Art is lucky to be gone. I stepped off the treadmill and my culture-shocked leg muscles recoiled in confusion. Were they supposed to still be working?

Dan and I strolled to the juice bar where café tables were scattered amongst gym bags and worn athletes. We grabbed a couple of seats.

I took a sip of some green mass of goo that turned out to be better than I thought. "This shake is delicious, Dan."

"Thought you might like it. Has spinach, banana, kale, and arugula. The extra kick is from cilantro they throw in last minute."

"Really? I probably wouldn't have tried it if you told me that before I drank it."

Dan chuckled. It was a nice sound, lacking the harshness of his criticisms. I smiled over at him. "Now, what was it about writing you wanted to talk through?"

Dan pulled his lower lip with his index finger and thumb. He gave me a measured look, and then seemed to make a decision. "Like I said earlier, Daisy, I honestly didn't think you'd show this evening. Your email came back so quickly. I didn't believe you thought it through before sending it. But here you are. That in itself is impressive."

"Thanks, I think."

"Don't look so upset. I meant that as a compliment. And here is another. Your writing, like your body, has good structure. You

250

bring tension about appropriately and you develop good characters."

My body had good structure? Cool! "But . . . ?" I prompted.

"But you're a little flabby."

I winced and tried to pull down my t-shirt so that my flab wouldn't show so much.

"Stop," said Dan. "I meant your *writing* is a little flabby. For someone your age, I think you're in pretty good shape."

For my age. Ouch. "Dan, stop trying to compliment me, okay? Not your forte. Not."

Dan chuckled again. "Sorry, friend. You're right about that. I keep a standing prescription with my pharmacist for the ol' foot-in-mouth disease."

"Chronic condition, eh?"

"Yeah." He gave me a wry smile.

It was my turn to laugh. So Dan Block wasn't mean. He was merely a little tactless.

"My mom was adamant about honesty in our house," said Dan. "We weren't nice very often, but when someone said you did good, it was a sure thing."

"Maybe we can keep the honesty but smooth it out with a little power shaking." I lifted my now empty glass.

"Deal. But right now, I want to show you how I edit my stuff, so maybe you can get where I'm coming from." Dan spread a few

251

pages across the table. I picked one up and recognized a piece he'd brought in a week or two back.

"But this is your work! You write so well, and now you've marked it all up. It was great when you brought it to group."

"I took everyone's feedback and used it to mark up another copy for myself. Here, see this sentence? *He stood off by himself, alone on the railroad platform.* Do you see the flab there?"

Honestly, I didn't. I shook my head.

"*By himself,* and *alone* are redundant," said Dan. "The sentence is stronger if I shorten it to *Charles stood alone on the railway platform.* Same meaning, same picture, yet shorter and cleaner."

"I wouldn't have caught that in a million years," I said, scooching in closer. "Can you show me another one?"

"Here. Attributions are often a waste. *"Sonya, I believe you," said Charles.* If I substitute a period for *said* and start the next sentence with Charles taking action, it will read better and be tighter."

I had a flash of inspiration. "Something like, *Sonya, I believe you. Charles winked at her and turned to refill his green smoothie cup.*"

"That's it." Dan patted my shoulder, and

I felt pride surging up my ribcage.

"Cool. Let's do it again." We ran through the portion of Dan's copy he hadn't marked, and as we worked, his pen slashed, dashed and chopped with the same ferocity he used on my writing each week. I noticed, though, that while the marks looked angry, when Dan talked them through, he was calm and confident. Interesting.

I couldn't resist. "Why do you use that red marking pen, and with such a big stroke?"

He shrugged. "I never thought about it much. Why?"

"Because I think you hate me when I see your editing."

"*Hate* you?" Dan shook his head. "You made me part of your critique group. How could I hate you?"

"But you cover my pages with those huge, red slashes. I feel like Janet Leigh in *Psycho* when I get my stuff back from you."

Dan laughed. "Jeez, Daisy. That wasn't my intention. I want to do a good job with critique and can't see if I write in blue or black. Plus, my eyes are going a little bad. Might miss something important without the size and color I use. Besides, it's fun to be so bold in my work."

"I can't see you ever missing a single

mistake I make." I hung my head.

"Sorry you feel so bad. Would you rather I not mark your stuff?"

I thought a moment. I'm the kind of person who usually blossoms under the occasional compliment, but did I like false ego strokes? "No. Now that I know what you're doing, I can handle it. But nobody in the group is thrilled with your critiques, even though they think you're right more often than not."

It was Dan's turn to look thoughtful. "I have to be honest. Don't know what else I can do."

"Do you like the critiques I give you?"

He made a face. "You're too soft. Fun to read how terrific I am, though."

"Okay, so how about Eleanor's critiques?"

"She's better."

"Yes. I like the way she writes a quick here's-what-I-like sentence before jotting down what she thinks is wrong."

"But she goes overboard. Tends to rewrite instead of edit."

"Great! You know what doesn't work in critique, so let's focus now on what does."

We talked about writing, critiquing, and self-editing for another few minutes then went on to the weight machines. Dan had me tired but happy within another half hour. At about ten o'clock I'd had enough. I stepped off a contraption that just about pulled my arms from their sockets.

"Dan, this has been a super evening, even with the flab-reduction torture chambers, but I'm done."

"No problem, Daisy. I need to get home too. My wife is a great woman, but not too patient when I hang out at the gym too long."

"I didn't know you were still married. You don't talk about your wife."

"Happily so, and for over twenty years. Tonight, Naomi's sister came over for the evening, and I didn't want to listen to girl talk, so coming here and meeting you was a good alternative. Anyway, Naomi's supported my love of writing ever since I gave up trying to become a lawyer."

"You wanted to be a lawyer?"

"Decades ago. I was more idealistic then. But we had no money and a baby on the way. I fell into the job with Express Plus Delivery Company, and that was that."

"So how did you end up wanting to join the wRite Stuff group?"

"Danny Junior grew up. He's off on his own now. I had time and looked for a critique group. Naomi said my work is good, so I decided maybe it's time to try a novel."

"Dan, I'm so glad we had a chance to talk tonight. You've been a very pleasant surprise."

"You too, Daisy. Now, you need directions to the women's lockers?"

I shook my head no, and we went to change. Dan met me on the way out through the reception area. Right as we were leaving, another couple came in. Gabe and Linda! My goodness! More police business?

Gabe's jaw dropped wide open when he saw me. I wished I had another health shake handy to stuff into that gaping hole.

"Daisy!" sputtered Gabe.

"We didn't expect to see you here," added Linda, who, with her totally sculpted thirty-something body, could just go investigate a grave as far as I was concerned.

I felt the health shake roil around my stomach. "After Wednesday, I thought I'd work on building some boxing skills. Never know when a good right hook could come in handy."

Gabe blushed deeply. Linda obviously didn't catch my joke. Guess maybe she and Gabe didn't share everything after all.

Still, my breath caught in my throat. I mean, this wasn't a lunch date turned down, but it was That Woman and *my* police lieutenant. "You're probably here on police business, right?" I took my time gazing at the couple from head to toe. Linda fidgeted near Gabe, who looked like he'd rather be out processing parking tickets.

I told myself I wasn't going to get upset. I was in control. *Sure. Control.* Just because my stomach had more butterflies than the Pavilion in Broomfield didn't mean I was upset. No way.

At that point, Dan stepped to my side. "Honey, are you going to introduce me to your friends?" He smiled down at me and gave a look that said he was in total love here. What game was he playing?

Linda found her voice. "Hi, Dan. Didn't expect to see you here tonight. This is Daisy's — er — my boss, Gabe Caerphilly."

"The police lieutenant?" Dan had a go at staring down Gabe. His was significantly better executed than my stare. "Heard all about you, man."

Gabe looked up toward Dan's towering height, stuck out his hand, and grimaced within Dan's grasp.

"Nice to meet you." Gabe squeezed the words out with some effort, I noticed.

"Now I know why Daisy hasn't introduced us before. She said you were a hunk. I

257

thought she was trying to keep me on edge." Dan actually snorted his contempt.

Linda suddenly found her gym bag was enthralling. She dug in it, presumably for a tissue, as she started a coughing fit.

"Look, you —" Gabe dropped his gym bag.

Dan grinned and held up his hands in surrender. "Only kidding, Officer. But Daisy seems so familiar with you and I'm a jealous man." With that, Dan put his arm around me. What the heck was going on? Gabe stared at me again. Linda's doe eyes bulged. Dan's grin spread to a smile as he walked me out of the gym.

"What were you doing?" I pulled out of Dan's embrace as we hit the sidewalk. "You're a married man, and we were only exercising together!"

"Precisely. You can thank me later."

"What?" I put my hands on my hips and glared at Dan.

"I saw you blush in there. Guessed the situation soon as I saw that guy was with Linda. He's supposed to be your man, right?"

"Right. And I don't blush anymore."

"You do, too. And I only gave him some of his own back. Like I said, you can thank me later." With that, Dan Block grinned again and swatted my butt with a gym towel, then disappeared into the night. I guess we were now officially good friends.

CHAPTER 24

So much for waiting to plant a garden until Mother's Day.

Today was that special day, and there was no way I was going to go throw seeds in my garden. I looked out my front window at snow dropping in big flakes on my yard. Weatherman promised this would be the last of the extraordinarily cold weather for sure. I contemplated my belief that there was no such thing as climate change, and then turned back into my living room.

There, Georgette sat in a tight ball of fur on my new reading chair. Art's chair had broken months earlier and for my birthday in April, I bought a new Lay-Z-Boy. I liked this much better, as it had a floral pattern in creams and sage green, with pretty delicate cherry blossoms dancing throughout the design. Much more my style than that 1960's gold and orange tweedy thing Art loved so much. When his chair broke, I clipped a small sample of fabric and stuck it in a memory box. The rest was hauled away. Would I ever stop collecting Art mementoes? It was becoming harder to picture him, to feel his spirit next to me at night. I didn't want to lose him, but my brain wasn't retaining all the details of my precious man any more. I sighed. It must be the weather. Gray days this late into the year were enough to make me sad. Colorado is known for its sunshine. I heaved another sigh and looked around again.

Queenie had settled her fat little Corgi tummy on the floor near my chair where she chewed on a peanut butter–filled rubber treat. Georgette snored in peaceful kitty slumber. My home was the picture of quiet contentment. Why I would want to disturb this feeling was beyond me, but after talking with Dan on Friday night, it was time to revisit his edits of my work. I took a deep breath, scooped Georgette onto my couch, grabbed my writing bag, and sat in my new chair. Perhaps the happy pattern would give me the courage to look at Dan's edits with a calmer spirit.

The phone rang. Thank goodness! Who wanted to work on critiques anyway?

"Daisy?"

"Hello, Sam." He sounded a little better

than the other night. Still, as a good friend, I would need to be prepared to listen more than talk. Didn't like that too much. "How are you feeling?"

"Better." He paused. "Thanks for your email."

"I'm so sorry about Rocky."

"Aww. I had some great years with that boy. And he lived a reasonably long time for a golden. Ten years."

"You're being very brave."

"Not at all. I loved that dog, and I'll be lonely without him. But I've been so focused on animals my whole life, maybe it's time to work more with people. I just don't know how I'm going to go on without a pet in the house."

"You won't get a new puppy?"

"At my age, Daisy? I'd probably expire before the pup grew up."

"A pup might keep you young at heart. And you're not so old."

"I'm old enough not to be messing with youngsters like you. I'm seventy-two, for God's sake."

"People live longer all the time, Sam." Me? A youngster? True, he was almost twenty years older than me. Funny, I hadn't thought about our age difference in terms of years before.

Sam laughed. "Damn! I don't want to hang around past my natural ex-pear-ation date! I'd turn into a fruitcake or something."

I chirped in response. "No, Sam, not you. You'd only go a little nutty."

And we were off with a string of puns that no other folks should have to listen to. Soon it felt like Wednesday's phone call was a small anomaly in an otherwise great friendship. We talked for at least an hour, neither Sam nor me wanting to hang up and face the snow and the dreary day outside. Finally, Sam said, "Daisy, my young friend, I can't use words as nicely as you do, but your email was very special. Thanks." The small hitch in his voice underlined his sincerity.

"I only wish words could help, Sam, but nothing will replace Rocky. I'll miss him too."

"Don't belittle your gift. I received cards and notes from the veterinary hospital and a couple of neighbors who knew Rocky, but you took the time to give my dog a proper eulogy. It was a big help. Closure and all that."

"Thanks, Sam."

"You said your writing group doesn't think much of your writing, but I can tell you, I'm impressed."

"Stop, Sam. You're embarrassing me. I

only wrote what I felt, what I feel. You and Rocky have been very important to me, and I will always love you both."

"Now don't go throwing that 'love' word around so easily, my dear. Could get you in trouble." Then he laughed. "I might become that kiss-and-tell guy you teased the other night."

Oops! Had I been leading Sam along? He wasn't getting hopes up for an affair with me, was he? "Sorry, Sam. I only meant that — that you are my best friend. Somebody I can tell all my troubles to without worrying about how I sound. I don't want to wreck our great friendship with romantic messes."

Silence. Then Sam's soft chuckle tickled my ear. "Of course. I was just pulling your leg."

"Well, in that case, wanna come over and pull a chicken leg out of the oven with me for dinner?" Goodness! I hoped I wasn't hurting Sam by keeping him firmly in the friend-only category.

"Deal. See you around five?"

"Deal." I hung up and felt my courage renewed. I pulled some chicken legs out of the freezer to thaw and checked to make sure I'd have enough dinner for three. I never knew when Chip would pop over, and as this was a Sunday, he might try for a game of Scrabble.

I came back out into the living room and spotted both my lazy pets lounging pretty much where I'd left them. And there sat my writing bag. It was time. I could and would address Dan's nasty notes bravely. They would be the first criticisms I'd look at today.

A half hour later, I had a much better idea of where to take my story. My heroine, Ruth, was over the top with her resolve to dislike her boss. She was sounding too much like the real me, and she needed to get her act together so both her career and the man of her dreams could fall in place. I needed to trim, trim, trim Ruth's inner thoughts and sniveling attitude. I also saw some of the same examples of flabby writing that Dan and I had discussed at the gym. Knowing his large red marks weren't projecting anger towards me helped a lot.

Suddenly, "flabby" wasn't an unflattering comment on my body or even such a bad comment about my writing. I finally began to realize that when Dan said "flabby," he was saying one word was over the top, or one phrase was passively written. I saw that "Ruth's attitude toward her boss was becoming muddled and unclear" could be cleaner if I simply said, "Ruth was confused.

Her feelings about Oliver . . ." I read through my pages and looked for "was" everywhere, because that word tipped me off to a passive phrase. Thanks so much, Dan! Suddenly, editing wasn't a chore of finding misspelled words. Editing became an invitation to make my story clearer, brighter, more fun. Of putting my story on a word diet. After working a little while longer, my back began to twinge. Time for a stretch.

I looked over to Queenie and Georgette. They hadn't moved at all. Suddenly, it looked like they had discovered the best way of going through a snowy Sunday afternoon. I put my writing down and stretched out on my couch next to Georgette. I sighed and let my eyes drift closed while I felt my body become one with the comfy couch. A little while later, a voice called out to me.

"Daisy, Daisy wake up," called my husband. "We need to talk."

"Art? Aren't you dead? We can't talk."

"I can talk in your dreams, if you're willing to listen."

"No! That is, I'm not willing. I'm sleeping."

Suddenly Art stood before me. I gazed up and saw nothing but gravestones around me. How did I get to the cemetery? There was Art's grave and Rose's. My family.

"Pay attention, Daisy," said Art.

"I can't see you, Love. Where are you?"

"Don't worry about that. You have some thinking to do. You're on the wrong track with your work and your boyfriends."

"I don't have boyfriends, Art. I just have one —"

"Don't try that with me, Darling. I knew you too long. I know you too well. You have become a flirt and you're headed for trouble."

I glanced around. Gabe, Joe Smaldone, Dan Block, and Sam were all walking toward Art's grave. Suddenly there was another hole next to it. My own gravesite! "Art, help!" I cried. My gentleman friends were stalking closer, none looking too pleased. An arm around my shoulders forced me to look up. Keith Johnson from the grocery store gazed down, smiled and gave me another kiss. I tried to push him away, when suddenly all the guys were piling up on him. Keith fell away and all I could see was a cloud with stars and hash marks around it, like the old cartoon fights I watched as a kid.

Then, that quickly, the fighting stopped. All the guys were laughing and pointing at me. I wanted to run away, but my feet were stuck, stuck in the open hole of my grave.

A breeze swept through the air and I felt chilled as never before. Art whispered in my head once more.

"Daisy, my love, you need to go on a diet. A date diet. These guys' fun will be your demise."

"Art! I miss you. Won't you come back?"

"No. Don't you hear the bells tolling for me? I need to go. You be careful, dearest. Fun and fear go hand-in-hand."

Then I heard bells, possibly church bells. My feet worked loose, and I ran toward the sound. My heart was pounding, but the bells kept ringing.

I woke with a start. Someone was at my front door. The doorbell chimed again.

Sam! Should I answer? Should I listen to Art and make Sam go away? I got up off the couch and straightened my hair.

Sheesh. Silly dreams.

CHAPTER 25

I tapped my finger impatiently on the steering wheel of my little Versa. I couldn't see the time on my dash, as I'd turned off the car a few minutes earlier, but I knew it was close to closing. More and more people strolled out from Gigantos, pushing shopping carts, hauling babies, some even holding hands. Why did people bring babies out this late at night? I guess it's better than leaving the darlings home to watch themselves, but still. Everyone looked worn and tired, and who could blame them? At ten forty-five, I was feeling less than perky myself. I waited for Ginny to appear.

Ginny. Even thinking her name made me smile. What a wonderful young woman she'd grown into. It was for her sake I was here, even though I wasn't really speaking with Gabe. Hmm. Speaking. He'd called mid-evening to ask me to pick up Ginny after her work. I'd almost hung up on him, especially when he said he and That Woman were going out on a call together.

"What did you do before I came back into your life?" I asked.

"I don't know, Daisy," said Gabe. "I don't remember having so many calls before. Look, I know you're upset with me. I know we need to talk about . . . about us. But I did apologize for the mix up over lunch. And I didn't press you about the date with that guy in the gym. Can't we be friends again?"

"I'm not sure, Gabe. It seems our friendship works only when you get all the benefits. What's in this friendship for me?" I couldn't believe I was being so bold, but the past few days had given me a lot to think about. The phone was silent for a bit before Gabe answered.

"I don't blame you for being upset with me. I've never been asked to leave a restaurant either."

"It isn't the restaurant, Gabe; it's your temper. These days I never know if you're going to yell at me or not over the simplest things."

"Ouch! You sure don't mince words, Daisy." He sighed. "To be honest, I'm not sure why I'm so angry all the time either. Trust me, I'm working on it. But for right now can you help out? I don't know who else I can call, and since that murder happened, I don't want Ginny riding the bus home alone so late at night."

The last thought caught me. I didn't want Ginny riding the bus home alone that late at night either. Not with a murderer on the loose. I loved Ginny. "Well." I drew out the word in order to make some think time. "All right. For Ginny's sake. But as for you, I think you should pay me. We're not friends right now, Gabe, much less partners."

He said he understood, and we agreed that he would give me gas money for the effort. It felt terrible making such a business transaction with the man who was supposed to be my guy, but who seemed more and more to be Linda Taylor's partner plus. I felt the itch of irritation creep through me, even though I knew this was the right thing to do.

I drew in a deep breath. Rehashing the evening was not a productive way to spend time waiting for Ginny. In the dark, reading was not an option, though I'd heard that writers could jot a few notes down even without looking at their notepads. I grabbed mine from my purse and posed a question to the air around me.

"What would my character, Ruth, say to a

trade show opportunity? She's never been and — hang on!"

I had been absentmindedly gazing out my window. A movement in the shadows caught my attention. What was that? I squinted into the dark. It looked like fifteen, maybe twenty people sneaking in the back door of Gigantos. No, they weren't sneaking in. Someone was ushering them in through a darkened doorway. Who was that? It was hard to tell, but the figure — slim and aggressive — shouted the identification. Roddy. What was that slime-ball up to now? I'd have to guess he was up to no good. Why couldn't Gabe see that Roddy was the man he wanted for the murder of Cissy Melato? If only I could prove that.

I gave a quick gaze around the parking lot again. Poor Cissy! The only time I'd seen her, and I didn't really see her at all, was when the medical examiner team was hauling her out in that black body bag. Ugh! It took four guys to put her into the ambulance that would take her away that night. That night when Ginny became a young woman with a boyfriend, and then that boyfriend became a murder suspect. It just didn't fit. Something about that night wasn't right. I pressed my forehead into the steering wheel. What was important about that night? What had I not seen?

A tap on my car made me jump. I whirled around to see Ginny's smiling face pressed against my passenger window. Her nose was smooshed into a pancake against the window and she stuck out her tongue. I laughed and unlocked my door. She hopped in.

"Hi, My Daisy! I so glad you camed tonight!" She gave me a hug and wriggled into her seat belt.

"Hello, good woman. You look completely suited for these night hours. Still smiling, I see."

"I like to work. I can work an' work, jus' like my daad. Are we goin' to the jail? Can we let Bri-Ann out now?" These were the words I dreaded. Lately, Ginny opened every conversation with me this way. Luckily, she wasn't prone to perseveration, so I could redirect her thoughts pretty easily. Still, my heart cracked a little.

"Sorry, Ginny. Not quite yet. So how was work?"

"Good."

The shadowy people caught my attention again. How could they stand around so, in the dark? I mean, it wasn't snowing like the day before, but our spring temperatures were quite slow in coming this year. "I wonder what those people are up to?" I mused out loud.

"Dem guys? They are jus' Roddy's 'legals,'" said Ginny. "We are not s'posed to talk about dem. I am not s'posed to know they come jus' 'bout ever night. But Bri-Ann and me. We know. We can keep secrets, so Roddy is okay we know."

" 'Legals,' Ginny, or '*il*-legals'?"

"I don' know. What's a 'legal?' "

This late at night, words escaped me. So that was Roddy's game! Had Cissy caught him letting illegal immigrants into the store? What were they doing there after the supermarket closed? Had she threatened to turn him in? Did he kill Cissy to keep his job secure?

Wait a minute. I remembered something nagging at the edge of my consciousness. Someone — who was it? Someone from the store said something. Ginny? Brian? No — Connie Allessi. She said, *Somehow, Roddy's night work is making my team look like slouches.*

At least I would be sure to let Connie know why her team looked like slouches. Roddy had help, and by the looks of it, lots of help. This needed investigation.

But I couldn't put Ginny at risk. I smiled at my young friend. "It's no one for you to worry about. Roddy's right, dear."

As we drove to her house, I wondered how long those people would be at the store. What I needed was to come back without Ginny, but with my phone. I could take pictures of all Roddy's "legals" and give the evidence to Gabe. Surely, this would prove that Brian was innocent, and that Roddy was the murderer Gabe and That Woman sought. What better motive than to cover up illegal actions with the death of a nosey accountant?

When we got to Ginny's house, the lights were on, and Gabe met us at the door.

"Got off a little earlier than I expected," said Gabe. "Thanks for your help all the same." He slipped me some money and I wanted to throw it right back at him. So he was okay with us being business acquaintances. How had this relationship gone so much awry?

"Thanks," I said, and a bitter taste chewed at the sides of my mouth.

"Uh, would you like to come in for a bit?" Gabe stood in his doorway, holding open his screen door.

"No. I have an errand to run before I go home."

"Errand? This late at night?"

"We romance writers have to research at all hours."

"With Dan?" There was a suspicious tinge to Gabe's question.

"Dan?" What was Gabe talking about — oh! Dan! Gabe thought Dan and I were dating. How messy my love life was becoming. I missed Art more every day. Father Wright be blessed, I still couldn't let go of my lifetime love of Art. "No, I'm not going to see Dan."

"Good. He isn't right for you."

"How would you know?"

"I checked him out. Daisy, I don't know what line he gave you, but Dan is a married —"

My jaw dropped open before I interrupted. "You checked out my date? How dare you!"

"I don't want you being taken advantage of." He gave me a what's-your-problem look.

"The only one trying to take advantage of me is you!" I didn't mention that Chip and Kitty had me running to take care of Thunder every time they ran off to the mountains for a quick ski. Or that Queenie and Georgette took advantage of every chance to get an extra snack. This was different.

"Me? I never!"

Ginny stepped past her dad and into the foyer of the Caerphilly house. "Daad. Be

276

nice. God loves you. No yelling now."

Gabe inhaled deeply. "Sorry, Ginny."

"An' what do you say a My Daisy?" Ginny had hands on hips in a perfect imitation of her dad. She even tapped her toe as she waited for his response.

"Go to bed, Ginny," said Gabe, firm but kind. Ginny had a magic touch that seemed to work on her dad as well as her boyfriend. I smiled.

She yawned. "Okay. But you be nice and not mad anymore, right?"

"Right, Ginny Bear." He kissed the top of her head as she passed by into the house.

I waited until she was well inside before speaking again. "Dan was pulling your leg, Gabe. I know he's married — happily married — and he was acting more like my writing coach than anything else the other night."

"So what's this research you're doing at eleven thirty at night?"

"More like evidence gathering. I saw something at Gigantos that needs checking out."

"Daisy, it's awfully late at night for evidence gathering. What are you up to?"

"None of your business!" I couldn't help it. I hissed the words. If this were a couple of weeks ago, my whereabouts on any late evening might have been Gabe's business, but not anymore. I put a hand to my head to ward off any possible headache and said, "Sorry. I need to go."

"Don't you dare go back to that store on your own, hear me? I won't stand for you running around playing at cops and robbers."

"Then you go and find out what's going on. Ginny said something about —"

"Leave my daughter out of this!" Again, the shouting was escalating. I didn't need the hassle, so I took a deep breath. I wanted as much cool, calm authority as I could muster.

"This isn't about police work, or Ginny, or anything more than that you're trying to control me. To be honest, Gabe, your tempers are no longer impressive or appropriate. Save them for your cop movies and your westerns. I am a woman who deserves to be treated better than this."

I didn't wait for any reaction from Gabe. Ginny had long since disappeared into the house, so I made good my escape. I didn't particularly want to go on this "errand," but I wanted Brian in jail even less. I dove back into my car and retraced my route back to Gigantos.

My stomach flip-flopped as I drove into

the parking lot. It didn't look like anyone was there. I slowed and did a creeping drive-by of the front of the store.

Gigantos at night and locked up was chillingly dark compared to the relative brightness of the parking lot. The store's grey brick facade turned black and the windows, while a mile high, did nothing but reflect back at me. I saw my Versa, and decided that if anyone were still there, I should park like I expected the store to still be open. Wait a minute. Had I just seen a flash of light in the store? Was the movement, the feeling of aliveness, real or only my overactive imagination? Could there possibly be twenty or more illegal aliens wandering around inside? Would they all be as frightened as that stock boy from a few nights earlier? Or, with so many, would I be in trouble for "stumbling" on them?

Suspense movies and cop shows montaged in my brain, mostly the openings, where the security guard or hapless witness (like me) is overwhelmed and killed for their commitment to good citizenship. I decided that parking right out front of Gigantos wasn't such a good idea after all. Even thinking about parking under the lot lights made me feel naked. I pulled out of the lot and back onto Carpenter, heading east away from the store.

Then, the sterner stuff in me took over. Danger be damned! I was investigating a case and I needed to do my job — my creepy job. I wasn't a schoolteacher anymore; I was Brian's hope.

I swung my Versa left onto a side street and backtracked to the rear of Gigantos. The street was dark and I turned off my headlights as I'd seen happen in so many private-eye shows. Then we slowed, my Versa and me, and crept up to a convenient parking spot where no one from the side or front of the store could see me, but from which vantage point I could see anyone who came or went. See and take photos.

Doggone! My phone was buried deep in my purse which was somewhere on the floor behind me. I fished for the thing in the dark. No luck. I hadn't left my purse at Gabe's and Ginny's had I? I popped open my car door for the dome light to help out. My purse sat with a smug look on the back seat. Not on the floor.

"You can bet I'll deal with you later," I admonished my errant bag. I grabbed it, found my phone and threw the thing back with more force than I normally use. Note to self — get a better-organized purse before going on any more stake-outs.

Then I waited. And waited. There were some more shadows, but I couldn't see much. Of course, with middle age, night vision isn't the greatest asset in the toolkit. Maybe my phone could capture more than my eye. I aimed the camera portion toward the shadows and snapped. A flash went off. I turned the phone over and reviewed what the camera saw.

The picture was not exactly ready for publication in *National Geographic*. A blurb of white reflected back at me and a sliver of the trunk of a cottonwood showed behind it. Nothing more. Silly me. What did Art used to say? *Don't try to shoot through windows. The flash catches on the glass and you'll never have a decent shot.*

This detective thing wasn't working so well for me. I heaved a sigh and got out of my car. Spring's evening air sent a chill through me. Perhaps the chill was more noticeable because emotional energy kept creeping up my spine. I tiptoed closer to the store and listened. The soft voices of people speaking Spanish reached through the dark to my ears. Why hadn't I ever learned a foreign language at school? Bet that what these people were saying was important evidence.

Hey, wait. I didn't know Spanish, but I

could record it. I pressed the wake-up button on my phone and searched for the recording app. What was it called? I flipped the screen back and forth a couple of times. At last! There it was — Voice Memos! Now all I had to do was creep closer . . .

The vise-like grip of two arms grabbed me from behind, locking my upper arms in place. The iPhone fell from my hands, and right as I inhaled to scream, one of the arms let go of my chest and repositioned a hand over my mouth. I smelled the rancid odor of cigarette breath, which fell hot on my ear as Roddy McKeague whispered: "I said nosey old girls like you oughtta be home in bed this late at night. Now, what am I going to do with you?"

CHAPTER 26

How does a nice special-needs teacher end up in such a pickle? I didn't remember having this frightening a life when Art was around. Of course, nothing much at all happened when Art was around. Still, here I was in the grip of a maniac, and panic threatened to fill my brain. I couldn't breathe. Roddy's grip was so strong.

My Art! What am I to do? Why didn't I listen to Gabe? Was I about to become another Cissy Melato? Saving Brian from jail was more than I ever was qualified to do.

Daisy. Sweetheart it's not your time. You've dealt with more than this before. What did you do when you substituted at that emotionally challenged classroom and that big boy tried to throw you around?

Thanks Art! I remember. I took control. I remembered that I used my self-defense training and put that boy in his place. I could probably control Roddy with a little old-fashioned ingenuity.

Instinct and self-defense took over. I took a chomp down on Roddy's hand. He let out a yelp and backed off. Instead of running away, I stomped over to him to launch a well-placed kick.

Roddy was too fast. He sidestepped the kick and backed up again. We stared at each other a moment, just enough time for me to realize once more how much trouble I was in, and for him to rethink my strength and aggression. I could almost see the wheels churning in his head.

Then he sprang at me. I tried to rabbit away, but the young man was too fast. I felt myself falling as Roddy tackled me to the ground. I rolled. He kept arms wrapped around me. My face slammed into the damp earth. Pieces of left over snow jammed into my nose and eyes. Roddy's hot breath poured a net over my head. He rolled me over and sat on top of me. The anger that fired in his eyes was terrifying. I opened my mouth to scream. My breath blew away without a sound as Roddy's hand slapped my cheek.

Anger inspired my wriggling and kicking. I found my voice and screamed.

Roddy hit me again. I yelled and arched

my back under him, but he only hit me again.

The world began spinning in my eyes. The evening's darkness reached my brain. I knew I was about to faint.

Suddenly, miraculously, Roddy's weight sprang off of me.

I looked up to see two figures in a fistfight nearby. Thank all the good spirits of the universe, someone had come to my rescue.

I sat up and my head swam some more. But soon it was Roddy's turn to be tackled by the larger figure.

"You're under arrest," gasped out my hero. Gabe! Of course he would come after me. My Gabe. I stood, ready to help if needed.

Gabe paid no attention to me. He handcuffed Roddy and arrested him.

Roddy growled in frustration as Gabe lifted the creep to his feet. The store night manager leaned in toward me and spat. I wanted to vomit, but managed to wipe my face with my sleeve instead.

Roddy yelled as Gabe started to haul him off. "Bitch! You bitch! You'll get yours. And you'll get it sooner rather than later."

Another police car pulled up, lights flashing this time. Officer Matt Hawkins stepped out. "Need help, Lieutenant?" called the younger policeman.

"Thanks, Matt. You can take this one in and book him for assault."

"Right." Matt took physical charge of the ranting Roddy. His large frame and cool professional air left no doubt about the outcome of Roddy's efforts to wriggle free.

"Thank you so much, Matt," I called. "How did you know I needed your help?"

The young man grinned at me. "Someone dialed nine-one-one for a suspicious car on the street. They said a strange woman was flashing lights in it. I have to guess that was you, right, Ms. Arthur?"

I returned the grin with a little sheepishness attached. "Right, Matt." Suddenly, my legs went weak, my head spun, and I plopped down on the ground. In a heartbeat Gabe was at my side.

"Daisy, what am I going to do with you? You could have been killed tonight." Gabe's face showed all the concern a damsel in distress could ask for. "Daisy? Are you okay? Your nose is bleeding."

My mind fuzzed over with grey thoughts, none of which I could properly put into words. "I don't feel so good, Gabe." My head lolled on his shoulder. "You're right . . . But Brian . . . Roddy . . . Illegals . . . Oww! Where's . . . my . . . phone?"

Gabe shushed me and scooped me up. "Want me to call an ambulance?"

"No. I wanna go home. Need ice."

"I'll take you." He gently put me in his passenger seat, latched a seatbelt on me, and gazed more deeply at my face.

"Ouch!" he said for me. "You'll need some aspirin to go with that jaw and the black eye I think you'll have soon. Sure you have what you need at home?" Then, a little softer, "Do you want to come to my house?"

Tears stung my eyes, but I willed them away. I wasn't Gabe's anything anymore. All right, maybe I was his babysitter, but there was no romance between us. "Thanks for the offer, but I'll be better off in my own bed."

Gallantly, Gabe found my phone and handed it to me as he got in the car. We drove home without further conversation.

At writing group Tuesday evening, my face caused quite a stir.

"Did that police officer hit you?" asked Dan. He looked ready to jump out the door and go fix "that police officer" for good. I smiled, and then winced. It was hard to form words with the lump at the side of my jaw, and I sure had no notion to open my mouth wide. Guess the make-up didn't cover as much as I had hoped.

"No, Dan. I had a run in with someone who ended up going to jail after. No worries."

"Okay, but I'm going to walk you to your car tonight. Whoever got to you might have friends."

I shuddered and nodded. For once I was glad for the size of my new companion. Heck, if nothing else, Dan could shake hands with whoever might harass me, and that person would know to stay away.

"Goodness, Daisy," said Kitty. "Let me look at you." She peered at my face intently. "Hang on a minute." She dove into her purse, the one almost as big as her, and came out with a make-up kit. "Let's go to the bathroom. I have some stuff that will turn your look into something fabulous. You poor thing."

Being mothered by this pixie was not what I needed this evening, great though it felt to be among such friends.

"I'll be okay, Kitty. Let's focus on the critique work for tonight." I tried to smile at her and she patted my arm.

Toni and Eleanor clucked and situated themselves on either side of me. They fussed and gaped at my wounds.

"This is what comes from pretending to

be an investigator," said Toni, but there was no harshness in her voice, only worry.

"I've heard of doing research for a book, Daisy, but you're not writing crime fiction," said Eleanor. "Tell you what. If you want to stay at my house for a few days, I'll make sure you're okay. I have a gun."

I'd seen that gun. Eleanor could hardly lift the thing. It was like a hand-held bazooka. Thanks, but no thanks.

Linda Taylor stared out the window, but I felt as though she were doing so to guard over me more than ignore the group. She reminded me of those pictures of secret service people near a president. I might be jealous as all get out of Linda, but she sure was a good cop.

I gave the group a lopsided grin, thanked everyone once more, and refocused us on our writing efforts.

After the meeting, Dan and Linda both walked me toward my car. We hardly spoke, but as we approached my Versa, Linda said to Dan, "I'll keep an eye on her. Thanks, Dan."

He gazed at both of us. A silent agreement seemed to flash between him and Linda, and the big man left with the admonition for me to be safe, and keep my doors locked.

Linda turned to me. "If you're not too tired, Daisy, I'd like to talk with you."

I looked around. "I'm not too tired, but honestly, I'm not fond of standing around in the dark right now." Didn't sense anyone nearby, but after last night's trauma, I wasn't about to push my luck.

"Want to hit Pete's Pub?"

"Sure."

"Good. I'll follow you." Linda smiled at me and moved to her car.

At the pub, we found a couple of seats in a snug booth. It reminded me of our old group leader, Sandra Martin. I wondered out loud what might be going on in Sandra's life.

"You didn't hear? She's done very well with Alcoholics Anonymous, and since she left her husband, she's blossomed. I saw her a couple of weeks ago at a shop in downtown Littleton. She works there, and got a special rate on an apartment above the store. Husband's being a bit of a pain in the divorce, but I think it's all going to work out."

"How cool is that?" I said. "I love a happy ending."

"Me too."

"Really, Linda? You surprise me. You write crime fiction, and your characters are rather unsavory most of the time."

She shrugged. "Hazard of the job, I suppose."

"You sound like Gabe. Always seeing the bad side of people. Is Littleton really that terrible?"

"Hmm. Good question, Daisy. I didn't used to think so. But look at you. You were assaulted last night. I guess you could say Littleton has the same kind of crimes as the big city — as Denver, I mean. We just don't usually have so much of it. Lately, though, things seem to be getting a bit rougher. Are you going to be okay?"

"I suppose. But you can be sure I'm going to be more careful about conducting a stake-out from now on."

"Daisy, why don't you trust the police to do our jobs? We'll find whoever killed Cissy."

"Will you, Linda? I don't mean to question your motives, but Gabe doesn't seem very anxious to let Brian out of jail."

"Did you ever consider that Brian may be safer in jail?"

"Safer from what? Special-needs people are never safe. People take advantage of them and use them for all sorts of criminal activity. And in jail, Brian is only going to meet the kinds of people who will look him up when they get out, and get him into more trouble. The longer he stays in jail, the less safe he is."

"Good point."

"I can't shake the feeling that Gabe has Brian locked away so Brian can't build a relationship with Ginny."

"I'll check into it if you want."

"That's nice of you, Linda, but until this murder is solved, Brian won't be safe no matter what, so it's not important what Gabe thinks about him and Ginny dating. I think Brian knows something the murderer doesn't want him to know."

I told Linda why I went back to Gigantos last night, and about seeing people Ginny may have been calling illegals coming and going. I told her about my suspicions with regard to Roddy, and meeting Joe Smaldone. She took out a notepad and jotted down some of what I said.

"You make a good detective, Daisy," she said finally. "If you had more training on how to stay out of trouble, I could see you succeed as a private investigator."

"Thanks, but no thanks. I merely want to write romance stories, and get published one day. Oh, and getting married again is still high on my priority list."

She grinned at that. "Speaking of romance, that's what I wanted to talk to you about. I need to talk to you about Gabe's intentions."

My heart skipped a beat, but brave Daisy decided to come out. "Go on," I said and leaned in.

CHAPTER 27

Linda sipped at her iced tea and nibbled some potato skins we'd ordered. I gulped at my water. Even while being leery of her intentions with Gabe, I felt good in her company. It was odd. I should dislike this woman, and when she wasn't around that was easy to do. I loved thinking of her as That Woman, but sitting across from Linda in the bar, I sensed she was a wise person, worthy of my trust. *Wise beyond her years,* isn't that how the saying went? This conflict caused a mess inside.

Suddenly, Linda laughed. "Daisy, you need to work on masking your emotions better. You're positively shouting skepticism with your face." She smiled again. There was that Renaissance beauty again. If only I could stop being so jealous of her.

"Sorry, Linda, but you mentioned Gabe's intentions with me, so I'm all ears." All ears, and a heaping pile of skepticism to boot.

"I don't mean to disappoint, but I don't really know his intentions. I only know that he's been behaving slightly off lately. Not quite sure what's come over him."

"What do you mean?"

"He's never been an even-tempered guy, but lately he seems on edge all the time. His fuse is really short, and I'm never confident about which Gabe I'm going to go out on call with — the smart, funny, and best professional I know, or the hard-driving, bad man with a badge."

"I see."

"Do you? In police work we have to know our partners quite intimate — well, quite well." She cleared her throat. "We have to be able to have each others' backs all the time. If I have to start tempering my actions because of Gabe's mood swings, I'm not going to be able to focus on my work. Perps will get away, or worse, off the hook because the Caerphilly–Taylor team screwed up." She fingered her tea glass and shook her head at some private memory.

Had they? Had the Caerphilly–Taylor team screwed up in this case?

"I hadn't thought about it from your perspective." And I hadn't. For the past couple of months I'd felt that Gabe's tempers were directed only toward me, and that his relationship with Linda was going on quite well — too well, in fact. "Do you know of anything that might have triggered this change in our — our friend?" I had to include Linda in Gabe's and my circle of friendship. As his partner she was, and probably always would be, closer to him than I could be, at least from a working perspective.

"No, not really. I began noticing changes right around the beginning of March."

"March?" Didn't ring a bell with me. March. Hang on — March! "March tenth is Gabe's birthday."

"Yes. So what?"

"So Gabe's birthday may have triggered it."

"Why? It wasn't a milestone year."

"No. You're right about that. He turned fifty-five. And yet . . ." I shook my head. In less than a year, I'd be fifty-five too. Even more than the hot flashes and mood swings, more than the stiff muscles, fifty-five marked an age I would probably start to see myself as *really* old.

"Yet, you think this has something to do with his age?" Linda pulled out a notepad and jotted in it. One day I'd love to see her notes. Copious.

"I've been reading more and more about

how men go through a kind of male menopause as they age too. We used to call it the mid-life crisis. You know. When guys go out and get a young girlfriend, buy a flashy car, generally go a little crazy."

"I thought that was just an old wives' tale." Linda tapped her notepad.

"Apparently not. And where Gabe is concerned, probably not."

"So Gabe's going crazy with his bad temper?"

"And his younger woman." I stared at her and raised my eyebrows.

Linda stared back, a look of shock covering her features. "Me? No way. All he ever talks about is Ginny. And you, of course."

Hmm. And me. Of course. That old skepticism crept into my consciousness again. Was Linda being honest, or merely polite? Could she truly be blind to the fact that she was the younger woman, the newer model?

I blew out an exasperated breath. "The fact of the matter is that he talks to you. Period. Right now, every encounter with Gabe is a trial for me. I still have strong feelings for him, of course, but I don't seem to get anything but arguments in return." Did That Woman's eyes light up? Was I being too open again? "Of course, this probably has more to do with me befriending

Brian than anything else."

Linda took a sip of her drink before answering. "You may be right there. Look, Daisy, I know we've never had a close-friend kind of relationship, but it looks like we're both going to be in Gabe's life for a while. Is there anything I can do to help us get along better?"

Yeah. Go away, far away.

"Thanks for being open, Linda. As long as I know your partnership is only work-related we'll get along fine. Deal?"

"Deal. And as for writing?"

"What about it?" I said.

"How 'bout you let up on me a bit, okay? Nobody else finds as much to complain about in my work as you do."

"I do? Goodness, I'm sorry, Linda. I met with Dan last week about the same thing — only I asked him to go a little easier on me."

She smiled at that. "The gym?"

"Yes."

"So he doesn't scare you anymore?"

I laughed. "That was downright stupid of me, wasn't it?"

She discretely dipped her gaze. Then she snapped up with excitement in those glowing eyes of hers.

"What was with his hugging on you? Did you set that up on purpose? Gabe was ready to tear the gym apart after seeing you there. He went right to the punching bags and pummeled away for a half-hour after you left."

"Really?" I let my eyes bulge. Gabe was jealous? Dan was right. How cool was that? Art had never been jealous. Of course, I'd never given Art reason to be.

"Daisy, I'm not an advice columnist or anything, but if I were in your shoes, I think I'd go easy on Gabe. You're as likely to lose him as drive him wild."

Doggone, she was right. His behavior with Linda was putting distance between us, and I had no proof that he might have kissed her or done anything really romantic with her. Unfortunately, my own behavior couldn't comfortably undergo the same scrutiny.

We talked for a little while longer on writing, the case, and Gabe, but it was unproductive girl-bonding stuff.

When the check came, I reached into my purse. In the bottom of the large compartment, next to my wallet, sat Cissy's address book.

"Linda, if I try to give this to Gabe, it's bound to start another disagreement between us." I handed the book to Linda.

She gazed at it a few minutes, flipped

through the pages and stared up at me. "We could have used this a couple of weeks ago, when we were first starting the investigation."

"But it's no help now?" A cloak of guilt began wrapping around my head and shoulders.

"Probably not, but I'll keep it just the same." She shook her head at me sadly, as if I'd disappointed her thoroughly. Great. Our budding friendship was already in jeopardy, and it was all my fault.

"I'm so sorry, Linda. I tried to give it to Gabe a few times, but there was never a good moment."

"I understand. Please don't do something like this again. No harm this time, but you still withheld evidence we could have used."

"I understand, too. I wanted so badly to help Brian. But I hope never to be involved in a case again. I wouldn't hold anything back if I were."

"Daisy, if you want to help Brian — or anyone else for that matter — work *with* the police, not around us."

I bit back the retort I had about being locked out of the investigation. Who was I to circumvent the police? Instead, I nodded my head like a chastised student.

Linda smiled. "It's really okay. We are onto

some good leads in the case. And I'll keep working with Gabe to keep an open mind on our suspects."

"Thanks, Linda. You're a champ."

She smiled, gave me some cash for her part of the bill, and left.

When I left the bar a few minutes later, I knew I needed to go visit Brian again. He had to know more than he realized. Special-education skills needed to surface again. Big time. At least the address book no longer burned a place in my purse or my guilty conscience.

CHAPTER 28

Ginny had dressed up again for her visit to the jail. Today's outfit was a brown pants suit and her hair shone with the long amount of time she said she used to brush it. Her make-up was subtler with the exception of the mascara that had been inexpertly applied.

Together we sat in the interview room. Brian came in, escorted by the security guard from our last visit. Ginny whipped out her comb and waved it at the guard. "Can I comb my Bri-Ann's hair?"

He swept a glance around the room and smiled at Ginny. "Very quick, okay?"

She bestowed her best smile on the guard and went to work. As she combed, Ginny hummed and whispered loving sounds to her boyfriend.

"I love you so much, Ginny," said Brian. "You visit me an' you make me feel good in my tummy."

"I love you too, Bri-Ann. You is my good guy. When My Daisy finds the bad guy, you an' me will be in love for-ever."

I gestured to Ginny. "Time to sit down, now. We can't stay long. You two both know that."

" 'Kay," said Ginny. Brian heaved a sigh in his seat. I noticed that there was something different about the young man. A profound sadness crept through every gesture, every movement.

"Are you okay, Brian? Are people being nice to you?"

Brian heaved another sigh, but didn't look at me. "I be quiet an' nobody hurts me. If I cry, then they all laugh a me, and call me baby, an' sometimes they hit me. If I look at 'em they hit me. If I tell the guards, they hit me more. I look down 'an I don't say anything. Den I am okay." He spoke all his words to the table top.

Every protective instinct in me jumped to high alert. I had to get Brian out of this place!

"Brian, I know this is very hard, but you are being brave. I am trying to find out who killed Ms. Cissy, so I can help you get out of here. But I need to know some things. Can you tell me, Brian, about the illegals at Gigantos?"

Brian and Ginny looked at each other. "No." They both said the word together.

"Why not?"

Ginny spoke up. " 'Cause Roddy said if we ever talk about dem, den the 'legals would come to our house and kill us."

I rolled my eyes. So Roddy had done a scare number on these kids. The question was, would they believe Roddy or trust me? "They wouldn't do that, Ginny. The illegals are probably more frightened of you than you are of them."

"But I wouldn't go to their house and killed dem. I wouldn't hurt anybody."

"Me eever," said Brian.

I smiled. "I know that, you two. But can we get back to what you know that others don't about Gigantos?"

"I don' know noffin," said Brian. He put his head on the table. "Do you have cookies, My Daisy? I like the cookies at your house."

"My Daisy, are you gonna be silly wiff Bri-Ann and me? Everbody knows stuff we don' know. An' Roddy tol' us not to talk 'bout the 'legals."

I tried again. "Is there other stuff Roddy told you not to talk about?"

"No," said Ginny, but Brian raised his head and looked at me.

304

"Brian? What doesn't Roddy want you to talk about?"

"He don't want me to talk about the freezer. An' no talkin' 'bout my sticker book."

I frowned. "Freezer? Sticker book? I don't understand, Brian. What do you know about a freezer?"

"I know it is cold. It is cold and dark. Pah! I no like da freezer, an' Roddy put me in it. He said stay quiet. He said 'Chill, dude.' An' he laugh at me when I couldn't get out. He laughed an' he left me. An' I gotted sick. Pah! An' Roddy gotted written up."

Oh how I itched to put my hands on Roddy. I'd show him how to chill. "How long were you in the freezer, dear?"

"I dunno. It was a long time, 'cause Mr. Jordan from the meat counter founded me sleepin' in da freezer. He put me in the amblance. After dat, Misses Sippi tooked me to work an' picked me up. She got reeally mad at Roddy."

I was liking Cissy more and more. "And the stickers, Brian? What could be wrong with a sticker book? Please tell me about that."

Brian shook his head and put it down on the table again. I turned to Ginny.

"Ginny, do you know about Brian's sticker book?"

"No. Is that baad, My Daisy? Should I know 'bout it?"

Brian looked up. "I love you, Ginny. I can tell you 'bout my book. But you gotta not tell Roddy you know 'bout it. 'Kay?"

"Oh. 'Kay," said Ginny. "Is your sticker book bootiful?"

"No. It is jus' fun. I made it wiff Misses Sippy. We put my stickers in her book, an' I telled her how I got 'em an' she wroted it down. In my book, she wroted 'bout my stickers."

I let the two friends talk, and sat taking notes of what they said. From what I could gather, the stickers were from fruits and vegetables at the store. It didn't make any sense. Who would care about fruit and vegetable stickers?

"So, Ginny. 'Case I don' get to come home, you can have my book," said Brian at last. "I putted it in a safe place. You know my safe place?"

"Yeah, Bri-Ann. I know. An' I know you will come home. I need you. You gotta come home wiff me. We will live together. I will marry you, an' we will work at Gigantos an' we will be very happy."

Brian teared up. "I wanna go home *now,*

306

Ginny. I wanna stop havin' to look down, and not cry, an' be quiet. I don' like it here. Please, Ginny. Take me home."

Ginny cried too. I looked over at the guard. His eyes were moist, as mine felt.

"Brian," I said, "I promise I will do everything I can to get you out of here. And I will take Ginny to find your sticker book and bring it to you."

Ginny stood up, as did Brian. Although I knew he wouldn't stop them, the guard turned so he wouldn't see the lovebirds hug once more before we left.

"Let's go, Ginny," I said.

The guard came up to me as I started to bundle Ginny toward the door. "He shouldn't be in here," said the man. "But I can't do anything about that. What I can do — what I promise — I'll try to keep him out of trouble here as much as possible." With that, the guard and Brian left.

"Come on, Ginny," I said. "Let's go find Brian's sticker book for him."

The drive to Brian's apartment complex was quiet. Ginny's normal happy demeanor had been wounded by her boyfriend's plight. I suggested ice cream on the way, but Ginny, looking older than I'd ever seen her before, said no thanks. We drove on.

Once at the Creek View Apartments, I stopped at the manager's office to borrow the key again.

"Do you know how much longer the police investigation is going to take?" asked Amber. "I'd really like to get both apartments rented as soon as possible. I can't see that retarded — that special-needs guy — paying rent regularly if he's stuck in jail."

"My Bri-Ann is a good guy. He will pay his bills. Maybe he will pay his bills at 'nother 'partment." Ginny stamped her foot, and Amber jumped back.

I stepped in. "If we can just borrow the key to Brian's apartment." I held out my hand and Amber dropped it in.

"Okay, but if you want into Cissy Melato's, you'll have to come back for that key. Some other investigator has it right now."

I stopped. "Some other investigator?"

Was Gabe doing more backgrounding? That didn't seem likely.

"Yes," said Amber. "A woman named" — she checked her registration book — "Ramona Jones."

I nodded and thanked Amber, and then hustled Ginny out the door before my friend could ask who Ramona Jones was. I had no idea. There wasn't a Ramona Jones on the police force that I knew of, and after seven months of wandering in and out of the Littleton police offices, I thought I'd met all of the staff.

We headed toward Brian's apartment. Cissy had lived below him in the two-story building. When we got to the stairs I turned to Ginny.

"You go ahead, sweet girl. I'll be right up."

Ginny started climbing the stairs. My stomach gave a quick flip-flop as I made the decision to see who this Ms. Jones was. I turned into the alcove with Cissy's door, which stood ajar. Quietly I took a peek. What I saw didn't seem right. When Gabe and I visited, Cissy's apartment was as neat as an elaborately documented spreadsheet. Even through the crack in the doorway, I spied a mess of monumental proportions going on. I pushed the door further ajar and called out.

Upon entering the apartment I went from surprised to shocked. The couch was turned over, the bottom slashed, as were the cushions. Lamps were pushed on their sides, books and magazines strewn everywhere. A glimpse of the kitchen showed all the cupboards open, much of the contents of food boxes spilled. This wasn't my place, but even so, I felt sick inside. Who would do this much damage to a poor accountant's place? It seemed so disrespectful of the dead.

A woman emerged from Cissy's bedroom, tissue to her face.

"Who are you?" we both demanded together.

We did the awkward "you first" thing for a second or two, but I gave up.

I put a hand to my chest and felt the comfort of my locket with Art in it. "I'm Daisy Arthur," I said. "I'm investigating Cissy Melato's murder."

The woman looked relieved. "Thank God you're here, detective. I came to start packing up my mother's things and found this mess."

"Your mother?"

"Of course. Who else would she be? God, will you look at this place? I should walk away. There's nothing here I want anyway."

My mind flew to the several other things I thought this woman could be. Daughter hadn't been one of them. I hadn't seen any pictures of her when Gabe and I looked around. And she had made quite a mess — but she said she found the place this way. As an amateur sleuth, why should I believe her? Or perhaps she'd found what she wanted here and would dump the mess part on me.

"I'm sorry for your loss, Ms. — er — Melato?"

"Melato was Mom's maiden name. Mine's Jones, Ramona Jones."

Ramona Jones. Why was that important? Ramona — hang on! Ramona Jones — R.J.! "You had an appointment with your mom the night she died."

Ramona's eyes widened. She was a stunningly pretty woman with voluptuous curves in all the right places. Joe Smaldone's description of her mother's younger years came to mind. *Bright, fun-loving and with a figure to make Raquel Welch jealous. Bella!*

"I did have dinner with her. How did you know?"

"I saw your mom's calendar."

"Oh." Nothing more than a defeated "oh," and Ramona slowly righted a toppled chair, then sat. "Mom was always meticulous. She kept records of everything. I can see the appointment note as if it were in front of me: *Meet with R.J. Cut her off. Queenie gets everything. Brian Hughes to be Queenie's caregiver and funds manager.*"

"I can't say I saw that much detail of the appointment — hang on! Did you say *Brian* will be Queenie's caregiver?"

"That's what Mom's will said. That's what she told me when we had dinner that night."

311

The woman's lip trembled.

"Want to tell me about it?"

She shrugged. "Not too much to tell. Mom and I had a rocky relationship ever since she and Dad split."

"You and your dad. I saw you at the funeral. He put his hand on your shoulder."

"I didn't see you, but you're right. We came together. I always liked Dad more than Mom. He's more understanding of my needs."

"So . . . your parents. Did they have an amicable split?" Was I getting another new suspect or two?

"I don't think so. The split was fifteen or sixteen years ago and I was only seventeen at the time. Something about another woman; fights, money. In the end, I chose to live with my dad. He was easier to deal with. Mom was always a stickler for the rules."

"What kinds of rules?"

"You know. She wanted to impose curfews and community service any time I made the smallest mistake. After a while, when I grew up, Mom and I had dinner together once a month. It was about all the nagging I could handle. She kept telling me to make the most of my college education and get a job." Ramona rolled her eyes, and I could envision the mother–daughter conflict.

"And you wanted — you want — something else?"

"I want to get married, have kids, and live in Cherry Creek. Is that so much to ask?"

"Seems reasonable. So what in all of this bothers you so much?"

"The will, of course. I spent my childhood with that Gawd-awful woman. I cleaned my room whenever she demanded. I did my homework and chores. Then she leaves Dad and expects me to follow in her footsteps. Wants me to go dig ditches or something." Ramona pouted like she might still be seventeen. I have heard that trauma can stunt a person's emotional growth, but this was over the top.

"I'm sure your mom wouldn't have wanted you to do something you disliked," I said.

"Detective. I have a degree in photography, for God's sake. Like what job can I get these days?"

"Okay. So what about the will would stop you from doing photography as part of your career choice?"

Ramona rolled her eyes again. "All you old women sound the same." She gave me the let-me-explain-to-the-dummy look. "The will wouldn't stop me from doing photography or anything else I want. But I didn't inherit, so all that time I put in being a good daughter means I get zip. I mean, Mom's estate has over seven hundred thousand dollars in it. And she only gave me a measly one hundred thousand. How am I going to land a rich husband on that?"

I wanted to step back from this woman. She was thirty-three years old, in good — make that great — physical condition, not damaged intellectually that I could see. But she had spent the last decade or so having dinner with her mom once a month so that she would inherit her mom's estate. Hmm.

"What happens to the rest of the money?"

"Haven't you been listening? The money goes to Queenie, and the stupid mutt goes to some guy I never met. Brian Hughes must be a smooth operator, if you know what I mean. Took advantage of my mom. Now all he has to do is take care of the dog, and he'll get over half a million dollars. Guy's got it made."

Ramona, suddenly energetic, got up from her chair and started throwing things around the apartment. Small objects flew against walls. Furniture tumbled about as Ramona let her temper take hold. "Damn usurper! If I ever meet that guy, he'll wish I hadn't. Taking advantage of a lonely old woman like my mom. He should be shot."

"Perhaps you could contest the will?" I asked softly.

"Contest? Are you kidding? I know my mom. She would have hired the best lawyer for this. There won't be any loopholes. Damn Brian Hughes. I hate that man!"

A soft voice cut through the frenzy of Ramona's anger.

"I love dat man. He is a good guy. He is my Bri-Ann. You be nice about Bri-Ann," said Ginny. She must have tired of waiting and came to find me.

"Ginny, dear, go back outside. I'll be done in a minute."

" 'Ginny dear?' " said Ramona. She turned back to me. "I thought you said you were a detective. Who the hell are you? And what's with the retard saying she loves Brian Hughes?"

CHAPTER 29

I quickly picked my way back to Cissy's front door and put my arm around my young friend.

"Ms. Jones, this is Ginny Caerphilly. Her father is the lead investigator on this case. I said I was investigating. You assumed I was a detective. Sorry for the confusion."

"Confusion, my butt!" screeched Ramona. "You probably made this mess. What were you doing? Looking for the will? Flipping lawyer has it. But you're right. I should contest that document. I will. I will. Brian Hughes stole my inheritance and I want it back!"

Ginny and I closed the door on the screaming woman.

"She needs a go in time-out, My Daisy."

I smiled back. "I think you're right, Ginny. Let's leave her alone. That will be time-out enough."

Ginny giggled for the first time in days. "I

like dat. She can scream till the walls come down. We will not be dare to see it."

Ginny and I climbed the stairs to Brian's apartment.

When we opened the door to Brian's apartment, a similar disaster met us.

"My gosh, My Daisy!" said Ginny. "Bri-Ann is a messy guy. I will have to look after him an' show him how to keep his house nice. Dis is baad. Dis is very baad of my Bri-Ann."

"I don't think Brian made this mess, Ginny. I think bad guys did this." I gulped. Were the bad guys still around? Surely we would have heard them making this disaster from Cissy's apartment below. Ginny started to pick up.

"Stop!" I shouted. She jumped. "Sorry, Ginny. But your dad needs to see things exactly as they are. Let's try not to touch anything, okay?"

"Oh. 'Kay. But my daad doesn't like messy places. He will be very mad at dis mess. He will yell until the walls come down."

"Does your dad yell a lot, Ginny?"

"Only when he is mad. An' when he watched the Broncos on TV. Go Broncos!" She punched a fist in the air.

"Go Broncos, Ginny." I smiled. It never

ceased to amaze me how the twists and turns of a conversation with a special student could cut to the most important points. Gabe yelled, but mostly in appropriate ways. He was hot tempered, but Ginny felt safe with him. I felt safe with him. I started dialing the Littleton police department.

"Can I get Bri-Ann's sticker book? It is in his bedroom." Ginny started back toward the room that in Cissy's apartment would have been called her office.

"Don't you think his bedroom is this way?" I asked, pointing in the opposite direction.

"No. It is in here." Ginny walked into the smaller room. A single bed lined the wall under the window, and a used-looking, Early American desk adorned the opposite side. If the place hadn't been torn apart, I could tell that the restricted space made organizing a little easier for Brian.

"Hello, Gabe? It's Daisy. Can you hang on a second?"

"Daisy, I'm swamped," said Gabe. "Can you call back?"

"No," I said and put my hand over the mouthpiece. "Ginny dear, I don't think you'll be able to find the sticker book." But she was already on her hands and knees,

318

reaching under the file drawer side of the desk. There was a small space between the drawer bottom and the carpet, and she could just slip her hands underneath.

"Gabe, there's been a break-in at Brian's apartment. Place looks like a war zone."

"What!" shouted Gabe. "What are you doing there? Get out as quickly as you can. If there's been a break-in, the perp may still be there."

"I brought Ginny over for something Brian wants her to have. And I'm pretty sure there's no one here now."

"Doesn't matter. You don't belong snooping around secondary crime scenes."

I thought for a moment, leaving my silence to scold Gabe for patronizing me. "And I think you'll want to check in at Cissy's too. There's a similar mess in that apartment."

"Daisy! Are you meddling where you're not supposed to be?" I could hear Gabe's teeth grinding through the phone.

"Gabe. I'm only a concerned citizen reporting what appears to be a break-in. Correction. Two break-ins. Though, to be honest, I think half of the mess at Cissy's is because of her bad-tempered daughter, Ramona Jones."

"Stay there, Daisy. I'll be right over."

"Like you said, Gabe. I don't belong here.

I'm sure you can handle this mess." I hung up. That man and his scolding were becoming more than tiresome. I turned toward the mess and Ginny stood looking at me with a triumphant smile.

"Got it!" she said, holding what appeared to be an old-fashioned scrapbook.

CHAPTER 30

I tapped my fingers on the top of Brian's scrapbook. My toes punctuated my fingers' rhythm as I looked around the law office of Morris & Wilson. It was a nice place with a stone fountain in what must have been a fireplace at one time. Lots of Littleton businesses were set up in buildings that had once held some of the founding families — Little, Louthan, and Spotswood.

The green walls and dark wood floorboards of Morris & Wilson gleamed with care. When I entered, the clerk showed me to a seat on a plush leather couch, made — I felt certain — to intimidate more than comfort. I sank down into the cushions feeling more like a child than a client or, in this case, a witness.

"Ms. Arthur?" The young woman strode toward me with more confidence than when we first met. "Heather Dunlap." She held out her hand. I looked at it skeptically.

Between Dan Block and this woman, my fingers were in danger of being crushed to dust.

"We've met before, Ms. Dunlap. At the jail? I'm Daisy Arthur, Brian Hughes's friend."

"Oh, yes, Ms. Arthur. I remember now. Thanks for coming in today. How can I help you?"

"You can call me Daisy. And I think I can help you — or rather, Brian." I held out the scrapbook Ginny found in Brian's apartment. "Ginny Caerphilly said I could borrow this, and I believe it's evidence that someone at the grocery store, other than Brian, might have had a motive for killing Cissy Melato."

Heather sat across from me. "I'd invite you into my office, but, to be honest, I think we'll have more quiet here." She casually flipped open the scrapbook and glanced at the contents. Then she flipped a page. And another. More rapidly she flipped pages until she came to the end of the book. Heather looked up and stared at me. "Can I keep this?" she asked.

"I've only been given permission to borrow it," I said. "But I think you can make photocopies if you want."

"Thanks. If I need to revisit this book,

will you be able to borrow it again?" We stood up and walked into the back where Heather began photocopying the pages of Brian's book. "And this belongs to Ginny Caerphilly?"

"Not really. It belongs to Brian. When we visited him in jail yesterday, he told Ginny where to find it, and that she could have it."

"I can really use this information. Puts a whole new perspective on the case."

"Not so open and shut anymore?"

"Right."

"Great! I had hoped so." I stared at the growing stack of photocopies, and decided to push a little. "May I ask a favor, Heather?"

She looked at me, a cautious expression stealing across her face. "What kind of favor, Ms. Arthur?"

"Daisy. I'm hoping — that is — can you possibly do something to help get Brian out of jail sooner rather than later? The poor young man is really suffering there. He's too innocent and gentle a person for that environment to be any good for him."

Heather shook her head. "Brian didn't have money to post bail, and so I can't really do much. The severity of the mutilation inspired the DA to ask for the highest bail amount possible, and the judge agreed. It also didn't help that your innocent, gentle friend assaulted all those officers at his arrest."

"But Brian only truly assaulted that stupid Roddy McKeague. And if you ask me, Roddy deserved it."

"Deserved or not, Brian behaved violently. Being put into jail was probably a good thing. But, like I said, this scrapbook will help build a great case for him."

"So the stories Ms. Melato wrote down for Brian make sense to you? I had a hard time with them."

"Yes. In the grocery business, relabeling is both an illegal, yet common, practice. But I don't understand why a big store like Gigantos would use this old trick. It isn't worth the trouble they'd be in if someone found out."

"So perhaps, when Roddy McKeague gave the stickers to Brian, it was to keep Brian quiet? A bribe?"

"Of stickers? Really, Ms. Arthur?"

"Brian, the special-needs man, is fixated on stickers. It makes sense to me."

"Or perhaps, if he's fixated, Brian took the stickers himself."

"Whose side are you on?"

"Brian's. But as his lawyer, I have to be able to think ahead to what the DA will claim. The DA may say that Brian stole the stickers, and when he got in trouble for it, turned his anger on Ms. Melato."

"No. See?" I pointed to the notes in the column next to Brian's sticker pictures. "Cissy wrote down every time Brian came to her with the stickers and wrote down how he told her he got them."

"You're right, Ms. Arthur. These notes do seem to lean toward Brian being an innocent dupe. But it doesn't point to any particular person as the potential murderer."

"I think, once you've had a chance to read Cissy's notes more carefully, you'll see that Roddy McKeague's name comes up frequently. He's the person who gave me this shiner, and threatened me on more than one occasion. I think he's the one you may want investigated."

"Did you press charges?"

"Only on Monday night." Monday night was when Roddy the store manager became Roddy the guy who was hiding illegals in the workplace, and then Roddy the monster who hit me.

"Would you be willing to testify, if this turns out to help Brian's case?" She handed me back the scrapbook.

I couldn't hesitate. "Sure."

Heather's look said I didn't know what I

was saying. "Sometimes witnesses have a change of heart. Things . . . let's just say things happen in murder trials that no one expects. I'll keep your name on file, and you let me know if you change your mind."

"Thanks."

"No, thank you, Ms. Arthur. Please keep that scrapbook in a safe place." She walked me to the door and shook my hand. I didn't wince even a little.

Then I remembered the destruction in Brian's and Cissy's apartments. "You can be sure of it."

CHAPTER 31

The knocking on my back door was soft enough that if I hadn't been in the kitchen, I might have missed it. Queenie picked up her head and scooted in between my ankles, a cute little *protect-me* move that made me reach down and scratch her behind the ears.

"Someone at the door, good girl?" I smiled and went to answer, Queenie staying a safe distance behind and barking at whoever had come to call. I'd read that corgis are supposed to be good watchdogs. Probably because they sure sound the alarm well.

"Chip!" I said when I opened the door. Since when had my half-adopted son started using real manners and door knocking?

"Hi, Daisy," said Chip. He looked down at his feet then up into my face. "May I please come in?"

"Sure. But tell me, who died? You look horrid, my friend."

Chip slumped into my kitchen table chair and dropped his backpack on the floor beside him. "Sorry, Ms. D. — I mean, Daisy. I wanted to come over to tell you what I found out about Joe Smaldone."

I sat in the other chair and pushed a bowl of strawberries toward him. "Go on, I'm all ears."

"Joe Smaldone runs a restaurant in LoDo. In a nutshell, while his family has an interesting past, Joe is legit. Throughout Prohibition and right up through the nineties, the biggest mob name in Colorado was Smaldone. There were several brothers in the family business, but just as many not. Eleven kids! Anyway, the bad boys were as well liked in the community as they were prime targets for the police. Guess Joe took after the Smaldone matriarchal branch of the family. Did you know it was Mamie Smaldone who set up and worked Gaetano's all those years before Governor Hickenlooper bought it, then sold it back to the Gaetano employees?"

"No. All I heard about was the bulletproof glass in front."

"That's all gone now. They did a remodel a couple of years ago and the glass shattered. To me, Gaetano's is a good, solid Italian eatery with mob stories and photos for fun. But Essence, Joe's place, is special. I hear the food is to die for. Get it? Smaldone? To die for?"

I rolled my eyes and giggled. "Chip, I'm rubbing off on you too much."

"Maybe you, Kitty, and I can go there sometime. To Essence. Their Chicken *Saltimbocca* is supposed to be very special." A stricken look crossed Chip's face. He looked away. "Maybe someday."

"Chip. Is there something wrong between you and Kitty?" I asked. "Is she okay? Are you?"

"I'm fine Ms. — Daisy. Fine. Kitty too." He'd been vigorously bobbing his head up and down. But then Chip looked into his lap at his hands.

"Chip? Friend here. What's going on?" I stretched across my table trying to reach Chip.

He ran fingers through his hair, à la Gabe's frustration give-away. "Whew. Can't get much past you, Daisy," said Chip. "I have a worry or two. That's all." Then he jumped up, like someone had lit a firecracker under his chair. "Maybe I should go." He whirled around and headed toward the door. Then he stopped, returned for his backpack, and stood to go again.

"Chip. You're not okay. I can tell. Now

how 'bout you share? The load is easier that way." I couldn't imagine what was on my young friend's mind.

He turned back toward me, eyes glistening. "I lost my job today." The floodgates opened and suddenly I found myself hugging Chip and leading him into my living room for a talk.

"Goodness, Chip! I'm so sorry!"

"*The Post* doesn't need someone who can only turn in a couple of stories a week. I'm not Pulitzer material in this day and age when newspapers have to keep trimming just to stay alive." He sat on my couch. I sat next to him, and again encouraged him into a hug. Poor dear. Chip kept shaking his head. He whispered "loser" in a mantra that couldn't lead to any good.

"There, there, Chip. I heard through a reliable source that you are a wizard with words. Maybe some better job will turn up."

"Better than *The Post*? What? You think the *New York Times* wants to open a Denver bureau?" The bitterness in Chip's voice hurt. I think it must have shown because Chip was immediately contrite.

"I'm sorry, Daisy. I know you're trying to help. Everybody's trying to be nice. Even my editor was great, but there isn't a full-time job for me anymore. Maybe a freelance piece or two, but no steady paycheck."

I handed the reporter a tissue. He blew his nose and dabbed at his eyes. "What am I going to do, Daisy? I just asked Kitty to marry me, and now I have to tell her we need to wait."

"But you two are so in love," I said. "Kitty won't mind . . . well, she may be upset you lost your job, but she won't blame you. These things happen —"

"They happen to other people. I was told to look for a promotion a few weeks ago — that changes were in the air. That's why I asked her — then I get the pink slip instead. How can a great woman like Kitty marry an out-of-work news geek like me?"

"Chip. You need a game plan, a way to get right back on your feet. Let's start with a good strong cup of tea."

"I think I need something stronger than tea, Daisy."

"Okay then, how 'bout I lace it with a little whiskey?"

"No, Daisy. Thanks, but no. I was just kidding. I need to think about this for a while. I can't marry the woman I love when I don't have an inkling of how I'll provide for her."

This old-fashioned sentiment seemed out of touch with the real picture I had of Kitty in my head. Perhaps Chip was still in shock.

A little food might help. "Fair enough. How 'bout I rustle us up some dinner?"

He slumped further in his seat. "Sorry. Kitty and I are supposed to go to her folks' for dinner tonight. How am I going to tell them all that I'm out of work? That I can't provide for Kitty? That we can't marry?"

I thought for a few minutes and let the sound of Georgette's snoring in my new chair and Queenie's watchful panting from the safety of her doggie bed fill the silence. Finally, I said to Chip, "I think you should enjoy a nice meal with Kitty's family. Then drive her home and tell her. This is something you and she need to share privately before you tell others. Chip, I believe in you. You'll figure something out."

"Thanks, Daisy. I appreciate the vote of confidence." He shook his head again. "The question is, will Kitty?"

Bright and early Saturday morning came with a pounding at my door. Chip and Kitty stood there grinning, handholding, and looking like yesterday hadn't happened at all.

"I have to guess that dinner went well?" I said, opening my door to them.

"It was lovely," said Kitty. Today's ensemble was a rose pink sweater set with blue

332

jeans and some gold-colored sandals. The outfit was completed with a gold headband to hold back her auburn curls, and crystal drop earrings. Behind his princess, Chip fairly glowed with happiness and pride.

"Daisy, you won't believe this," said Chip. "Last night, when we went to Kitty's folks', Jonathan — that's Kitty's dad — he asked me if I could help produce an eBook for his company. They sell software."

"And that's when Chip, my hero, stepped in and made the project seem like it would be a snap," said Kitty, beaming at her fiancé. "Before dinner, he and Dad had outlined a series of books that are really going to help sell Dad's accounting package. I was so impressed."

"Then, Jonathan, he says, 'How much do you charge for your business copywriting?' "

"And Chip says he couldn't charge a nearly family member. Dad says 'nonsense,' and before dessert, they have a contract outlined too." Kitty rubbed Chip's shoulder. He blushed.

"It gave me an idea," said Chip. "I told Jonathan I'd been thinking of going free-lance for a while, and would trade the first eBook copy for a couple of introductions around town. Now I'm set to sell Beaumont Technologies six books by the end of the summer and Jonathan says we'll have lunch at his golf club next week, where he'll introduce me to his friends."

"Chip! I'm thrilled for you. Nice work. And *The Post*?"

"I told Kitty what happened after dinner, like you said, Daisy. She was great about the whole thing. In fact, Kitty helped with this idea — I'm thinking of writing a book on the Smaldone family — maybe a 'where are they now?' kind of exposé."

"Terrific! Maybe we should celebrate losing *The Post* job."

"I love *The Post,* and always will. But now that I can do some freelance work for them and Beaumont Technologies, with room in the schedule for other writing opportunities, I think my writing career will soar."

"As for celebrating," said Kitty, "Chip and I are heading down to Colorado Springs today, to look at the Broadmoor for wedding plans. That's why we've stopped by."

"You want me to come with you? But what about your mom?"

"Sorry, Daisy. I didn't mean that. We were wondering if you wouldn't mind taking Thunder for a walk for us."

"Oh!" I recovered quickly. "Of course, Thunder needs a walk. We want to keep that Colorado Spring in his step, don't we?"

Chip and Kitty laughed in unison.

"You're a champ, Ms. D.," said Chip.

"Champ? Probably more like a chump." But I smiled and held out my hand for Thunder's leash.

CHAPTER 32

Chatfield in May is breathtakingly gorgeous. Hawks and eagles sit proudly in still-bare branches, Canada geese haven't left yet for cooler climates, and the wild grasses are lush and green. Behind them all the foothills of the Rockies glow in a purplish-blue, and the bright skies make it seem like there couldn't be such a thing as trouble in the world.

I parked my Versa, clipped leashes onto Queenie and Thunder, and stepped toward the dog park gate. It was late afternoon and cool enough for a nice long walk. I planned to let the dogs roam while I thought through what was forefront on my mind, the Cissy Melato murder. Each dog was anxious to get inside to sniff and run to his or her heart's content, and I was looking forward to a nice quiet walk. Thank goodness the leashes would come off as soon as we were in the gate, as Queenie wanted to go one way and Thunder seemed determined to go off in another direction. They would work things out. The couple of weeks I'd had Queenie in my charge had produced a growing friendship between the two canines.

It always amazed me how dogs got along so well. Yes, there were the occasional tiffs, but these usually ended quickly with one dog succumbing to another's idea of proper hierarchy and that was that. They didn't lie in wait to murder and rob each other as people sometimes do. There was no subterfuge, no victimizing, and no plotting of revenge for real or imagined slights. Dogs are straightforward kinds of creatures.

Of course, I did hear of the fight a few years back that turned deadly. A little guy was playing with a bigger dog and things got out of hand. A large pack of dogs was around, and some people, the owners, I think, started screaming. The screaming, too high pitched a sound for dogs, encouraged the frenzy that followed, and in the end, a few dogs had stitches, and the smaller dog died. The story still gave me shivers and I looked around for Queenie. She chased Thunder, nipping at his heels, but they seemed to be enjoying the perpetual chase game hard-wired into a dog's definition of fun. I went back to my musings.

I was pretty certain that Brian would be let out of jail soon. Heather said the sticker book was enough evidence that, along with an "expert advocate" letter from me, would encourage the DA to drop the murder charges Ginny's boyfriend had been held for.

I was thrilled for Brian and Ginny, but it still left the question of who killed Cissy Melato. I'd invested myself in this to get Brian out of jail, but after investigating for the past few weeks, I couldn't just walk away from the challenge. I asked who would have enough rage to stab a woman more than twelve times? Who would be angry enough long enough to lie in wait, drag her into the bathroom (or follow her in), and nearly decapitate her? What would an accountant do to inspire such intense fury?

Something at the edge of my brain argued against rage as the sole reason for so much horror. I couldn't quite bring the thought into focus, so I counted suspects off on the fingers of my hand. I tried to attach motive with means and opportunity for each.

Of course, Roddy popped in my mind right away. Heck, a guy willing to assault a middle-aged woman like me would have no problem killing one. I really wanted him to be the killer. I'd like his butt in jail forever.

But to be fair, he seemed a bit small for the job. I mean, I had almost gotten the upper hand in his and my altercation. If I hadn't chickened out or had refreshed my self-defense training . . . I rubbed my chin, where I was definitely on the mend.

Cissy had outweighed me by a good hundred pounds or more. She would have presented a formidable opponent for Roddy, unless he was able to take her completely by surprise. Roddy had motive all right, and opportunity, with her shopping late at night and all. But means? Brian had gotten the better of him, and I had managed, at least short term, to hold my own. No, something wasn't quite right about Roddy as the murderer. Much as I really wanted him to be it.

Thunder came up to me, wagging his tail. I gave the dog a quick pat and a biscuit. "Run along, Thunder. I'm thinking here."

Next on my list was Joe Smaldone, but no, he was out too. Chip said he was clean. Wasn't part of the better-known mob portion of his family. Of course, anger doesn't necessarily inhabit one side of a family and not the other, so I supposed it was possible. He had a dangerous feel about him, and he did sort of threaten me, but I couldn't see it. What would be his motive? He wasn't in her will or anything — though Cissy's daughter was, and she had enough anger and greed for motive. Plus she and Cissy had had that fight.

But, like me, Ramona was average height and weight. I'd have to get back to thinking about her. As for Joe, when he talked about his and Cissy's business relationship, what did he say? *Made my taxes sparkle for the IRS man, and never asked too many questions . . .*

Dan Block came to mind. I wasn't sure why. Dan didn't know Cissy, had no motive to kill her, much less kill her in a rage. But something he said about anger was sticking with me. Something that made the anger in this murder not quite right.

Thunder came up again.

"What is it, good boy?" I asked, plunking another biscuit into his mouth. He stared and panted at me. Then he barked. I laughed, because sometimes it felt as if the dog really was trying to talk with me. "You are such a good boy!" I said, ruffling the thick fur around his neck. I bent over and kissed the top of his head before moving on.

Now, where was I?

Hang on! Where was *I*? *Where was Queenie?*

My goodness! I had been so lost in thought that I forgot I'd brought Brian's dog with me. I looked around the park. Seventy-six acres of prairie swept before my eyes, but I had no vision of Queenie. I called and called.

How could I lose a six-hundred-thousand-dollar dog? My stars!

I started running and calling to Queenie. No response. How long had she been gone? Where should I look for her? Who could I call for help?

I thought of Gabe. The case had him bogged down, but I had to find Queenie. Poor Brian would never forgive me. I dialed Gabe's number.

"Hi, Daisy. What's up?" Gabe's deep voice was a salve, and I tried to respond calmly.

"Gabe, I'm sorry to drag you out, but I seem to have misplaced Queenie."

"The dog?"

"Yes."

"Don't worry. Dogs usually come home on their own. She's a little thing, so maybe you'll find her behind your garage or something."

"I'm not at home, Gabe. I'm at Chatfield."

There was a silence. Then, slowly, as if he were weighing his options, Gabe said, "I can't really drop everything right now, my girl, but I'll call you when I wrap things up here. If she's still lost, I'll come over after work — say in an hour?"

Inside I sighed. I knew his police work was important, but so was Queenie. "Okay, Gabe. Thanks. As soon as you can, please call."

"I will." Silence again, then, "Be careful, Daisy." Gabe probably remembered I'm not much of an outdoors kind of woman.

"Thanks. Will do," I said, happy he should care.

Reluctantly, I dialed Sam. We'd had a great time at dinner a week ago, but I didn't want to give him the impression I was looking to him for a boyfriend relationship. Thunder came up to me again. This time he sat in front of me, panting as if he were laughing at my stress.

"Thunder, good boy, where's Queenie?" I said. "Can you show me where she is?"

Thunder barked and bounded off. I started running after him, but Sam picked up the phone.

"What's up, Daisy?" he asked. "You want another beating at gin rummy?"

I tried to force lightness into my voice that I definitely didn't feel. "I let you win. Next time you'd better watch your nickels."

He gurgled. "When's next time?"

"We'll make a plan later. Right now, Sam, if you're not too busy, I have a favor to ask." I told him about Queenie and being lost at the dog park.

"I'll be there in ten minutes," he said. There was no edge in his voice. No annoyance. Only the helpful friend he'd always been.

True to his word, Sam pulled into the Owl Glenn parking lot after a short while. He had a leash strung around his shoulders, and a bag in his hand. "These are the best dog treats you can buy," said my friend. "I purchase 'em on-line and haven't ever had a dog do anything but go hog wild over them."

"Thanks, Sam. Unfortunately, I don't know which way Queenie went, so it isn't really a matter of coaxing her out, but where to look in this great expanse."

Sam pulled a whistle from his pocket and blew. I didn't hear much, but Thunder started dancing around Sam's legs, barking and jumping like a restive colt. Sam put the whistle down and gave Thunder a pat and a treat. "At least you have one of your charges."

"Thunder's the best."

"Did you try asking him to find Queenie?

Dogs can be pretty smart that way."

"I did, but then I got on the phone with you and lost Thunder for a bit."

"Which way did he run off?"

"Eastward. Down that path," I said and pointed in the direction.

"Then that's the way we'll start. Lucky this is spring. We'll have light for at least an hour or so longer."

"Thanks for your help, Sam." I put my hand on his arm.

Sam smiled at me and patted my hand. "What are friends for?" Then he turned and blew his whistle again. This time, even Thunder didn't come. We walked on for a bit, Sam asking questions about Queenie, most of which I couldn't answer.

"When's her next meal scheduled?"

"With Queenie, she eats all the time. The better question would be, when isn't she planning to eat?"

"Ah, the old corgi downfall. They are very food motivated, and will take eating to the extremes if you let them."

"Kind of like Cissy Melato."

"I see the challenge. Not so much a dog-eat-dog world for them, but an owner-feed-dog-constantly thing, right?"

I smiled. "Right."

Sam shook his head. "If only owners

would learn that nonstop feeding or feeding people food is so bad for their pets —"

Sam stopped mid-sentence for a high-pitched yipping sound.

"Think that was Queenie?" I asked and started to trot away. Sam grabbed me from behind. "Careful, Daisy. That wasn't a dog. That was a coyote."

"Coyote!" I jumped and searched around. Ooh! I so did not want to be here. Thunder came bounding out of some scrub bushes near one of Chatfield's ponds. He charged the park fence. Sam and I followed his gaze. Sure enough, a coyote stood on a ridge overlooking both the dog park and Chatfield Reservoir. A chill ran through me. "Stop, Thunder!" I was trying to be calm but the sound that came out sounded angry with fear. Thunder, hackles up, turned his head to me. "Come," I commanded in that over-authoritative voice. He looked back at the coyote, growled once, then came trotting up to me.

"Well done!" said Sam. "Get a leash on him right away. We'll put Thunder back in your car, and then find Queenie. Safer that way."

Safer? I wanted to get in the car with Thunder and let Sam go find Queenie. Coyotes! My goodness.

After making sure Thunder was safe, we returned to our search for my smaller dog. It took about twenty minutes of searching around, asking other owners and caregivers about her, and generally whistling and calling, but eventually Queenie came bounding up from the reeds surrounding the eastern edge of one of the ponds.

"Queenie!" I said. "Will you look at yourself? You're filthy! And what, in heaven's name, have you gotten into? Eeew." I covered my nose, my eyes watering. Sam was chuckling beside me, but he stepped away as Queenie ran up and wove her fat little belly between my legs. "Eew! Queenie. Off," I cried.

Sam let out a belly laugh. "Smells like she found a dead fish," he said. Queenie turned her attention to Sam. She let out a few barks and ran toward him. "No you don't," he said, bent on one knee and put his hand out stop-sign fashion. Queenie stopped. Sam raised the palm of his hand and said, "sit" with a tone of authority. Queenie sat, her big eyes never leaving Sam's face. Her tongue lolled out with a happy, albeit, dirty little grin on her face.

"You've had quite the adventure, my dear." Sam pulled a special doggie treat from his pocket and gave it to my truant.

Deftly, he clipped a leash onto Queenie and, with no more ado, stood up and started walking away.

"That's it?" I asked. "She runs away for almost an hour and she sits, so she gets a treat?"

"She's a dog, Daisy. Only did what came naturally to her. Even if she remembers she ran away, I think she knows it's more comfortable to live with you than without." As if she wanted to confirm what Sam said, Queenie gave a sharp bark. He laughed and gave her another treat.

"Come on," said Sam. "We'll take her to the south side of the pond where there's a beach and wash her off a bit before she gets in your car."

"My car!" My dear stars! That smell in my car. Yuck!

Sam laughed. "Guess you could say that you can't teach an old dog new tricks, but you can teach him to fish. Heh, heh, heh." Sam's laugh was full of wicked fun. I couldn't help but laugh in reply.

We got Queenie washed off a bit in the pond and walked back to our vehicles, where Sam had a towel in the back of his truck. As he wiped down my charge, Sam said, "Thanks, Daisy."

"Thanks? Thank me? Thank you, my friend."

"No really. After Rocky" — he paused his rubbing of Queenie — "well, after Rocky, I didn't think I would ever come here again. I was done with walks and dog parks. Thought I'd simply sit at home and watch TV. You and Queenie here have changed my mind. Don't care if I am an ancient. I'm gonna go to the Humane Society and adopt a new dog. I'll do it tomorrow. So yes, thank you, Daisy. You'll always be a good friend."

I smiled. Right then, my phone rang. Gabe. I smiled at Sam and excused myself.

"Daisy? I'm finished with my notes. You still need help with your dog?"

"No, thanks, Gabe. Sam helped me find her."

Silence. "Oh," said Gabe. "Okay."

"Gabe, I really appreciate your follow-up. Let's talk later. Queenie's a mess and I need to get her home now."

"Sure." He hung up. I wondered if I would ever get used to that. I turned and smiled at Queenie and Sam.

"She could go home with you, you know," I said.

There was a mischievous twinkle in Sam's eye as he said, "No, I think I'll leave the dog bath adventure to you."

"Thanks," I said, hoping every bit of my sarcasm flowed through my word.

He laughed again and reached into the back of his truck. "Here. You'll need this," he said, tossing me a plastic bottle.

I read the label: "Nature's Miracle — Skunk Odor Remover" it said. What joy.

CHAPTER 33

Monday afternoon dragged on with me being good about sitting at my desk writing. My character, Ruth, was struggling in her relationship with her boss. She knew he was attractive and she wanted more than a business connection, but were the feelings reciprocated? Thoughts of Gabe sprang to mind. More than a business relationship? Wishful thinking?

I re-read the next day's sample pages, and struck out more superfluous words. At last, I was beginning to understand what "tighten" means to authors. I didn't need to stop putting in descriptions, but needed to get rid of words that didn't move the story along. Especially fatty adjectives. I crossed out a few exclamations like "Oh!" and "Well," and left the juicy dialogue to my characters.

Tightening could be compared to dieting. I wondered if Cissy could have lost the weight she wanted, if only she'd cut out a few of the superfluous snacks, instead of trying so drastically to change the way she ate. Balance is the key. Then again, I didn't know her. Maybe she had tried. Maybe she struggled and food became her over-the-top coping mechanism. A real demon. I knew balance was hard for me to find in life. Why not for Cissy?

My fingers hovered over the keyboard, as my thoughts wandered to the accountant, her murder, and my adventures in trying to figure out who killed the poor woman. Were so many stab wounds necessary? Could he or she have done the job with less mess?

Daisy! This is murder. One wound is too much.

What was I thinking? Good thing Gabe and the police were working the case. I had made very little headway on it. Would Cissy become a cold case? I hoped not.

Suddenly, my back door started banging like it was Paul Revere warning that the British were coming. Queenie started barking and yapping, as if I hadn't heard all the commotion. Georgette jumped off my desk and ran to the shelter of my bedroom.

That Chip. I appreciated he was remembering to knock these days, but did he have to be so enthusiastic? I hoped he wasn't

351

having problems already over his new free-lance writing career. No way I could help there.

I reached the back door and flung it open without looking at Chip. I was too busy turning to tell Queenie hush. My back door pounded open against the inside wall. I turned to scold Chip and found myself staring into the very angry face of Roddy McKeague.

"Roddy! What in heaven's —"

"Shut up, you bitch!" spat out Roddy. He grabbed my upper arms and shoved me against a wall.

My limbs tingled in fear as the furious young man invaded my personal space, pinning me where I stood. I gasped, as he shifted his hold into a forearm against my neck.

"You thought you'd never see me again, didn't you? You meddlesome old cow. Did you think I wouldn't come after you when you and that smug Connie Allessi made sure I got fired from Gigantos? When you pressed those assault charges? When the Department of Homeland Security paid me a visit over those people I gave jobs to at night? Guess you thought wrong." Roddy's ragged breath blasted in my face with the smell of cigarettes and alcohol. He must have been drinking before he came here.

The ex-night manager released me suddenly, and shoved me further into my kitchen. I stumbled but managed to keep my feet under me.

"Roddy, I didn't do all those things," I said. Placating an angry student usually helped. Usually. "You want to talk about it?"

"Shut up, cow. You and Connie are real gone, now." Roddy glanced around my kitchen. His gaze lingered on my knife block. Dear heavens! What was he going to do?

"How 'bout you sit down? Maybe we can talk this out." I hoped to stall for time. Maybe I could signal Chip that I needed help.

"Talk what out? You lost me my job, had me thrown in jail, and put me at outs with some important friends. What's there to talk about? Women! Fuck 'em all! Cissy got hers, Connie's going to, and you —"

"Connie's going to? What do you mean? Maybe I can help. Maybe I can —"

"Can what? Get me my job back? Make this mess go away? I've been told that before, by better people than you."

"What do you want, Roddy?"

"I want my life back, you stupid woman! I

want my life back." His face was almost purple with rage.

A small blur of fur streaked across my kitchen. Queenie! She charged in at Roddy and sank her sharp little teeth into his ankle.

"Yeowww!" cried the young man. He began shaking his leg, but Queenie was out for blood. She clung to Roddy's leg, growling and shaking her head with a mouth full of Achilles tendon.

"Get it off. Get it off!" screeched Roddy.

Queenie growled more. Roddy raised a fist and brought it down on Queenie's head. She let out a yelp and was flung backward against my dishwasher. The plucky little thing got up and began circling for what I could only guess was another attack on the other ankle. Roddy hobbled to my wooden block and withdrew my butcher knife.

"Wait!" I jumped in to catch Queenie. "I'll put her outside." I strode quickly to the back door, Queenie still struggling in my arms to get to Roddy. I let Queenie out, not bothering with the back yard. Remembering old dog hero television shows, I whispered, "Go find Chip, good girl. Find help!"

As I receded into my back door again, Roddy came up behind me and grabbed my hair. The pain seared through my head. He dragged me back into my house, the butcher knife at my neck. I just had time to fish for a hold on my door jam and fingered on my back porch light. Hopefully Roddy didn't see that. Hopefully Chip did. Hopefully Chip would sense something was wrong. Maybe come over. Art! I need help! Outside, Queenie was going berserk with her barking. Good girl, Queenie!

Roddy flung me away again, and I settled into a kitchen chair. He waved my knife around in the air.

"You're not so brave now, are you, cow?" He hobbled to the kitchen sink and wet a rag to put on his profusely bleeding ankle. Queenie scratched at my back door. Her barking sounded frantic. I could hear Thunder in his yard begin to bark too.

Roddy returned a wild gaze in my direction. "Get that thing to shut up! Do it now, or else I knife it. Move!"

I jumped and ran to the door again. I grabbed Queenie up in my arms. She was frantic with ferocious barks. Maybe she knew Roddy was Cissy's killer. A dog's sixth sense and all that.

But if I let her go, and she went after Roddy once more, he'd kill her for sure. "I'll put her in her kennel," I said and went toward the crate under my kitchen table. With a little struggle, I was able to calm

Queenie enough to get her in her kennel. I slipped in a treat to thank her for her protection.

"You got any booze?" Roddy was opening and slamming closed my cupboards. "Where you keep your bandages? Damn! I oughtta kill that mutt!"

"She won't do you any more harm. Here. Sit down and I'll put a wrap on your ankle. You scared Queenie, that's all. She won't hurt you anymore."

I found a glass, poured some sherry, and handed it to Roddy. He stuck his foot up on my other kitchen chair.

"Ow! Be careful, you clumsy cow," he said as I tried to pull his sock down to look at the dog bite. Queenie had done a number on Roddy's ankle. I would have given her another treat if I could.

"You really ought to see a doctor about this. It looks pretty bad. You'll probably need stitches." *You dumb miscreant.*

"Shut up and bandage it." He waved the knife at me again. I felt perspiration break out on my forehead. Focus, Daisy. This guy is past being able to reason. Why would he be so out of touch with reality?

I looked at Roddy. So I had been right all along. He did kill Cissy, and now he was going to kill me too. A wave of sorrow swept over me.

"Why, Roddy? Why did you kill Cissy? Will you at least tell me that?" *Tell me before you kill me.*

Roddy stared at me for a long minute then broke out in a snorting sound. It was a cross between laughter and bitter snarling. I wanted to throw up.

"Kill Cissy? I only wish I had. I wanted to. The fat bimbo found out about everything. Came in threatening to go to immigration and health services. She somehow made sense of the ramblings of that boob, Brian. I said I wanted to kill him too, prove my worth, but no. My friends said they would take care of both Cissy and Brian at one time."

"What friends, Roddy?"

"Never mind about that. We had a good thing at that grocery store until the stupid accountant butted in. The illegals helped me get more done in a night than I ever could with the small budget I had for staff. I paid them Mexes half what I had to pay union guys, and they worked all night, even in the dark."

"But how did Cissy know?"

"Must've coaxed it out of Brian. I told that kid not to talk to nobody, but he did. Can't trust those retards at all. Can't keep a secret if their life depended on it."

I reflected how Brian's life, thankfully, didn't depend on keeping that one secret. At least, not so far. But he had been in jail. Maybe Gabe putting him there was better than I'd thought.

"And Brian's stickers?"

"Ah, they were the clincher. We needed to re-label some cucumbers a year or two ago. Remember the salmonella outbreak? We couldn't lose all that money jus' because some people don't wash their veggies when they get home. That's how it started. Had to save the profits."

"So you re-labeled more than once?" My stomach churned.

" 'Course. It got easier and easier. Fruits and veggies come in from all over the place, some good, some not so good. I replace the bad stickers with good ones. Change dates. Change place of origin. Simple. The really bad stuff, I put on sale. Didn't want the old stickers around in case someone had suspicions. Gave them to the kid when he did a good job."

"And Brian went along with this?"

"Why wouldn't he? He didn't understand, and I didn't have to pay him bonuses. Just gave him the stickers I didn't want around the store." Roddy went from looking pleased with himself to a deep scowl in a single breath. "But he went and shared them with the accountant. She brought in the stickers in a scrapbook one day. Said the health department would be shutting us down if we didn't put things right. Said she'd go to the press with her information. I told my friends they'd find that book in Melato's apartment. She was too sharp to trust the dimwit to hold onto 'em. Do you have that book?"

"No," I said, crossing my fingers behind my back.

"You're lying. I need it. Give it to me."

"Did someone you know kill Cissy? You could tell the police, and that would help get you out of this mess."

"Are you kidding? The friends I have don't let you out of any messes. Best thing to do is disappear. That's what I'm going to do. And if you knew what was good for you, you'd disappear too. You know too much. Now, about that book —"

Sirens came up my street. Police!

Roddy jumped up and hobbled to the front room. He pushed back the curtains and swore. Then he hobbled back past me through my kitchen. For an injured man, Roddy could move fast.

"You say anything . . ." he said, and

brandished my knife in my face. Then he was gone. I caught a glimpse of the young man racing through Chip's backyard, and a few seconds later, in hot pursuit, Matt Hawkins ran after him.

At about the same time, a pounding at my front door said the police had arrived. Thank goodness! Queenie started barking again, but she was safe in her kennel, so I went to open the door to them.

Before I could get there, Gabe burst in looking like a wild bear, his gun out of its holster, his mouth set in a grim line I'd never seen on him before. My heart quickened. I raised my hands then froze in place. Would he recognize me or shoot first and ask questions later?

CHAPTER 34

"Gabe," I said. "He's gone. Roddy's gone."

It took a moment to register, but at last Gabe's gun pointed up and not out in my direction. He holstered the thing, and in two swift strides scooped me into his arms.

"Daisy," he said. "Daisy. I thought I'd lost you! There was a call —"

"Chip called? Thank goodness."

"No, not Chip. Call came from a disposable cell. Caller hung up before we could trace it, but he said Roddy was out to kill you. Thank God you're all right." Gabe hugged me close and kissed my face all over. I could hardly breathe, but it didn't matter. My guy, my nice strong police guy, came to save me once again.

Reluctantly, I pulled back. "Gabe, Roddy didn't mean to kill me. He was mad enough, all right, but I think there was something more. He was frightened, Gabe. Really scared."

"Tell me about it, my girl. Something isn't right here," said Gabe.

Gabe walked me over to my couch and sat me down.

"Now, Daisy, I need those special observation skills you have. Tell me what happened."

I told Gabe all about Roddy's intrusion. I told him how Roddy had pushed me against the wall, and threatened me with the knife. How Queenie tried to come to my rescue, but Roddy hit her, too.

"Thing is, Gabe, he was a little drunk and a lot scared. Kind of like a guy who is haunted or something. I know that's a silly analogy, but —"

"No, not silly at all, Daisy. You said he was involved with some very shady workings in an otherwise good store." Gabe got up and paced the room, thinking.

"Yes." I rose too. "I used to work with the people at Gigantos. They often helped me place students. Until now, there hasn't been any hint of questionable ethics. You must know this, with Ginny working there. She loves it."

"Yes, she does. But Ginny isn't great at judging good from bad."

"You don't give her enough credit. Even when you put Brian in jail, she was steadfast in her belief he was innocent. And look how that turned out. She thinks deeply, Gabe, if not quickly, and uses her judgment based on what you've taught her."

"Okay. So Gigantos is not a hotbed of undiscovered criminal activity. But that Roddy guy has a lot of explaining to do. And we can add another assault charge for what he did to you today."

"Roddy is a twerp, Gabe, but —" I stopped. I was using words to describe him that were too familiar. *Roddy is a twerp.* Roddy is a twerp. Who said that?

"Daisy, what is it?"

"Some memory I can't pull up. Somebody said Roddy is a twerp, but a small fish in a big pond. Now, why oh why, does my brain have to choose now to short circuit?"

"Don't worry about it, my girl. It'll come to you. Right now, I have enough on Mc-Keague to go after him big time."

At that moment, Gabe's cell rang.

"Matt? . . . Yeah? . . . Lost him? . . . Okay, I'll be right out." Gabe disconnected and turned to me. "We lost Roddy, but the way you described his bleeding ankle, I'm sure we'll catch him soon enough. Meanwhile, do you have anyone who can come stay with you? I want you safe."

My heart melted. Even with all that was

going on, Gabe found time to think of my safety and me.

"I'll call Chip. Maybe he and Kitty can come over for a while."

"Good. Have 'em stay with you until I call, got it?"

"Roger that," I said with a quick salute.

Gabe rolled his eyes, then grinned at me, leaned over and gave me another kiss. Then he was gone.

I dialed Chip's number and he came right over. For a guy I so often thought of as a mischievous manipulator, Chip always seemed to come through when I needed a friend.

"I tried Kitty, but she's gotta work tonight," said Chip.

"Even on Memorial Day?"

"Especially because it's Memorial day. Bars do brisk work on the holidays. Even you should know that, Daisy."

I guess I did. Still, I would have been much more comfortable if Kitty had been here, too. She had a black belt or some such martial arts thing, and Chip? Chip had good intentions.

"Let's order some pizza and play a game of Scrabble," said my young friend.

Fifteen minutes later we were engaged in a heated debate over the use of the word *um* that would've given Chip a double triple word score when my phone rang.

"Daisy? Daisy Arthur?" The voice had a familiar tone, but I couldn't quite place it.

"Who is this?"

"Joe Smaldone. Cissy's cousin."

A chill ran through me. Joe's voice had an urgency that made me nervous. I had been only too glad to keep clear of this man. Okay, so Chip said he ran a legitimate business with Essence Restaurant, but when we talked that day a couple of weeks back, I was left with the distinct impression that Joe and I would not ever be close friends.

"What can I do for you, Joe?" I tried to keep the wary feeling from reaching my voice. Chip looked up and raised his eyebrows. I mouthed "Smaldone" to him and he ran to listen in on my other extension.

"I'm looking for your boyfriend, Caerphilly. Tried at the station, but he's out on call. Thought he might be with you."

"How'd you get my number, Joe?"

"For a private eye, you're pretty clumsy, Daisy. I looked you up online a couple of ways and was able to piece together everything I needed. I have your address, phone, email. Everything. You oughtta be more careful."

I was on the Internet? I'd have to Google

myself sometime. But Joe was right. I wondered who else had my information. Roddy seemed to have it, and that was too scary by far.

"Anyways," continued Joe, "I need to talk to your police lieutenant."

"Like you said, he's on a call right now. Can I give him a message?"

"No . . . Well, yeah. Tell him it's me. Tell him I'm hearing things. Bad things. Never mind where I'm getting them. In the food industry you hear a lot. I'm no snitch, but word is Littleton's going to light up tonight. Your cop is a straight shooter, so I thought I'd give him a little heads up. I think what Cissy did stirred up a wasps' nest."

"What exactly did she do?"

"Right before she died, Cissy asked me for a meeting with a friend of mine — a friend in the Food and Drug Administration. I didn't think the meeting took place, so I never mentioned it to anyone. But now she's dead and you made me think more about it, there may be a connection."

"Thanks, Joe. You're a good man."

There was a short silence. "Just tell Caerphilly to keep his Kevlar close tonight."

"I will."

"And Daisy?"

"Yes?"

"Your name's flying around out there too. Jus' so you know."

Suddenly I heard a scream at Joe's end of the line. Joe must've turned away from our conversation, because I could hear him calling someone. Just before the phone went dead I heard him shout, "Oh, my God!"

CHAPTER 35

I stared at the dead phone in my hand. Breathing took all my concentration. Joe's call had chilled me to the bone. Chip came out from my office and wrapped a throw around my shoulders. "Come on, Daisy. Come sit down."

A ring on my front doorbell encouraged me to jump. Chip went to get it. Gabe came into my living room, with Chip in his wake. I ran to my police officer.

"Gabe! I'm frightened."

"We'll catch Roddy, Daisy. You'll be all right."

"Not Roddy, Gabe. I know you'll get him. But I had a call a minute ago."

Gabe put his hands on my shoulders. "A call? From whom?"

"Joe Smaldone. He said you should keep someone or something called keppler close tonight."

Chip broke in. "That's Kevlar, Daisy.

Bullet-proof vest?"

"Okay. Kevlar. Whatever. It sounds serious." I told Gabe everything Joe had said, Gabe's face growing more and more somber as I rattled on.

After peppering Chip and me with questions, Gabe turned directly to me. "I don't like this," he said at last. "I don't like it at all — especially the part where your name is flying around. You're going to stay with me tonight. I'll call this in and —"

The phone at Gabe's hip went off. He looked down. No softening of features for what must have been Linda's call. Chip and I could only hear Gabe's side of the conversation, but it was enough to let us know things were bad.

"Another murder? . . . Louviers? . . . Who was she — Gigantos employee? . . . Spell that, I'm taking notes . . . A-L-L-E-S-S-I . . ."

"Allessi? Has Connie been murdered, Gabe?" My heart wrenched in my chest. It was all I could do to keep from screaming. Roddy said Connie would get hers, and I would too.

Gabe held up his hand and cupped the phone with his other. "Yeah, I'll be right there . . . No. No McKeague yet, but Hawkins will keep on him. Keep your head down, partner. Word on the street is we're in for a long night." Gabe hung up and put his phone away.

"Gabe. Connie Allessi? She was a manager at Gigantos. Oh, my God! Please, don't tell me she was murdered!"

He shook his head sadly. My knees went weak, so Chip helped me to a chair and took over asking questions.

"Louviers. Isn't that where Smaldone lives, Lieutenant?" he asked.

"Think so. Place is in the foothills. Know more when I get there. Thing is, I'm not comfortable with this Roddy character running around. Can you keep an eye on Daisy, young man?"

Chip seemed to grow an inch. "No problem, sir. Daisy and I have pizza ordered, and other than that, these doors will stay locked tight."

Gabe patted Chip on the shoulder in that "man-to-man" kind of fashion, gave me another kiss, and whispered that he would return as soon as possible. And then he slipped away. I realized at that moment why police spouses have abandonment issues.

CHAPTER 36

Scrabble game forgotten, Chip went back to my office to text Kitty. For a very young man, he was trying to pull himself in a couple of protective directions, and with admirable success. I felt better with him in the house.

My doorbell rang and I jumped before remembering we'd ordered pizza. But then my mind went to all those criminal movies where the bad guy has mugged the pizza delivery person and stolen the uniform as a way to break in to the victim's house.

"Who is it?" I asked from behind my door. I could hear the old, wimpy, and avoid-conflict-Daisy-voice creep forward.

"Pizza," chirped a friendly reply. It wasn't enough for me to be able to tell if the pizza person was Roddy or not, but the silhouette in the glass panel had a ball cap of some kind on.

"Can you leave the pizza on my porch chair?"

"Yes. I can do that. But what about signing the receipt?"

"How much is the total?"

The guy gave me an amount. By this time I was pretty sure it wasn't Roddy, but I wasn't particularly in the mood to take any chances. Especially as Gabe was headed to Louviers, twenty minutes away. "Just add a ten-dollar tip and sign the receipt yourself," I said.

"Thanks for the tip, lady, but it's against the rules to sign customers' receipts. I could get fired for that."

I rolled my eyes. In Littleton, people didn't usually have chains on their front doors, and I was no exception. Dare I risk opening my door to a complete stranger? I looked around, and saw my front closet where Art kept his bowling ball and the golf club he used for protection. I dragged the ball behind the front door. It didn't offer a whole lot of safety, but it was at least as good as one of those silly door chains.

"Pizza's here!" I yelled back at Chip, so if I went missing, he'd know where to start looking for me. Then I opened my door a crack and took the receipt. The pizza delivery guy looked all of about sixteen, without

so much as any facial hair to belie his innocent, and very confused, look. I scribbled
my name and handed him back the receipt.

"Hey," he said. "I thought you were going
to give me a ten-dollar tip."

"I thought you were going to give me my
pizza hassle-free."

"Sheesh," he muttered and retraced his
steps leading down to the curb. "They said
I'd see some weird people on full-moon
nights. I sure did."

I waited until pizza boy got to his side of
his car. No sign of Roddy. Looked like the
Nelsons were having company, with an extra
car in front of their house, but other than
that, the street looked pretty clear. I scooted
out to grab our dinner, and ran back inside
with my treasure.

Chip came out from my office and I put
the pizza box on my dining table.

"This is silly, Chip," I said with a grin. "I
think I just freaked out the pizza guy all
because my nerves are on edge."

"No one can blame you for that," he said,
picking up a slice and stuffing it in his
mouth in one swift movement.

"No plate?"

"Adds to the feeling of adventure tonight."

I smiled, but eating was beyond me. Cissy
dead. Roddy's fear-riddled assault. Connie

dead. Joe Smaldone. It was all too much for my middle-aged digestive system.

With Queenie locked up in her kennel, Chip's pizza crumbs fell safely to the carpet. As a bachelorette, I could relax the housekeeping rules a bit tonight. "Wanna soda to go with that?" I headed toward the kitchen to grab a bottle.

I opened my refrigerator and stopped.

"Chip," I called out. "Are you expecting company? Thunder's going crazy in your yard again."

Thunder was making quite a racket. His barking sounded almost frantic. I was used to that. Thunder found life an adventure and was constantly barking at something.

"Some watch dog," said Chip, coming in to take the soda from me. "Must have spotted a fox. He goes crazy after them." Chip stepped to my back door. "I'll go put him in the house, so he doesn't bother the other neighbors. Be right back."

"No, Chip! You said you'd stay with me. It's dangerous out there. That might be Roddy or his friends. It might be —"

Chip poked his head outside and looked around. "No, Daisy," he said, turning back toward me. "Don't worry. If I know anything, McKeague's far away by now. He knows the police are after him. The noise has to be a fox. And old man Nelson calls and yells at me every time Thunder barks more than once, so I have to go. Just to be safe, though, lock the door behind me. I'll knock three times when I get back to you, so you know it's me." And then Chip was gone, whistling and calling to Thunder as he went.

Thunder quieted almost immediately after, so Chip must have put him in the house. A chill ran down my back. I put a hand to my locket and scolded myself. *Daisy, you have to grow a spine one of these days. Roddy is just a little fish . . .*

I returned to my dining room and fingered a piece of pizza. My over-active nerves were getting the better of me. I kept reminding myself how foolish I'd felt in dealing with the delivery boy. Chip was right. Roddy was long gone. But Connie had been murdered. I thought about the last time we'd seen each other. It was a day or two after Cissy had died. I could envision her on the bench outside of Gigantos. What had we talked about?

Then I remembered. We sat on that bench in the sun, but I felt cold with our conversation. *"Roddy is an arrogant little twerp . . . but he has very powerful, nasty friends."* . . . *"Business can be cut-throat at times,"* I imag-

ined Art saying, and Cissy's throat had been enthusiastically cut . . . Dan Block said, "Besides, it's fun to be so bold in my work." Next to Roddy, at Cissy's funeral, stood a good-looking man. "So you think Brian's being framed," said Joe. A chill climbed up my spine again.

I picked up my phone. I knew who killed Cissy, and probably Connie too. I knew he would be after me next. Or was I, after all, being silly? I put the phone down. Chip would be right back and I could tell him my newest theory.

The tingling inside me wouldn't go away. I dialed Gabe's number. Two, three rings, then voice mail. No, I wouldn't leave a message. I was braver than that. I hung up and at the same time, there came a single knock at my back door.

Then two. Then three.

Must be Chip. Thank goodness.

CHAPTER 37

I got to my back door and saw a strange face pressed against the window inset, the eye area covered with a Zorro kind of mask. The kind of mask I'd find at Reinke Brothers' Halloween shop downtown. It startled me and I screamed and jumped back, grabbing for the locket of Art around my neck. Then I yelled at the face.

"Not funny, Chip! Not funny at all. So that's why you were so long. I ought to —" I reached toward the door handle.

Then I realized I was looking up toward, and not directly at, my short friend's face. And then I saw the bloody palms pressed against my windowpane. They were a ghastly white color under the blood. Surgical gloves. Whoever was at my door was leaving no fingerprints, only bloodstains.

And whoever was behind that mask wasn't Chip. Or Roddy. I felt my eyes widen in horror. A heartbeat later, I noticed the masked man's grin. It looked too familiar. I'd seen that grin before. It was a beautiful curve of lips. Very Russell Crow. I was right — Keith Johnson! I stopped thinking, turned and ran.

Queenie started barking in her kennel. Who knew where Georgette was, let alone Chip?

The glass from my back door shattered. Where could I hide?

I looked around me. At my age, I didn't exercise enough to contort my body into any tight spot or unusual places. All I could hope for would be a call to Chip on my cell. Chip! Why didn't he come back? Why had Thunder stopped barking? I crouched behind my living room couch, hoping the curtains wouldn't swish too much and draw attention. I heard steps in the kitchen, and dared a glance across to my dining nook. There on the table sat my pizza and my cell phone.

The steps from the kitchen became softer as my assailant stepped onto my rug. He was a large man, larger than Gabe. The posture was very confident.

Keith stopped and looked down at my dinner. There was that grin again. I couldn't believe I'd allowed that man to kiss me. Then he scooped up a piece of pizza and, without so much as taking off his blood-dripping surgical gloves, sat down to eat. My stomach lurched.

A couple of bites later, Keith fingered my phone, and said, almost to himself, "You've stolen my heart, Daisy." He chuckled at that.

Stolen my heart! I stood up.

"You!" I said and let every piece of loathing I could muster drip into the word.

Keith rewarded me with that sad smile of his and took off his mask. "Me. Don't tell me you didn't know."

"How could you? First Cissy, and then my friend, Connie?"

"It was only business, Daisy." He glanced down and then back up at me. "Pizza?"

He offered a slice in my direction.

CHAPTER 38

It all fit in a gruesome sort of way. Roddy got in trouble because Cissy figured out how he was using Brian and the illegals to make Gigantos — or more likely himself — more profitable. Roddy had that gangster wanna-be attitude and had intended to kill both Cissy and Brian, but didn't have the know-how to do it himself. Maybe one of his less than appropriate friends was indeed standing before me. I could tell Roddy hung on the man's every word. Keith had to be the leader of the two. But why would Keith get involved? Why would he risk his career to help Roddy the Twerp?

"What does Roddy have on you, Keith? How could he have talked you into murdering Cissy? The risk, the violence, it doesn't make sense."

"Roddy doesn't have anything on me anymore. And besides, every murder must have a killer, wouldn't you agree? Every murder has to have the right story in order to solve it." Keith shrugged and took another bite. "Only, the killers I chose wouldn't cooperate. They kept claiming their innocence. Now there's you. Who would've thought you'd take the side of some retard? That one threw me for a loop. If you had only let him take the fall for the Cissy killing, everything would be back to normal. He'd be nice and safe in jail — at least for a while." Keith waggled a finger at me. How could he tell the difference between the pizza topping and his blood-covered digit?

Keith grinned. "Tsk. Tsk. Busy little bee, Ms. Daisy. Too busy by far."

I was finding it hard to breathe. What did he mean *these killers wouldn't cooperate*? Had he chosen Brian to be a killer? How? "You need to leave Brian alone. He never hurt anybody."

Keith snarled. His striking face transformed instantly, and I realized that in the few times I'd seen him, I had always sensed something calculating in his actions. Even when he kissed me and used that line about stealing his heart, I knew it wasn't true. But that it was something I'd always wanted to hear. How did he know?

The persona of confidence slipped into

place immediately. Did he know he'd shown himself too clearly? "You are a puzzle, my girl. Sorry. That's what the police officer calls you, isn't it? *My girl.* But tonight, I think he and I have traded places. Tonight, you are truly *my* girl."

"How did you find me?"

He snorted his contempt. "Oldest trick in the book. I stirred up Roddy. Gave him a description of your car and sent him to follow you. Then I followed him. Parked right down the street. Easy. Police will think Roddy murdered you. He'll be your assassin, but my brave girl, you will have succeeded in striking a fatal stab in your adversary before you succumbed to your wounds. You'll be a hero, Daisy. You will have done the world a favor by killing Roddy in self-defense."

With that, he pulled a little box-like thing from his pocket and pinched it. A small clicking sound bounced around the room, and a knife blade appeared. The object glowed in the light of my dining nook like a tongue of fire.

I gulped. Was Keith saying he was going to kill both Roddy and me, or had he already killed Roddy? Too many ideas. I couldn't think clearly.

I couldn't think, but Keith could. He

turned to me, all business. "Now that I'm finished with my meal, how would you like your police officer to find you? Would you like to be at the kitchen table or lying on the couch like an Egyptian goddess?"

"You wouldn't!"

"But I would."

I glanced toward my front door, then back toward my kitchen.

Keith looked at me with a cat-like stare. Then he said, as if reading my mind, "There's really no escape, Daisy, but run if you must. It will make my work — shall we say — more engaging?"

A shiver ran through me. "You *enjoy* killing people?"

"Women, mostly. Men grunt and groan and fight until the end, but I find killing women a warmer, more sensual experience. Their wide eyes. Their soft, sweet breath. Their screams. Their helplessness —" He closed his eyes and breathed deeply. A small groan escaped his mouth and his eyes rolled slowly open.

"Men grunt and — what men have you killed already?"

He looked at me and tilted his head as if measuring the risk in telling me his exploits. "Too many to name them all right now. You might even say I was name-dropping. I know you like puns. Was that a good one?"

I couldn't even force a smile. "Who, Keith?"

"Not your precious lieutenant." He shrugged. "Some others."

"Who?"

Keith sighed. "The hardest part of what I do is to do my work without taking credit. I'd like to be able to tell someone. Maybe even you."

"But I thought you were a grocery store man."

"Today I am. That's what my set-up required. I came into the grocery business to trim a little fat, is all. Profits are measured by pennies in this business, so things get cut-throat fast."

"So you *planned* to kill Cissy? It wasn't an act of passion gone awry?"

He laughed outright at that.

"I put an overweight diabetic out of her miserable life, and saved some people a lot of money in the process." He shook his head. "Vegetarian, my ass. Nosey bitch who threatened to go to the news." He looked hard at me. "There is never passion in my work beyond the enjoyment of doing it well."

Dan Block's red slashes across my writing came to mind. *Might miss something impor-*

tant without the size and color I use.

"Actually, I do understand." I saw where Keith was coming from, and it repelled me as nothing I'd witnessed in my life had ever done before.

Keith nodded. "I think you do. Shame you're on my to-do list. I like your spirit. But, if you want, I'll make yours a quick job. You'll hardly feel a thing." He smiled that disgusting smile of his again. "It will be interesting to watch the glow of life seep from your gaze. I think I'll kiss you as I put in the knife. You'll like that, I'm sure."

Barf city!

The idea of this blood-drenched psychopath kissing me was too much. "Wait!" I cried, putting my hand out and searching for a stall tactic. "What about Roddy? Don't you think he'll squeal on you? He said he was a little fish. Are you the big one? The big fish?"

Keith smiled again. "Alas, no. You have the wrong analogy. It would be better to think of me as a chess king's knight, and Roddy as the pawn. But a fish? Come, come, Daisy. A fish stinks."

I could smell his aftershave and something harsher — blood. Somehow, my predator had crept closer to me.

I made a move to run away. Upstairs,

down to the basement, anything but here.

Keith caught me by the nape of my neck.

"Chip!" I yelled. "Chip! Help!"

Keith smiled again. "Your friend is a bit tied up at the moment. By the time the cops find him I think you two will be sharing the same fate."

"You killed him?" I couldn't believe it. "Chip?"

"No. Just cut him enough that if he doesn't get help in the next hour or so, he'll be in real trouble."

"Keith, please. Chip didn't do anything. Let me get to him. Help him."

"Sorry, Daisy. He got in the way. Seeing me when he went out for his dog was the guy's downfall."

Tears sprang to my eyes. Keith's grip had tightened around the back of my head and the pressure made me want to faint. I wished with all my heart I had never had a kind thought about this man. That I had kept a narrower focus on this case and really investigated before getting my friends in danger. I'd been so caught up in testosterone gazing, I hadn't really looked at the dangerous men I'd been talking to. Gabe's partner in crime-solving, my eye — wait a minute.

Faint. That was it! If I went limp, Keith

would have to hold me up while trying to stab me. When my kids went limp in class, we teachers had the devil of a time trying to get them back into wheel chairs. I couldn't think of another option. It wasn't like I was going to overpower this guy.

Keith loomed over me. I closed my eyes and dropped in his arms, a surprise dead-weight package.

"What the — ?" Keith had to grab me with both arms. My weight threw him off balance.

We fell to the floor. I rolled away, but Keith caught my ankle. I kicked at his hand, but he held tight, dragging me closer. I kicked again and connected with his head. He yelled out and his grip loosened. I kicked once more, this time on the arm that was holding me. Just enough to get out of his grasp.

"Bitch!" he cried, all pretense of the smooth, suave flirt falling away.

My breath came in struggling gulps. Sweat boiled around my ears and forehead. I scooted backwards, warily watching Keith as I made my way toward the front door.

Keith got to his feet. His own breaths were coming hard, and a look of satanic joy crossed his face. "So," he said, "we make it a game, eh?" He licked his lips.

I didn't waste any energy on talking. Needed to get to the front door. Had to escape. Scooted backward on my butt, stare never leaving Keith. Upper arms tingled with adrenaline.

Keith picked up his knife from the floor. "Tsk. Tsk. I was going to be kind, but you're a more worthy opponent than I thought."

My nostrils flared. I had reached my front door and pushed my back up against it. I grabbed for the door handle to help me up, almost to my feet. I stared at Keith, willing him to keep back.

He inched closer. He was toying with me.

I grabbed Art's bowling ball from its bag and rolled it toward Keith who easily side-stepped it. He smiled and advanced.

"Where to now, my friend?" Keith shifted weight from one foot to the next, like a tennis player before a serve.

I blew a slow steady breath out and mirrored what I could of Keith's actions. I would not go quietly into Keith's plan of destruction and death. I swung around and grabbed my door handle. The door was dead-bolted. There would be no escape this way.

Keith advanced again. I could hear him. He grabbed me around the waist and pulled

me back from the door.
I screamed.

CHAPTER 39

The light in my bathroom was too bright. I saw the terrified woman in the mirror and realized this might be the last I'd ever see of myself. Keith had dragged me to the bathroom, though I kicked and screamed all the way. He only laughed at my meager efforts for freedom, and whispered how he wanted to do me like he did Cissy, in front of a mirror so he could watch.

I didn't want to look anymore. To see the fright that was so clearly written across my features. The glee that fired his eyes. He started kissing the back of my neck and bit me along the nape. I screamed again, and tried reaching back to pull his hair. It only made him laugh more.

"Shall I slit your throat first, my dear, or puncture you so you can watch too?" Then he whispered, "I'm really getting off on this. The policeman's girl and me."

He pinned my hips against the sink front,

and began showering more kisses up and down my neck, nibbling my earlobe. I could even feel him growing hard with excitement, pressing against me in a rhythmic motion. My goodness! My pain and fear were bringing him to sexual arousal. I closed my eyes and tried to think. There must be a way out.

Keith was going to "do" me. Exactly like Cissy Melato. And everyone would think Roddy McKeague did this. No one would look for the sociopath behind Roddy. Keith would make sure of that.

My head swam. I debated whether fighting to the end would be worthwhile, or if I would be better off keeping my eyes closed and opening my mind to my happier memories. My hand flew to the locket around my neck. *Art, looks like we'll be together soon.*

No, Daisy. You have to fight. You were always the strong one between us. You can do this.

How, Art? How?

Fight, my love. Fight. It's not your time.

Suddenly, I was pushed forward harder. The sink bit into my hips painfully and my cheek flew into the mirror. I opened my eyes to see a blur of eyeballs and nose. Then all pressure came off of me and I found myself flinging backwards.

"What the fuck?" cried Keith.

CHAPTER 40

"You keep your hands off of my woman!" shouted Gabe. He landed a heavy blow onto Keith's cheekbone.

Gabe! He'd come to my rescue again. How had he known I needed him?

Keith flew back against the tiles and crumpled against my toilet. His knife flew into my bathtub. Thank goodness!

But Keith wasn't through. He lifted his leg and kicked hard right toward Gabe's torso. Gabe flew backwards out of the bathroom and into the hallway wall opposite.

Keith took advantage of the break and jumped up from the floor, reaching into the tub as he did.

"Knife, Gabe!" I screamed from a protected spot between the sink and the bathroom entry.

Keith charged.

I squeezed harder against the wall to keep

out of the way.

Gabe started back into the room drawing his gun.

Keith was too fast. He knocked Gabe's arm and the gun flew down the hallway.

My house shook as the two men wrestled and fought. It wasn't like in the movies. I didn't hear any talking or threats. The fist blows didn't so much as sound like slaps. Amazingly quiet, but for the grunts of pain that each man let loose involuntarily.

Queenie, stuck in her cage in the kitchen went wild. Her barking was the only accompaniment to the deadly battle the two large men were executing. Neither Queenie nor I could do anything to help Gabe.

Hang on! I could help. Where was my cell? I'd call for backup. Where was Matt Hawkins? Where was Linda Taylor?

Keith and Gabe rolled toward my dining nook, fists flying and bodies dancing in an evil choreography of rhythmic destruction. I saw Keith's knife flash as light struck it. I screamed but neither man paid attention to me.

They fell against my dining room table. That's where I'd left my phone.

Art and I had bought the table when we first married. It was an antique oak pedestal design that had been the center of so many happy times together. As the men landed on one side of the table, it crashed to the floor. Gabe's upper arm got pinned under the table's heavy rim and he cried out in pain.

Keith grimaced in pleasure. Breathing heavily he raised his own arm — the arm with the knife.

"No!" I yelled and dove into Keith's side.

He stumbled sideways and tripped over Gabe's prone body. Gabe took advantage and locked feet with Keith. The two men wrestled on.

How could I help? I ran toward the front entry area. Maybe I could find something in my closet. Keith let out a chilling laugh. I turned in fascinated horror.

The monster was on top of my Gabe again, his knife recovered. He brought the evil blade down, precisely as Gabe raised his now freed left arm. Blade connected with bone and blood spurted high in the air. The blood seemed to inspire Keith, who smiled through his spattered face, and licked at the drops of red liquid closest to his mouth.

Gabe let out an anguished cry, but kept fighting. He rolled beneath Keith, heaving and lurching.

Keith was bigger, heavier. Gabe stretched

his right arm trying to reach something on the floor nearby. His gun!

Keith brought a knee down hard on Gabe's arm. Gabe yelled again. Then Keith pinned Gabe's left arm with his other knee. Though winded, the monster held fast to his knife. He grabbed Gabe's hair with his left hand and started to bring his knife down toward Gabe's throat.

"No you don't!" I cried, closed my eyes and swung. Art's golf club closed on Keith's head. There was a sickening crunch as the seven iron connected with the back of Keith's skull.

"Wha —" said Keith, then he slumped over and fell onto Gabe.

Gabe pushed the monster off and immediately checked for signs of life.

"I didn't . . . did I, Gabe?"

"No. He's alive. Though, to be honest, I wouldn't have minded if you had killed him, Daisy." He rolled Keith onto his stomach and cuffed the criminal's hands behind his back. Keith groaned.

I covered my mouth, forcing my stomach to hold itself together. Gabe smiled at me. "You did good, my girl. Real good. I didn't see it until you reached for it. But remind me never to get you mad at a round of golf."

At that point I began shaking. I knew

Gabe was trying to help me relax, so I tried to laugh, but it came out as a howl. Tears streamed down my face. I ran into Gabe's arms. He held me with his right, but the left arm was still pumping a scary amount of blood.

"You're hurt badly." I remembered the fight and shook more, but tried to focus on Gabe's arm. There was a large, deep gash that would definitely require stitches. "Let me get a tourniquet on that. Gabe, I'm so sorry. Should I dial nine-one-one and get you an ambulance?"

"Good plan, but here." He righted a chair and sat down as he handed me his phone. "Speed dial number one. It'll cut through even quicker."

Gabe was looking paler, more tired by the second. He was losing a lot of blood. "By the way, how did Keith get in here? I thought you were going to sit tight with your neighbor."

"My neighbor! Gabe! We have to go find Chip! Keith said he'd bleed to death soon."

"That guy is good at knowing where to strike." With that, Gabe too, lost consciousness.

CHAPTER 41

I speed-dialed the number on Gabe's phone. Linda Taylor answered.

"Partner, am I glad you called," she said before I could tell her it was me. "It's a real mess down here in Louviers. Called in the state police for backup."

"Linda, this is Daisy. Actually, it's a mess up here at my house too."

"Daisy! Are you okay? Where's Gabe?"

"He passed out in my dining room. Linda, I'm frightened. Keith Johnson will be coming to soon —"

"Keith Johnson? Why is he there? What's going on?"

"Keith's the murderer. He killed Cissy Melato, my friend Connie, and he tried to kill me, then Gabe."

"Are you okay, Daisy? Give me a complete update."

"I will, but first we need an ambulance here right away."

"On it," said Linda. "Putting you on hold, but stay with me."

So I did. And when she came back on the line, I told Linda about Keith breaking in and trying to kill me. How Gabe saved me, how Chip was possibly bleeding to death somewhere.

"And so Keith is handcuffed and lying on my dining room floor, and I've propped up Gabe in the chair he's in."

"Okay. Think I have the particulars. Help is on the way."

"Should I go find Chip?"

"Not until Gabe regains consciousness. Johnson will probably come to first. Make sure he knows you're the boss."

"Me? The boss?"

"Pretend, Daisy. You know. Fake it till you make it? You're braver than you realize."

I gulped, still not feeling all that confident. "Okay," I ventured. Nope. No confidence at all.

"It's only for a couple of minutes. I have squad cars going to you."

"Thanks, Linda."

"Thank you, Daisy. Is my — is Gabe okay, do you think?"

I looked over at him. Gabe was stirring even as we spoke. "He's lost some blood, and it looks like he's already got a bruise on his cheek starting, but yes, I think he'll be all right."

There was a tense silence, then Linda heaved a sigh. "Good work."

"Hey, Linda. Do you have any idea how Gabe decided to come back to my house?"

"That one's easy. You called."

"But I didn't leave a message."

"Your number was automatically recorded, and when Gabe didn't receive your message, he got worried and left me in charge down here."

Thank goodness! But all I could manage in response was an inarticulate, "Oh."

"Gabe thinks you're special, Daisy. And I guess I do too. Now, can you get his cut raised above his heart?"

I hopped to, following Linda's instructions for propping Gabe's arm with pillows.

On the floor below me, Keith started coming to with moans. A second later he was vomiting full force. "God, my head," he cried. Part of me wanted to hit him again, to get him to go back into an unconscious state so I wouldn't have to worry about him breaking free and coming after me again. I waited. He turned his face to me.

"Who are you?" he said, "And why am I lying on the floor here? And oh, God! What is that?" He stared bug-eyed at the puke before him.

"It's all right, Keith," I said. "You banged your head, and I think you have a concussion. Do you remember anything of this evening?"

He frowned. "Not at all. Something about following Roddy somewhere, but no. And my head feels like it's going to explode."

"Hmm. Definitely concussion, all right. I'm the one who's going to help you." *Help you right into jail, you slimy rattlesnake.* "You lie still, right there. Help is coming."

"But why are my wrists tied? What's going on?"

"There will be people along soon to explain it all to you." I turned to Gabe, who was also coming to. I put his gun next to him and fed him a few sips of orange juice. "Ambulances and more police are coming, Gabe. I can hear the sirens now."

Sure enough, the doorbell rang at that moment. I opened the door to firefighters and emergency medical technicians. They went right to work. One EMT didn't look very busy so I grabbed his arm.

"I think there might be someone else in need of your help," I said and practically dragged him through the kitchen and out my back door.

CHAPTER 42

There were no lights on at Chip's house. I banged on his front door a few times, but to no answer. Thunder kept barking a warning from inside.

"You sure about your neighbor needing help?" said the EMT. "No offense, but I don't like going into houses with large dogs unless the owner is there to control them."

"Thunder is okay," I said. "He's just saying hello."

The EMT looked at me like I was crazy. I shrugged. "Okay. How 'bout we knock on the back door? Chip was coming back here to get something when the guy at my house apparently knifed him."

"You sure about that? Do you think there is another suspect in the area who could have done it?" The guy started gazing around, apparently ready to run if need be.

"Look. I'm only sure that my neighbor headed home, didn't come back, and the bad guy in my house is being treated better than my friend. Will you or won't you help?"

The EMT stepped back and let me pass into Chip's back yard.

There, on the back steps lay Chip's crumpled body. Oh, my stars! Chip's hands were tied behind his back. He couldn't have helped himself with his wound. If Keith lived and Chip didn't, I might step on over to the wrong side of the law. Luckily the EMT was calmer than I, and dove right in to work.

"Is he — is he?" I couldn't bring myself to say the words.

"He's alive. Good thing you brought me, though. He looks in bad shape. Any chance you can get some light on here?"

I ran onto Chip's back porch and flicked a switch. The backyard flooded with light. Thunder went crazy at Chip's back door.

The EMT freed Chip's hands and stretched my friend on the ground. Chip's face was pale and more stoic than I'd ever imagined possible. "Chip," I called, "Chip! Chip!"

He opened his eyes. "Who'd have known you had two guys chasing you, Daisy? You're too popular." Chip rasped the words out but grinned.

"Chip, I'm so sorry."

The EMT pulled me back. "He'll be okay, but it's best not to get him stirred up. Let him rest. We'll send him in the next ambulance to Littleton Hospital."

Linda Taylor came running up. "Daisy! What happened here?"

"I wish I knew. Roddy came and threatened me. Then Gabe came to be sure I was all right. Chip was going to stay with me, but then Thunder started making too much noise. Then Keith barged in and now everybody's hurt." I so wanted to break down and cry my eyes out.

"Okay, okay, Daisy." Linda's voice was calm and professional. I fed my own confidence with the persona she was using.

"Have you seen Matt Hawkins? I still can't raise him on his phone."

"Matt went charging off after Roddy McKeague. I haven't seen either for almost an hour."

Linda looked thoughtful. "EMTs are transporting Gabe now. I don't think you or I could be a lot of help here. What say we take a walk around your neighborhood and look for Matt and McKeague."

"Great idea," I said. "Let me grab a coat. With the evening, it's getting chilly out."

"You can say that again."

"You need a wrap too, Linda?"

"Thanks."

I wasn't sure how we were becoming friends, but I felt all the better for being with Linda just then. She was right about not being able to help anymore. I grabbed a flashlight as well as a couple of jackets and headed back to Chip's place. I didn't even want to think about what my house looked like. The quick traverse through showed a set of rooms in complete disarray, with overturned furniture, scuff marks, and of course, the blood. I shivered at the thought of even beginning to clean up the mess.

In Chip's house Thunder continued to bark.

"Mind if we grab Thunder? I feel like keeping as much protection around me as possible."

Linda shrugged. "As long as he stays on a leash and doesn't cause trouble."

I hooked up my best friend from next door and the three of us took off. Thunder behaved differently than I'd ever seen before. His hackles weren't exactly up, but every inch of his classic breeding showed. Thunder sniffed the air and suddenly seemed on high alert. His chest widened and his ears stood at point. He seemed to grow to a full-blown specimen of raw courage and strength. How cool was that?

As we walked, I had to find out more. "I heard about the murder in Louviers, Linda."

"It's a mess out there, but the state police have it covered. Apparent murder-suicide."

"No!" I almost shouted the word. "Sorry. I mean no, it probably isn't what it seems."

"What do you mean?" Linda turned to me.

"That slimo, Keith Johnson, said something about the assassins being patsies. That every murder needs a murderer. I think he's the one who killed Connie. Whoever else was involved was probably a patsy in Keith's words."

"You sure about this?"

"Absolutely. Who was killed? Joe Smaldone?"

"No. His bodyguard. Some sort of cousin, I think."

Inside I wanted to burst. Linda must have been referring to Stone Face. Poor guy would have made a great patsy. And it seemed that Keith did enough research to know that too. "How awful," was all I could think to say.

Suddenly, Thunder's head dropped and he sniffed on the sidewalk. I shone my flashlight at the spot. "What is it, boy?" I asked.

"It's blood," answered Linda. "Good dog."

"Find more, Thunder," I said. "Find more."

Thunder took off at a trot, practically dragging me along behind. It wasn't long before he made a sharp right into another neighbor's yard and behind their garage. There, nestled into a bed of newly emerging hydrangeas lay Roddy McKeague. I recognized the leather jacket and slim figure, but had no desire to see more. I hung onto Thunder as Linda went to investigate. She came back, cell phone to her ear. "Mac, we found the perp. Yeah . . . No, not the one from Smaldone's. One from old town Littleton . . . Yes, the Arthur place . . . No, not at that address precisely. Four houses down . . . East side behind the garage. Dead."

She swept her flashlight around the back-yard.

A man came out in his pajamas, a shotgun in hand. "Who's out there?"

"It's me, Mr. Nelson. Daisy Arthur."

"Daisy? What you doing in my hydrangeas this time of night?"

I looked to Linda for an explanation. She supplied it. "Police business. Please stay inside, sir. This is a murder investigation."

"Oh?" said Mr. Nelson. "Oh!" With that he went in and turned on the backyard light. Linda and I smiled at each other as sirens sounded from a short distance.

In the flood of Mr. Nelson's lights I could gaze clear around his yard. I avoided looking at Roddy, but beyond the hydrangeas Mr. Nelson had a nice setting of garden furniture, rock formations, and a large vegetable garden. He even had a scarecrow in the garden. Funny, I didn't remember seeing that before.

My stomach nose-dived. "Linda," I said and pointed to the scarecrow. She flashed her light on the figure. "No! My God!" she cried and ran toward it. Thunder and I came up in time to see that the scarecrow was not some fake stuffed thing with button eyes and a rough stitched mouth, but a man. A dead man. And the face belonged to the boyish police officer, Matt Hawkins.

CHAPTER 43

It had been less than a month since I'd come to the cemetery to witness Cissy Melato's funeral. At that time there had been only a handful of family and friends to mourn the loss of the accountant who seemed larger than life, as I'd investigated her murder.

Today, for a young man half Cissy's age, the cemetery was bulging with mourners. They stretched far and wide across the hill that overlooked Littleton's railroad and the Rocky Mountains beyond. Wind chimes accompanied the thoughts and prayers of the police department heads, the Littleton dignitaries, and Matt's family. A cadre of motorcycles lined the lane in Littleton Cemetery where Matt would be laid to rest near so many I knew, including Cissy, Art, and my daughter, Rose.

A reverend from the local Presbyterian Church gave a touching eulogy across the flag-draped casket.

The chief of police stood and took the flag, folded in the traditional triangle of military and police officers, and handed it to Matt's mother. She took the flag, drenched it with her tears and leaned into Matt's dad. I had to guess these folks were my age or younger, but today the weight of the world etched deep lines in their faces.

How short life is! I looked around the cemetery and wondered at the history before me. How many people buried here had been known as heroes in their time, as Matt was in ours?

I had met the young officer only a handful of times, but my mind fought to keep the memories clear — his open smile, sharp deductive skills, his willingness to believe in the good that was Littleton. Who knows why he was "called home" so soon in his life? It made no sense to me.

I looked over at Gabe and Linda. Matt's partners. Linda, ever lovely, stood in dark dress uniform, her eyes hidden behind sunglasses. I wouldn't speculate why they were in place. And Gabe. My favorite police officer in the world, stood shoulder to shoulder with his partner. Again in dress uniform, but no glasses, and his arm was in a black sling. No doubt of their partnership, their closeness in solemn loss. But no jealousy raised itself in my mind. These partners lost one of their own and it created an invisible wall around them. I didn't want to witness their pain. It felt intrusive, and the hundreds of others here would poke and prod their feelings more than enough.

I walked away to let the community mourn. My feet took me to my own family's graves once more.

Art, this death thing is so hard to deal with.

Yes, Daisy, but it was Matt's time.

I looked across the field of headstones. So many came before me, so many would come after when I would be little more than a name on a marker. The pine trees that were so small when I buried Art towered over the lanes that wove their way through the cemetery.

When will it be my time, Art? When will we be together again?

Soon enough, my love. Soon enough. But you can stand on your own now. You're growing stronger, braver all the time. You have a life to live, Daisy. I'll be there if you need me, but I think you aren't so needy anymore.

He was right, of course. I grabbed the locket around my neck.

I am a habit right now, Daisy. You need to let go.

No! Art, how could I do that? It would be so disloyal.

I will love you through eternity, but I think there are enough men in your life now without me.

I will love you always too, Art. You have always been my hero.

A breeze blew through the trees, and with it the scent of lilacs from somewhere across the street. Something in the smell and the movement gave me a feeling of peace. I listened to my heart and heard Art once more.

We let go of those we love, and when the moment is right, our loves reunite. Good luck, Daisy.

At that moment I knew what I had to do. I took off my locket of Art and Rose, and put it on his grave. Then I squared my shoulders and walked away. It was time to do what good I could on my own.

Before I could reach my car, a man in dark glasses and trim suit approached. Joe Smaldone.

"Joe," I said. "I heard what happened at your house . . . Connie and your cousin, I think? I'm so very sorry."

"Yes," said Joe. "Thanks. That's partly why I'm here. Sal woulda wanted me to talk with you. He liked you."

411

So the man's name was Sal, before he became Stone Face, and then dead. I swallowed a bit of grief for the man who scared me, but whom I sensed held a small heart of gold within his spirit. I remembered him the last time I saw him. It was here, at the cemetery — a big hulking guy with tears streaming down his face for Cissy Melato.

"Thank you, Joe."

Joe spent a few minutes telling me about Sal. His cousin, like himself, was a transplant from New York. He and Joe came out west so as to get away from family business in the big apple, and stay out of trouble. Joe's degree in restaurant management from Cornell allowed him to get Essence started.

Sal had always been a bit slow, so he needed family to watch out for him. He had lived with Joe for the past twenty-five years, and the arrangement worked well. He could lift everything from trays of food to office or cleaning supplies, and never seemed to hurt his back. Great to have around. He'd also fallen in love with the more tame of the gangster movies, so Joe allowed Sal to wear the sunglasses and call him "boss."

"But to me," said Joe, "he was the one who should be called boss. He made everyone who got to know him feel good. He cared about people in his own way. Had

412

spot-on intuition about who to trust and who to keep away from."

"I'm sorry I didn't get the chance to know him better," I said, and felt the truth of the statement.

"Yeah, so when he told me I could trust you, I believed him. We were talking about you the day he died."

My stomach dropped. "Talking about me?" I wasn't sure I liked that.

"He said I should watch out for you. See, we're expecting that as Littleton goes through this latest growth spurt, things are likely to get rough. Too much need for more and more around here. This grocery business stuff is likely only the beginning. And by helping the police with Cissy's murder, you've drawn attention to yourself."

I stared at Joe as a chill crept up from the graves around me.

"Attention to myself?"

"Yeah. Guys like Roddy McKeague and that Johnson slime. They're a dime a dozen. They do the leg work, take the consequences. But the ones you have to watch out for are the ones you can't see coming."

I thought I hadn't seen Keith Johnson coming. There were worse people than him?

Gabe walked up at that moment.

"Hello, Smaldone," he said, his temperament nothing to be toyed with. "What are you doing here?"

"Offering condolences." Joe stuck out his hand. "Sorry for your loss."

Gabe stared at Joe's hand for a long moment before taking it in his own. Not the friendliest of greetings. "Likewise," said Gabe.

Joe turned to me. "Hoping we don't have to see each other again, Ms. Arthur. No offense, but I suspect you attract trouble."

I shook hands with Joe and he was off.

"No truer words," said Gabe. He turned to me. "Daisy, I think we need to talk. Platte Canyon Bar and Grill?"

I nodded.

Yes. Gabe and I needed to talk badly.

CHAPTER 44

The noise at the restaurant was same as always. No one seemed to notice that I was all in black and Gabe had on a dress uniform with black armband, not to mention his arm in a sling. Heck, between the bikers and the Goth college kids, we seemed to blend right in. Funerals happened across the street and up the hill often, so the patrons here wouldn't even notice if someone came in to drown their sorrows.

We settled into what looked like the cut-off end of a 1960's Thunderbird, but was actually a booth bench, and ordered hamburgers off the American side of the menu.

"Thanks for coming," said Gabe. He shook his head at some thought.

"What is it?" I asked.

"I was thinking it's been a rough month."

"And not exactly a diamond in the rough either, right?" Gabe didn't even flinch at my poor pun. I lifted a glass of lemonade to him. He covered my wrist and I put my glass down once more.

"I have to be serious for a few minutes," said Gabe. "You see, Keith Johnson was killed in his jail cell last night."

I thought over this a minute or more. How did I feel about a man's murder when that man came so close to killing me? To killing Chip and Gabe? A man who seemed to know so much about me, yet who lent no real feelings to his actions. "Is that such a bad thing? I mean, I wouldn't want to kill anyone myself, but Keith was a terrible human being."

"I'm not concerned so much about Johnson as I am about what he was paid to do."

"What do you mean?"

"The guy was a hit man, plain and simple, Daisy. People hired him to get rid of their problems in the grocery business. Very powerful people, I should think. There isn't any proof, of course, but wherever Johnson's been living over the past several years, there have been a string of suspicious deaths and outright murders."

I kissed a hit man? This was very creepy in a thrilling sort of way. "But now that he's gone?"

"I hope the killings will stop. But Daisy, I think you need to be more careful."

You have no idea, Gabe. I raised my glass to my police lieutenant. "I will, and here's to hoping for better days ahead."

He smiled at that. I loved Gabe's grin. It was a mixture of boyish charm and rakish seduction, and I always felt free to respond with whichever feeling I wanted. Today, I went for the boyish charm.

"Daisy, you are one special friend," said Gabe. "I only wish I'd met you sooner and kept you in my life. I think things could have been a lot different."

My heart sank. He was going to tell me that he and Linda were dating. I knew it. "Is this the official brush-off?"

"Not exactly, my girl. It's just —" he hesitated and gazed out toward the west. "Just I think we're not in synch with our emotions. When I'm interested in taking us to the next level, you seem to go distant on me. And vice versa. I'm not sure why we can't get our relationship on a better footing, but . . ."

I stared west too, across the biker parking spaces to the wilds that lead to the Platte River. "But something keeps getting in the way. Something like murder, opposing opinions . . . Something like — Linda Taylor?"

"What do you mean, Linda? She's my

partner."

"Right. Your partner and your friend. Heck, she's my friend too. But I think she and your work are a higher priority than me, and Ginny is even higher on that list."

"Isn't that how it should be?"

"No, Gabe, it isn't. At least not to me." A tear threatened to pop out, so I faked a cough for a quick eye wipe.

"You okay?" asked Gabe. His concern for me was always so attractive. Goodness, he made the perfect hero for somebody's novel. I smiled at him and sat as tall as I could in the car-seat booth.

"I'm fine, my friend. Just fine. Gabe, you have a set of priorities that worked for so long, it's not a wonder you'd like to keep things as they are, with me fitting myself in around them. But I played that role with Art. I know this probably sounds harsh, but having been there, done that, I'm not ready to fling myself back into an old-fashioned relationship and put myself in last place on the priority list."

He looked thoughtful, as if I'd given him something to think about. "I could change that."

"No doubt. But change takes time. Now that you're aware, I'm going to step back and let you think through what's important to you."

Gabe's cell tingled with a text message.

"Excuse me, Daisy, I have to get this." He stood and walked away, dialing Linda no doubt.

Less than a blink of an eye later he came back, a sheepish grin on his handsome features.

"Oops," he said. "I see what you mean. Sorry."

"Don't be. But do understand that I'm jealous. Jealous of your work, of your partner, of the time and energy you don't have to make me feel important."

"I don't want to lose you, Daisy."

"Nor I you. But maybe we should concentrate on our friendship for a while and not push the exclusive relationship thing quite yet."

Gabe's face relaxed. Then he gave me a wicked grin. "Perhaps friends, with benefits?"

"Don't push your luck, buddy." I fake scowled, but the thought of a little exercise in a prone position seemed like a lot of fun to me. Healthy too. Much better than loving a gallon container of ice cream, like Cissy had.

"Daisy, I'm sorry things have been so rough. I've thought a lot about our dinner at that Italian place —"

"Please don't mention that place ever again. I think I owe them an apology letter a week for the rest of my life."

He laughed. "We'll go back sometime, after they've forgotten who we are. We'll have a nice dinner and they will never know we were the ones who caused such a stir in their establishment."

"Maybe, Gabe. Sometime."

"How about after I finish a course I'm taking at the community college?"

"You're going back to school? For what?"

"Anger management." He said the words simply, his eyes challenging me to go all gushy on him. His face flushed red and my heart melted.

"It's a plan. And my treat for your graduation."

Gabe reached around me with his good arm and gave me a quick hug.

"I knew you'd understand. Now, I have a proposal for your own personal growth."

"Goodness! They don't do a course on growing a backbone, do they?"

"No, and you wouldn't need it if they did. You are much braver, I think, than even you know, my girl. Daisy, you saved my life with Keith Johnson."

"No, I don't think so. We stopped a bad

guy — together."

"Yes. We make good partners."

"Gabe, I think you said your partner is Linda Taylor. I want — I need more."

"You're right. And you are more. You're . . ." he searched for the right word.

"I'm your friend."

"You're my special friend."

I smiled. "I like that."

"So, special friend, I'm thinking that if you are going to get involved in any more murders —"

"Never! I don't make a good detective at all."

"If you're going to get involved — and I know you will — I'd like to see you at least take the next Littleton Citizen's Academy police course."

"What's that?"

"It's six weeks of meeting at the police station to get to know how our police force works. Mostly it's public relations, but some of our graduates have gone on to apply for jobs in the force. I'd like to see you do this, and enroll in the community college's program for women's self defense."

"Now you're asking me to do two courses for your one."

He smiled again. "A fair deal, sounds like to me."

The man would never stop taking care of me, no matter what he said. I laughed. "Deal."

"And Daisy, I'm supposed to ask if Brian and Ginny can stop by this afternoon sometime. They have some news they want to share."

"And I'd like to give Queenie to Brian. She's been a great house guest, but she and Georgette will never be friends."

He chuckled. "You sound pretty frazzled every time you step out of your house."

"Let's just say I have a growing sympathy for the Secretary-General of the United Nations. So you're reconciled to Ginny having a boyfriend?"

"I'm going to have to. Brian's about to become my son-in-law."

"What? Gabe. That's so exciting! I'm thrilled for you."

"You may be thrilled, but I have to live with Ginny gone from my house. I can't watch her so closely. And that boy has a police record!"

I laughed. "Which you gave him. Seriously, you can get used to all of that."

Gabe sipped from his glass. "I probably can, at that. At least the apartment manager, Amber, is willing to look in on them regularly. Them and Queenie. But I think I'll

still send a squad car around at least daily
—"

"At least weekly . . ."

Gabe grinned and nodded. "At least weekly, just to keep an eye on things."

"Gabe, you'd be an easy man to love."

"Do you think so?" His eyes shone the special periwinkle color that stole my breath away.

"I do. Maybe. Someday." He smiled again at that. *Friends with benefits* sounded pretty good in his company.

CHAPTER 45

Tuesday night. My favorite night of the week.

I had just changed into a flowered drape dress for the group meeting when my doorbell rang. Queenie started barking, as usual, and Georgette dove under my bed. I went to answer the door.

"My Daisy!" cried Ginny, as she bounded inside. She gave me a big hug, then went back on the porch and dragged in Brian by the hand. He smiled shyly at me, then gave me a big hug too.

"I gotted out of jail," said Brian. "I no bad guy no more. Pah!"

I smiled across the group hug toward Gabe, who had brought Ginny and Brian over, and now leaned on my porch railing, that devilish grin firmly in place. I could have stared at his face all night, but Queenie was barking like the whole world should know Brian had come to our house.

"Come in, come in," I said. "I have sparkling apple cider and cookies to celebrate. Brian, I am so proud of you!"

The young man beamed at me. "I don' getta wear the pretty orange suit no more, but Mr. Care-filly — I mean Daad — gaved me a orange shirt. I like it, an' Ginny likes it lots."

Brian was indeed brightly colored, with a nice button-down collared shirt tucked into navy pants.

"You will be ready when football season starts, won't you?" I said.

Queenie continued yapping and barking. I could tell she was excited to see Brian. She jumped up on him, and he went down on one knee to kiss his dog — his very wealthy dog. "I love you, Queenie," said Brian.

The dog went wild. She ran to the kitchen, fetched a doggie bone and brought it back. Then she jumped on Brian again. He laughed and scratched her ears again. Then the pooch zeroed in on Brian's ankle.

"Ow," said Brian. "Queenie bites too much. I love you, Queenie, but you gotta stop dat."

Ginny put her hand on Brian's arm. "Queenie is a good doggie, Bri-Ann. We will train her, and she will stop biting you."

"You f-ink so, Ginny? I no like Queenie

biten' me lots."

"She will learn to be good, Bri-Ann, 'cause we love her. And My Daisy will help us." Ginny turned to me with a shining look in her eyes.

Oh, goodness! What could I say? "I'll be happy to try, Ginny. Yes. I will visit lots and we will teach Queenie some very royal manners. I hear corgis are very smart dogs."

Ginny smiled again. Then she looked like a totally new thought popped in her head. "My Daisy! I 'most forgotted. We love Queenie, and Bri-Ann an' me love each ovver. We is going to be married an' we will be a family. Is dat a great idea or what!"

"Ginny and Brian, I couldn't be happier. Congratulations!" I looked over to Gabe, who seemed more comfortable with the thought of Ginny and Brian as a couple with each moment.

We went to the dining nook where I had put out cookies and the apple cider. As Ginny and Brian nibbled their treat, Queenie kept jumping at Brian, and wriggled between his feet. He kept reaching down to pet his dog, and I knew the little corgi couldn't have been happier.

At last we bundled the young people and their dog into Gabe's car. He stepped over to me.

"I can't thank you enough, Daisy," said Gabe. "If you hadn't believed so firmly in Brian's innocence, I might have put a very good young man into jail and lost my daughter's trust forever."

I nodded, a little too choked up for words. In the back seat of Gabe's car, I could see Ginny and Brian playing with Queenie and knew all was well for them. I turned back to Gabe.

"Well," he said, shuffling a toe against the sidewalk, "I'd best get these guys home. I'll keep Brian with us until we can fix up the apartment for them."

"Sounds like a plan, Gabe." There was a tension in the air. We weren't partners, certainly not lovers, but friends? Pals? What?

Suddenly, Gabe took hold of my upper arms. "I know we're searching for a good definition of our relationship," he said, "but, while we do, let's not be total strangers." With that, he kissed my cheek and dashed off to his car.

I stood on the sidewalk, hand to cheek, until they drove out of sight. Yes, I could love that man. Someday. Maybe.

Then I remembered writing group. Had to get ready or I'd be late.

The whole writing group made it for our

first Tuesday in June.

Toni waved at me from the door. "Daisy, may I have a word?"

We stepped aside from the others, and Toni lowered her voice. "Daisy, will you speak to Dan? He keeps slashing my work to bits, and I can't write for almost the whole week after one of his critiques."

"I know Dan's reviews are harsh, Toni, but he means well."

She sighed. "I know, but he doesn't have any filters, and doesn't write a single nice thing about my work. He's not nice to anybody else, either. I checked."

You gossiped. "Let's see how tonight goes, and I'll think about it. But Toni, you are the one who has to believe in your work. Kudos from Dan, or anyone else for that matter, aren't what writing is all about."

She didn't look precisely satisfied, but she nodded. "All right. As long as you know."

I knew. I knew what it was like to be in Toni's shoes. Her self-confidence needed shoring up, not tearing down. But I also knew that Dan Block's thick skin encased a heart of gold.

As I had been last to arrive, I read last, and when I finished, had the chance to look around at my group. These friends — and yes, they were friends — offered so much through their writing. Fiction or no, their stories all held a bit of themselves, and a lot of truths that are hard to face without story.

Toni's narrative was good, but even when she read her pages out loud, I could hear the extra verbiage and understood where Dan was probably coming from. There was room for compromise, as we couldn't all write with Dan's precision.

Kitty read next. Her story sparkled with the same spirit of fun that she infused into everything she did. Kitty, the newly engaged young woman. Thank goodness we got Chip to the hospital in time. She stayed by his side for the few days he had to spend there and brought him home, where Chip's mom had moved in. That was a fun dynamic to watch from across our properties, and it looked like Kitty and Mrs. McPherson would be tightly knit forever over the Chip incident.

Eleanor and Dan had offered, as always, very polished work. I had a "someday" wish for my own work, and then smiled at our group.

Next was Linda Taylor. For the first time in months I hadn't listened to her writing in hopes of hearing something wrong in her work. For the first time I truly heard her story. She had given up on the Raymond

Cruz story and started something new. It was about a young crime scene investigator who was best friends with her boss until he died in a drug bust. Then the investigator had to find the bad guys on her own, with the upper echelon of the force accusing her of being "dirty." She knew they did that because, even in her world, female cops had a bad time of it. I made a commitment right then to stop thinking of Linda as That Woman, and start thinking of her with the respect a police officer and writer deserved.

I wondered how much of her story came from her own personal experience. Linda always looked neat as a pin, came prepared each writing group session, and had an air of professionalism that extended beyond her years. In the past few weeks I'd been a part of what Linda had to live with daily, and the thought made me shudder. I couldn't live with so much crime in my life.

A small voice inside me, my own voice, argued back. *Yes, Daisy, you could. You've learned to be over-dependent, but you can unlearn that. You know you can handle whatever life throws your way. It's time to stop being afraid of the world and start believing in yourself.*

Where the heck had that thought come

from? Hmm. I'd have to journal about this one.

Kitty waved a hand in front of my face. "Daisy. Whoo hoo. Are you ready for your critique?"

I shook my head. "Sorry, everyone. Wool gathering."

And they were off. I was criticized for plot problems and details gone awry. Then Eleanor's time to critique came.

"Daisy, I'm surprised at you," she said. She smiled the brightest I'd ever seen. "This is the best writing you've done to date. Yes, you need a couple of plot point revisions, but those are easy to fix. I think you're jumping to the next level. Your writing is clean and tight, without superfluous words or get-to-the-point paragraphs. Nice job." She sounded surprised even saying what she did.

My chest was ready to explode. A compliment? From Eleanor? Unheard of. I glanced over at Dan and smiled. He winked at me. What a good friend.

Then I turned back to Eleanor. "Thank you," I said. "I went on a new diet . . . a word diet."

"Well done," she said and repeated, "well done."

ABOUT THE AUTHOR

Liesa Malik is a freelance writer and marketing consultant originally from Bloomfield Hills, Michigan, but currently living in Littleton, Colorado, with her husband and two pets. She has always enjoyed reading mysteries, from *The Happy Hollister* series, through *Trixie Belden* and into Reader's Digest's *Great True Stories of Crime, Mystery and Detection*.

A graduate of the University of South Florida with a degree in Mass Communications, Liesa has built on her writing interest with long-standing membership in Rocky Mountain Fiction Writers and recently joined the board of Rocky Mountain Mystery Writers of America. Most days you can find Liesa either at her desk, at a local ballroom dance studio, or on the web: www.liesamalik.wordpress.com.